BOOKSTORIES

BOOKSTORIES

Sarah Tollok

BALANCE OF SEVEN
Newport, VT

Bookstories

For information, contact:
Balance of Seven
www.balanceofseven.com
info@balanceofseven.com

Cover Art by altocello (Andrea L. Farley)
www.altocello.com

Cover Design by Fictional Services
www.functionallyfictional.com

Developmental Editing by Katryna T. Seto
www.ktseto.com

Copyediting by Leo Otherland and Ynes Freeman

Formatting and Proofreading by TNT Editing
www.theodorentinker.com/TNTEditing

Publisher's Cataloging-in-Publication Data

Names: Tollok, Sarah, 1977 - .
Title: Bookstories / Sarah Tollok.
Description: Newport, VT : Balance of Seven, 2024. | Summary: To learn the identity of a mysterious author of brilliant, unfinished stories, a retired publishing house editor and a young playwright seek the "perfect reader"—someone who can empathically understand a person just by reading their writing. The lives they touch in the process are more intertwined than they realize.
Identifiers: LCCN 2023952506 | ISBN 9781947012585 (pbk.) | ISBN 9781947012592 (ebook) | ISBN 9781947012608 (Itchio)
Subjects: LCSH: Empathy - Fiction. | Books - Fiction. | Storytelling - Fiction. | Book editors - Fiction. | Dramatists - Fiction. | BISAC: FICTION / Literary. | FICTION / Magical Realism.
Classification: LCC PS3620.O45 2024 (print) | PS3620.O45 (ebook) | DDC 813 T65- -dc23
LC record available at https://lccn.loc.gov/2023952506

28 27 26 25 24   1 2 3 4 5

For Kris.
I love our life together.
Can't wait to see where this story
we share takes us next.

Contents

Contents

Unfinished

New York City, 1960

I got one!"

Bobby's exclamation resulted in turned heads and several groans rising from the cramped rows of desks in the smoke-filled bullpen of Tandem Bike Publishing. Most of the junior editors went right back to work, thumbing through towering stacks of thick manilla envelopes, trying to decipher whether they had a submission worth passing up the chain to the assistant editors. However, a few bowed heads shot up. Those editors dropped what they were doing and made a beeline for Bobby's desk.

Dottie was the first to arrive. Of course she was. She'd known exactly what Bobby's announcement meant. Although her looks were unassuming, Dottie had a presence about her. She was highly focused and no-nonsense, especially when it came to books. Only those not scared off by her intensity knew Dottie also had a sensitive soul, relentless curiosity, and a razor-sharp sense of humor.

"Is it them? Are you sure?" Dottie's cigarette nearly singed the paper as she reached for the slim stack in

Bobby's hand. His mother-of-pearl cuff links caught the light, capturing Dottie's attention. Bobby was always fully buttoned up, stylish, and perfectly coiffed, even on days it was unlikely he'd have to make an appearance in any of the wood-paneled executive offices upstairs.

"Of course I'm sure, darling! Here, I'll trade you." Bobby exchanged the manuscript for her cig, only to dramatically gag after the first puff. "Ugh! How do you smoke these things? Filters are ridiculous. It's the smoking equivalent of getting a hand job with a woolen sock."

Still frowning, he tore off the lipstick-stained end of Dottie's L&M and sucked down half the tobacco in one long drag.

"I thought you were quitting," remarked Ted as he pulled his chair up next to Bobby's desk.

Bobby smiled. "It's a special occasion. I finally got one!"

Gail, the last of the fan foursome, deposited herself on Ted's knee. Dottie gave the mismatched pair a quick smile before diving into the story. Gail was a transplant from a wealthy Connecticut clan; her family had been rich longer than Ted's family had even been in the country. Her perfect patent-leather shoes rubbed against Ted's pant legs, hand-hemmed by his Baba. He smiled up at her with his chipped-tooth grin, and she beamed back. Gail ran her red fingernails through Ted's shaggy brown hair, trying in vain to make it neater.

"Just don't tell my mother you caught me smoking," Bobby quipped, taking another drag.

"Your secret's safe with us," Ted assured him. "Now, catch us up! What's this one about?"

"Sailors and boats," said Bobby, wagging his eyebrows and loosening his collar.

"Shipyards and longshoremen," Dottie corrected, already turning to the second page.

Gail began humming "Ships Ahoy!" Bobby joined in.

"Shh! All of you, shut it," snapped Lorn, an editor one row over. "I'm trying to read here. You're all crazy to waste your time with the crap that guy sends in."

"You have no vision, Lorn!" Ted yelled. "Besides, we all know you hide torn-out pages from *Playboy* in the manuscripts when you get bored. Nothing wrong with a little *Playboy*, Lorn! Good articles! No need to hide it!"

"And the author could be a woman, Lorn," Gail added in a scolding tone. "We exist beyond the centerfolds of your girly magazines."

Turning beet red, Lorn grumbled and closed the top drawer of his desk, giving the four a guilty sidelong glance.

After this, they all fell silent as Dottie read. Turning to page four, she sighed and shook her head.

"The part with the imagery of the coiled rope?" Bobby asked.

"Yeah," she responded in a whisper.

The writing was so brilliant, it required reverent silence. Reading this author's work made Dottie feel as if she were standing near the huge bank of votive candles at St. Pat's Cathedral, surrounded by soft, warm illumination. Each flame was an intention all its own, but together, they created something beautiful: a whole greater than the sum of its parts. Enough to warm someone looking for more than physical warmth on a cold, lonely day.

Dottie flipped through the pages faster and exponentially faster, like gravity tumbling young Alice down the rabbit hole. Yet like always, just when she was thoroughly lost in the story, she reached the end of a page, and there was no more.

Her descent into Wonderland abruptly halted, and she was left hanging, suspended among the teacups and pocket-watch gears, unable to set even one silk-slippered foot into the Mad Hatter's party or anywhere else.

The story didn't have an ending.

None of them ever did.

Dottie handed the manuscript off to Gail and Ted, then slumped onto the corner of Bobby's desk. The story, like the author's other submissions, was incredibly real and immersive. Dottie felt like she could hear the water of the Hudson lapping against the pilings below the dock and smell the oily smoke from the ship engines.

But any sense of the author themselves?

Nothing.

It was maddening.

"Wow, right?" Bobby asked.

Dottie nodded, then walked back to her desk to get a new cigarette. As she dug one out of the pack, she glanced down at the submission she'd been reading before Bobby sounded the alarm.

The story was a romance set on some island in Alaska. The writer's cover letter spoke of how everything Hawaiian had become a fad since the island's recent ratification as a state. She felt that Alaska, also having just officially joined the USA, was equally deserving of some love and attention.

Dottie thought the writer had a point. The Alaska angle could be a good hook, and what she'd read of the story so far was a fun romp in the Alaskan wilderness with a GI and a local tomboy of a gal. The earnestness of the author's words showed how serious she was about wanting others to fall in love with Alaska as she had.

Compared to what Dottie had just read, though, the Alaskan romance felt flat. But at least it would have an ending. And at least she knew something about the author. Even without the benefit of the cover letter, Dottie was always able to pick up an . . . understanding of a writer as she read their work.

Every time Dottie read, she got brief glimpses into the mind of the author. It had always been that way, even when she was a little girl. She'd once thought everyone felt and knew such things, and only as she got older had she slowly realized they didn't.

Immersed in a story, Dottie could tell the author's gender, even when the given name was just a first initial. She could tell whether they were writing from their own experience, they were inspired by reading about something, or they were making everything up for the sheer love of it. She could even tell how the author felt when they were putting pen to paper.

The knowledge just came to her, a mist of understanding that crept in from the edges of the page when she took in the story. Sometimes, insight rolled in quietly, becoming more detailed the further she read. Other times, the flashes came fast and intensely: lightning from a thunderstorm that blew in on an otherwise-sunny day.

As a young girl, Dottie had learned that some of the saddest people wrote the funniest prose. Those who were the most fearful of the world wrote the bravest characters, and those who were lonely wrote about family and love like no one else.

Fumbling to light a cigarette, Dottie looked over at her friends as they passed the pages of the new story around. Watching the three of them, she tried to grasp why and how the author of the unfinished stories was different from every other writer whose work she'd read. She took a long drag from her cigarette, held it between her pursed lips, and straightened the pages of the Alaskan story that she'd thrown aside when she'd run to answer Bobby's call.

It was easier to fall back into the swirling eddy of details she'd picked up about the young romance author than to try in vain to decipher anything about the mysterious writer.

The Alaskan author was a young transplant, probably in her late teens. Dottie could feel the younger woman's appreciation for Alaska—not as a first home but as an adopted homeland—and she intuited that the girl was from a military family. The bits about the GI rang true and were written with ease and confidence, handled in a way no amount of research alone could have produced. As for her age, Dottie could feel the girl's youth in her moments of self-consciousness around the romance, with which she had very little personal experience.

Oh, and the author was used to being an outsider of sorts, in a way that extended beyond being a military kid. Dottie couldn't put her finger on exactly how but felt she would be able to by the end of the story.

Yet when it came to the writer who never finished a story, Dottie could barely pick up anything about them. She didn't know their gender, their emotional state as they wrote, or anything else. Not even the smallest detail presented itself to her when she read the author's words. She wasn't used to having to guess at things.

Dottie and her three pals in the editorial pool—all fans of the mysterious author—guessed that the writer was a fellow New Yorker. The postmarks on the submissions were from all over the city, and almost all the stories were based somewhere in the Five Boroughs. Not only that, but the detail in each story spoke to someone who knew the locations intimately.

The author was also probably well educated—or at the very least, well read—because the quality of the writing was remarkable. If it hadn't been, the unfinished short stories would have been quickly tossed aside to the gals who sent the courtesy rejection letters.

Yet even that would have been problematic. The stories never bore a return address. They were also never signed. Even if anyone at Tandem Bike had wanted to publish the stories, they had no way of getting in touch with the author.

Who sends something they wrote to a publishing house with no hope of getting an acceptance letter and contract in return?

Probably the same type of writer who never finished a damn story.

And they never wrote the same kind of story twice. There was never a common theme between the stories beyond the locations always being in or around New York.

One story followed Maria, a young mother from Argentina who ran a little grocery store with her husband but secretly harbored dreams of being an inventor. Every week, she would lug her kids to the library via public transportation so she could read periodicals about engineering and mechanics and check out vehicle manuals. She tinkered with their store's delivery truck and with the appliances at home, sketching out her thoughts about how to make them work better. In Maria's imagination, she built a child from metal, wires, and small hydraulics that could run and play like the children of her own flesh.

That particular story cut off right as the young mother was picking her way through the aisles of a hardware store, with no good excuse for being there save for dreaming.

Another piece followed Albert, an older man in love

with his young milkman, Jerry. He thought about Jerry all the time and tried to find ways to make his life easier. Albert gave Jerry gifts he would pass off as casual, like quality long johns for cold mornings that he said were a birthday gift that didn't fit. Or the box of chocolates he claimed were from a client but that he didn't care for because they had peanuts, knowing full well that Jerry had a fondness for peanuts.

When Jerry mentioned the diner he liked to go to on payday for the Friday-night pot roast, Albert worked up the courage to go, planning to pass it off as a chance meeting. If the younger man invited Albert to sit with him, Albert would insist on picking up the tab.

It would almost feel like a date.

But Albert never went into the diner. He only stood across the street and looked through the window, through which he watched Jerry blush and respectfully flirt with a waitress.

After standing on the street for an indefinite amount of time, Albert went home. He saw Jerry the following Monday morning, and they talked about the ball game—their familiar routine. Then Jerry got back in his truck, and Albert walked to the corner to catch the bus to work, still thinking about Jerry.

That was where the story ended—with no indication of whether the two ever had that pot-roast date.

Even if the story had been finished, no one would ever publish a one-sided love story about two men. It didn't matter that it was one of the best love stories Dottie had ever read.

So many unfinished stories. Yet Dottie still couldn't sense anything about the author who wrote them all.

Her frustrated fascination with the mysterious author

made Dottie the obvious choice to be the keeper of the stories. They resided in a thick brown folder tied up with string, which she kept in the bottom drawer of her desk.

Well, all except the story about Albert and his milk-man. Bobby held on to that one. Over a few too many drinks one night, he'd told her how it made him cry—with hope.

"Knowing someone out there can understand what it's like—and can write about it that beautifully—it makes me feel like someday . . . someday it'll be okay. It'll be okay for the Alberts of the world—and for me too."

All the unfinished stories were so real and alive, they seemed to have lives of their own. The new one about the longshoreman was no different.

Shaking her head, Dottie snuffed out her cigarette and returned to her friends, who had just finished making plans to meet up after work at a local burger-and-beer dive.

"Bring the whole folder, Dottie," Ted exclaimed with grandiosity. "Tonight, we are going to figure this mystery out once and for all!" He nearly spilled Gail from his lap in his excitement, and she swatted his arm.

Smiling at her friends' antics, Dottie told them she'd be there, folder in hand. Then she returned to work.

That evening, before heading out to meet her friends for dinner, Dottie stopped at home to change out of her work clothes. She deftly dodged her father's newspaper-shaking tirade about the US needing to be less worried about what Russia was doing in space and more worried about what it was doing in Cuba. However, Dottie found it harder to dance around her mother's not-so-subtle attempt to set her up on a lunch date with the son of a woman from their temple's ladies' auxiliary.

"Think about it, Dorothy!" her mother was yelling as

Dottie closed the door between them. "He's a med student at NYU!"

Although Dottie's mother was bent on finding her only daughter a husband, it was the last thing on Dottie's mind. She could only think about the unfinished stories. Sometimes the pages she carried, tucked under her arm in a manila envelope, seemed more real to her than real life.

As Dottie's sensible wedge heels clicked on the subway steps, thoughts of the young mother, Maria, marched through her mind. Ted theorized that Maria's tale was influenced by science fiction, possibly even *The Twilight Zone*, but to Dottie, the robot details were not the focus of the story. The core of the piece was Maria's incredible mind and her dreams.

As she swayed to the rhythm of the train with her fellow passengers, Dottie thought of another incredible mind—that of the unknown author. To write the way they did, they had to be not only brilliant but also compassionate and empathetic. How else could they have created so many diverse characters and have the reader feel like they knew the workings of each of their hearts? How else could they have captured Albert's unselfish love for Jerry and the expansive longing he kept neatly buttoned up and tucked away, day in and day out? Who else could have envisioned a sailor, anchored by his responsibilities, who wanted to run away on a freighter and never step foot on land again?

The stories—especially the characters within them—were so real to Dottie, she felt that if she were to ever meet them, it would be like resuming a conversation with an old friend after spending time apart.

Dottie was so wrapped up in her thoughts that she missed her subway stop. Getting off at the next, she walked the extra few blocks, cursing her lack of attention the whole way. She was going to be late meeting her pals.

As it turned out, though, her worry was for nothing. Ted arrived a half hour later than she did, dropping into their usual corner booth and wedging himself in next to Gail. "I had to stop at three different newsstands to find a decent street map of the city."

Ted was quick to order himself a burger and fries, eager to spread out the map and begin solving their mystery. They all had to pick up their plates and glasses to make room for it, and Gail grabbed the monogrammed hankie out of her handbag so she could wipe away the circles of condensation left behind by cold beers. The map wasn't all Ted had brought with him, either; he retrieved a handful of colored drafting pencils, a ruler, and a protractor from his deep pockets and dumped them on the table.

They spent the next hour in uncharacteristic solemnity, pouring over the stories and marking up the map with any locations that were mentioned. A napkin became the Jersey Shore, where one story took place, and another became the Pocono Mountains in Pennsylvania, the setting of a story about a couple on a train.

By the end of the evening, all the four friends had to show for their work was a map covered in dots, a bunch of empty beer glasses, and two pitchers with foam dissolving at the bottom. Undeterred, they gave up on trying to make sense of the map and fell into a conversation they had had many times over already.

Bobby had his arm around Dottie, absentmindedly playing with her curls, and Dottie leaned into him, listening to the reverberation of his voice in his chest.

"I swear, those pages smell like shrimp fried rice sometimes when they first come out of the envelope."

Dottie, Gail, and Ted each lifted pages to their noses and took a long whiff.

Bobby dissolved into giggles. "I just got three grown adults to sniff paper!"

That earned him a few crumpled napkins and an empty cigarette pack flying at his head.

When Ted and Gail settled back on the other side of the table, Dottie nestled against Bobby's chest again. Gail restarted the conversation.

"I still think it's some intellectual trying to make a point about the nature of fiction. You know, trying to say something about the structure of narrative or about the expectations of the masses." She shrugged. "Stein talked about how writing should move toward a 'continuous present' in 'Composition as Explanation.' Maybe the lack of conclusions is the author's take on Stein's nonlinear style."

"Well, we didn't make it through the night without Gail quoting good old Gertrude again," Bobby teased. "I feel you're overthinking it and getting way too technical there, Vassar College."

After a moment, when no one said anything else, he added, "I bet it's someone normal, like a quiet older lady who lacks confidence and knowledge of publishing, and she just wants someone to read her work. I mean, off the top of my head, I can think of references in the stories to crocheting, embroidery, a fondness for cats, and tips on how to mend baby clothes. Old-lady things."

Gail tapped a finger on the table. "That's narrow-minded of you, Bobby. In my hometown, Daddy was friends with a local judge, and that man and all his brothers knew how to embroider; their mother taught them how. He worked on a recreation of some famous Flemish tapestry for over fifteen years."

"Now, now," Ted said, adopting a placating tone. "I think Bobby is on to something with the 'regular person' angle. Maybe the author is some high-school gym teacher who coaches Little League on the weekends and doesn't know how to properly tie a tie but reads a lot and writes in his spare time. Or maybe it's not PE; maybe he's a science teacher. I mean, there were references to moon phases and some chemical reactions. It went beyond common knowledge, and it was all correct, so . . ." He shrugged.

"Well, if you know enough about those science-y topics, then it's somewhat common knowledge." Gail rolled her eyes. "That means someone wouldn't have to be a science teacher to know. Or maybe—oh!" She grabbed Ted's necktie, long-since untied and hanging loose around his collar. "We all know you can't tie a tie to save your life and that your mother has to do it for you. Maybe it's been you all along!"

The mock seriousness of the accusation held for a moment, then they both broke into smiles and gave each other a comically loud kiss.

"For that matter," Dottie chimed in after lighting another smoke, "it could be any one of us. Then the author could sit back and watch the others respond to their work in the office." She took a long drag. "On second thought, nah! None of you morons could write like that!"

Her declaration set off a round of laughter and well-meaning jabs, but in the end, the other three kept bouncing around more ideas.

"A beatnik who's trying to make a point about being antiestablishment but is really just lazy about finishing stories and is not living up to his potential."

"A Buddhist monk who doesn't feel endings are important because, you know, impermanence and all that."

"A veteran with a plate in his head and no long-term memory!"

"A hunchback!"

"Seriously? A hunchback? Like from Notre Dame?"

"No! Like from the Bronx. And it doesn't have to be an actual hunchback, maybe just bad goiter . . ."

Dottie smiled and chuckled and nodded along as her cigarette burned down. None of her friends' guesses rang true for her. None of them felt right. She kept hoping that if they ran through enough scenarios, one would reverberate with something she had picked up from the stories, something just beyond her grasp of awareness. A piece of the puzzle that would allow a portion of the fog to clear around the unknown author of unfinished stories.

While her coworkers joked and tossed around ideas, Dottie looked at the map. She squinted and crossed her eyes, hoping some pattern would jump out at her. None did. There were little clusters of dots here and there in the areas where the stories took place. But they were ultimately just blank signposts pointing nowhere. It was as if the writer spent time visiting each place, but only just enough to be able to write about it accurately.

Dottie sat up straight in the booth. "He's been to all these places!"

The words came out louder than she had planned, and three sets of eyes landed on her.

"Or maybe 'she,'" Gail added, breaking the silence left behind by Dottie's declaration.

"Shh! I'm thinking." Dottie let her hands hover over the map like a phony psychic trying to get a reading from a dead spouse's favorite shirt. "Whoever wrote these stories had to have visited these locations. They wrote the settings with too much accuracy to not have seen them for themselves." She paused, looking around the circle of her friends. "Why are we being so passive? Why don't we go find them? Why don't we let them know that we love their stories? Why don't we invite them to come visit us?"

"Uh, because we don't know their address? Remember?" Ted twirled his finger in the vicinity of his right ear.

"But we know where they've been. And they may go back again! We can put up posters in all these places." Dottie's tone rose with excitement. "We can even take an ad out in the classifieds, say we want to meet them!"

"That's actually not a bad idea," Bobby said, matching Dottie's surge of energy. "Reading the newspaper was mentioned more than a few times in the stories. It's a small detail, but it could indicate that it's a habit of the author's. Which one was mentioned the most? The *Times*, the *Tribune*, or the *Post*?"

Gail and Ted looked at each other, then flipped through a few stories. The *Tribune* was the winner.

The call to take real action sobered the foursome up right quick. Turning over the map, they started to compose a classified ad in the margins. After that, they worked on wording the flyer and figuring out who at work they could call in favors with to run off a bunch of mimeographed copies.

A few days later, the four young editors set out across the city to different locations, posting the flyers on telephone poles, in store windows, and in specific places mentioned in the stories. Gail and Ted made a day trip to the Jersey Shore to put a few out on the Boardwalk.

Dottie clutched her stack of flyers to her chest as she rode the trains and buses. In between stops, she read bits of the stories, trying to find clues about where exactly she should put up the signs. Did the writer describe a certain fountain in the park? Didn't they mention a newsstand near Times Square?

It was as she traveled and read that Dottie finally felt a little something. A bare flicker of the author brushed against her consciousness, as if her traveling and seeking echoed their own.

After almost all her flyers were posted, she took out her copy of the longshoreman story to read as she walked along the docks, letting the catcalls of the rough sailors slide off her without acknowledgement. It wasn't until she'd read the last part of the unfinished story that she realized her feet were sore from all her walking. Wanting to rest, Dottie stopped by a seafood shop, grabbed a bottle of Coke, and lit up a smoke on a bench facing the water.

She sat in silence for a while. Then she pulled out the last of her flyers, a ripped one she hadn't wanted to post.

To the unidentified writer who has been mailing stories to Tandem Bike Publishing:

The junior editorial staff would like to get in contact with you. Some of the stories in question are titled 'The Mother of Invention' and 'At the Docks.' This is not an offer for publication but has the potential to lead to a future partnership.

The rest of the copy asked the author to call the switchboard and ask for Dottie or to show up at the Tandem Bike Publishing offices at a set date and time, just under two weeks from now.

We look forward to meeting you! the last line proclaimed with cautious optimism. Dottie's heart fluttered at the thought of someone actually walking into their lobby on the decided day.

She was staring off into nothing, trying to picture the

mystery author's face, when the small bell on the seafood shop's door tinkled, oddly delicate among the heavy, heaving sounds of the rest of the docks. The thick beams beneath her feet seemed to demand that everything around them also have gravity and mass enough to keep from floating away with the tide.

Dottie froze, the bottle of soda just barely touching her bottom lip. That line about the thick beams of the dock wasn't her own thought. It was from the story about the longshoreman. Fingers shaking, she pulled the manila envelope of stories from her handbag and flipped through to the page with the description.

As she looked around, her fingers traced the words the unknown author had used to talk about this place. There was the one shiny, red boat bobbing among the older, weathered crafts. A coil of rope had been hanging from a pole for so long, birds had built their nest in it. It was all so familiar. It was just how the author had written it. It was just as they had seen it.

Dottie sprang up, turning round and round. "He was here!"

Her shout rang out too loud, and a nearby long-shoreman glanced at her suspiciously. A pretty, well-dressed gal was meant to be admired and whistled at, not popping off with crazy exclamations in the middle of drinking her Coca-Cola.

Dottie barely noticed the looks she garnered, though. She was too intent on gathering her things and darting off to the nearest phone booth. Her hands shook as she attempted to load coins into the slot so she could call Gail. Her excitement kept her heel tapping against the metal floor as she waited for one of the other girls in the all-female apartment building to call her friend to the phone.

When Gail finally picked up, complaining that she had been in the middle of applying a box of red dye to her hair, Dottie's words tumbled out in a rush. Gail first told her to slow down, then moved on to asking Dottie about other things she could check for.

"Is there a boat named *Diana*? And is there a little stray beagle running around?"

Gail had an excellent memory for anything she read, and the details she quizzed Dottie on made Dottie start to doubt her conviction. Maybe she'd gotten ahead of herself when she saw a few details that matched the story and she hadn't let herself see the differences.

Worrying her lip, Dottie allowed herself to be talked down and then let Gail get back to her hair dye. But for good measure, she went back to the bench and put her last ripped flyer right on it. The paper strained against the masking tape holding it down in the rising wind, and Dottie hoped it would stay in place long enough to be seen.

Despite her doubts, Dottie couldn't entirely shake the feeling she was right. The unknown author had been there.

The feeling reminded her of when she was a little girl, realizing she got more from stories than the other kids, or even her parents, did. She'd thought everyone knew that the author of *Winnie-the-Pooh* wrote for his son and that everyone could picture real trees as Christopher Robin and his friends tramped through the Hundred Acre Wood. Over time, Dottie had learned that the feeling of knowing a location with a familiarity akin to knowing her own childhood backyard was not something other readers could sense.

Now, at the docks, it was as if she were seeing everything through her own eyes and the author's eyes simultaneously. It reminded her of a television program she had watched about how cartoon animators used transparent cells, laying one over another, to set a scene.

Standing in front of the bench, Dottie opened her hinged handbag and shuffled through the pages of the dock story again, careful that they didn't blow away in the process. She reread the passages describing this place, then closed her eyes and let herself see the space as it was described in the story.

When she opened her eyes, there was no beagle and no boat named *Diana*. However, she knew that the empty boat slip was where the *Diana* belonged. And when she spotted a well-worn box with a burlap lining tucked away from the wind, Dottie knew that was where a certain beagle curled up to sleep.

She knew in the way only she could.

On Monday morning, Dottie arrived late to the bullpen—an unheard-of occurrence. Bobby, Gail, and Ted were already bent over their newest rounds of manuscripts, weak coffee from the office urn in hand. At the sound of her entrance, Bobby looked up and smiled, but his expression quickly turned to one of concern. Abandoning his reading, he followed Dottie to her desk.

"Darling, you look ghastly! What were you up to this weekend? I'd suggest something salacious, but let's face it, you don't do anything salacious. At most, you skip Shabbat at your grandmother's house to go to a reading at a hole-in-the-wall bookshop and treat yourself to a piece of pie on the way home."

"That's ridiculous," Dottie quipped, tugging off her hair scarf and inspecting herself in her compact mirror. "You know I prefer cake over pie."

Bobby was right, though. Despite her best efforts, Dottie's fatigue showed through. She sighed. She was tired, but it had been worth it.

"I spent the weekend going all over the city, checking all the places where the stories take place. I'm nearly broke from all the subway tokens, my bus pass is frayed at the edges, and my shoes will need to be checked in to the repair shop as soon as possible."

Bobby's eyes widened, taking her in with deeper concern. "Why would you do that? We all took an area, remember? I mean, Ted can be flighty, but I got my flyers up in the park and the Village, and you know you can count on Gail—"

"I know, I know! I came across the flyers you all put up. Even Ted's! I wasn't worried about that. I was looking for *them*!"

Bobby caught one of her hands and held it. "I don't follow, Darling. Do you have a flask hiding in that bag of yours? If you do, I'd say lay off the sauce."

"I was looking for the people in the stories," Dottie protested. "They aren't just characters that *feel* real; they *are* real! Some of them we won't be able to find, of course. I mean, there were no specifics given about the location of Albert's home or the diner with the good pot roast or where he worked.

"But I know I sat on the exact bench where the dock story took place. And Bobby." She gripped the hand holding hers. "I found the grocery, and I found her! I found Maria! She's as beautiful as he wrote her and just like he described. She's so quietly smart and inquisitive. I asked her if I could put up a flyer in the store, and she agreed; she even asked about it. She said she couldn't recall any customers who were writers."

Bobby stood still for a moment. "Did you tell her that he wrote about her?"

"No." Pausing, Dottie released Bobby's hand, lit up her first cigarette of the day, and took a long drag. "I told her we had someone sending us stories and we wanted to track them down, but I just told her that her store was used as a location in one of them. I mean, how do you tell someone that a stranger wrote about them? Much less, tell them that stranger wrote about them in such an intimate, fond, and revealing way? I didn't think the author would want her to know that, you know?"

"Well, it could have been a fictionalized version of her," Bobby said slowly. "They could have just fancied the grocer's pretty, smart wife and made up the other stuff about her."

"Nope!" Dottie grinned from ear to ear and counted the details on her fingers as she fired them off. "Maria had machine grease under her fingernails. There were kids running around the store, one of whom rode a blue tricycle in the alleyway where the old delivery truck was parked. And the pièce de résistance?" Dottie bounced on her heels, tapping so loud that several folks turned to see what the commotion was about. "The latest copy of *Popular Mechanics* was tucked away under a stack of mail on the store's counter!"

Bobby sat down hard in Dottie's chair, where he crossed his arms and nibbled on his thumbnail. "So our fiction writer may be more of a biographer of the every-man . . . and everywoman. Dottie, they might actually show up. This could actually work."

Ted and Gail had been watching the exchange from their desks, but after seeing Dottie's bouncing and Bobby's dumbfounded-but-happy smile, they came over to share in the enthusiasm. Plans for the day of the possible meeting were made in a flurry, and excitement ran high.

When the day arrived, they each dressed in their best professional attire. Ted was the most laid-back of the group, but he asked Bobby to tie his tie for him. "I never get it quite right."

The excitement had hit its peak, but anxiety stole in as the appointed time approached. Sitting at their desks, they pretended to read, even as they threw glances at the clock, counting the minutes as they ticked away. Between 4:10 and 4:15, they staggered leaving their desks so as not to arouse suspicion, as if anyone cared what they did. Dottie took the stairs, walking slowly and breathing deliberately to calm herself.

The four of them met in the lobby and spread out to watch for their guest. Ted and Gail stood by the door, Bobby sat with a newspaper by the big front windows, and Dottie leaned on the reception desk. She casually mentioned to Beth, the receptionist for the day, that a potential client might be coming in to talk with her and that she'd already told the switchboard operators to route any calls she received around this time to reception.

As they waited, 4:25 came.

Then 4:30.

The few folks who entered the reception area all asked for someone other than Dottie.

Time ticked on: 4:35, then 4:45.

A few stray tears fell from Dottie's eyes around 5:00.

At 5:15, Bobby put his arm around her. "They're not coming, kid."

"They could just be late," Dottie protested. "There could be a traffic jam."

"Okay." Bobby nodded, sympathy in his eyes. "We'll wait a bit longer."

By then, the whole building was emptying out for the day. Waves of people flowed toward the street, though a few stragglers went against the tide and entered the lobby. Gail nudged Ted and shot Dottie a look when an unfamiliar woman came in around 5:25, glancing around but not approaching the reception desk.

Dottie had a feeling the woman wasn't who they were waiting for, but she wanted to hold out hope that she was wrong. Yet she couldn't make herself go over. Gail was about to introduce herself and ask the woman if she was looking for someone in particular when Hal from the fact-checking department came bounding out of the elevator and instantly apologized to the woman for being late.

They all crumpled a bit at that disappointment and huddled together in quiet solidarity.

At 5:40, Dottie broke the silence. "We've been waiting for over an hour; they're not coming. They don't want to be found."

"Maybe they didn't see the signs," Ted ventured, loosening the knot in his tie. "I mean, this is a big city. You can walk and ride around for a week straight and never go down the same street twice. And if they do see a flyer later on, they can always still call, right?"

Gail nodded, and Bobby gave Dottie a one-armed hug. None of it changed Dottie's certainty that the author was not going to come forward. Not now, not ever.

There was no story the next month.

However, one did come the month after that.

The story was based in a jazz club in Harlem but was more about the boy who shined shoes out front. He had a bad foot and a limp, and he was saving up for something. The reader never found out what that something was, because the story ended before he had the money he needed. The point seemed to be more about his desire to have something for himself, rather than his accomplishing his goal.

The envelope the Harlem story came in was addressed to Dottie. After that, all of them were addressed to her—the only name listed on the flyer.

Thump

New York City, 2018

Thump!

The heavy noise came from the ceiling right above Jim's head—or rather, from the floor beyond it. He instinctively looked up, as if that would help him determine the cause of the sound, though he understood how silly it was. It wasn't like the shape of whatever had made the sound would bulge down through the plaster, as it might in an old cartoon.

The humorous image was quickly replaced by worry as Jim remembered his elderly landlady, who lived on the first floor of the brownstone, just above the basement apartment Jim called his own.

To be completely accurate, Jim occupied a corner of the brownstone's basement level. The rent was reasonable—by NYC standards—and no wonder! His living area was wedged next to a unique storage space that the building manager had told him was a book depository.

Because of fire codes and the need for multiple exit routes in the case of an emergency, his apartment had two doors: the main one leading out into the hall and one that would take him through the storage space to an exit that opened onto a recessed stairwell leading up to the back courtyard. In case his apartment door was inaccessible during a fire, he had been given a code to open the door to the storage space, but doing so would also set off the security system, alerting both his landlady and the building manager. He had been sternly warned against using that door outside an absolute emergency.

The secured storage room piqued Jim's curiosity, but not enough for him to risk setting off alarms. Its existence, however, left him with a small studio, a closet of a bathroom, and one window that gave him a ground-level view of the dingy alleyway between his building and the next.

He had been told he didn't have to worry about flooding because there were twice as many sump pumps than were needed for a basement this size—extra security for the book collection. There were also dehumidifiers running nonstop. Notably, though, none of these were in Jim's corner of the basement. Despite the building manager's assurances, he would have to sink, swim, or bail water out the little window if matters ever came to it.

All in all, the books were living large compared to Jim.

Even so, Jim didn't resent his landlady for the disparity between the book collection's accommodations and his own. If anything, he thought she was probably lonely. He'd only met her in passing, but he knew she lived alone. And while she hadn't struck him as fragile or infirm, she had to be in her midseventies.

The startling thump replayed over and over in Jim's mind, and he couldn't stop picturing commercials he had seen as a kid: an old woman lying on the floor, clutching her hip, and yelling for help in an empty house.

He knew the old bookworm liked her privacy, so he stood on his bed and strained to hear through the ceiling whether she was calling for help or moaning in pain. There might have been some shuffling footsteps overhead, but the barely there sound wasn't enough to convince Jim she was okay.

His mind made up, Jim jumped off the bed and headed toward the door. Catching sight of himself in the mirror on the door, Jim realized he looked like a wreck. His wavy brown hair was overdue for a haircut, he was in dire need of a shave, and he wore a too-small cast T-shirt from a high-school production, complete with stains from last night's ramen.

There was no helping the hair or beard, but Jim quickly changed into a cleaner shirt before heading out the door and up the stairs.

Passing a door marked *Private: Not an Entrance*, which led to the office of the bookstore that took up half the first floor, Jim stopped a few steps later in front of Ms. Barber's door.

He listened at the door for a minute before knocking loudly and listening again. When the door flew open as far as its two security chains would allow, Jim blushed; he'd had his face practically pressed up against the wood.

"Who?" his landlady exclaimed. "Oh! You're the boy from downstairs. The playwright! What's wrong? Are my books okay?" As she asked the last question, her voice pitched higher with near panic.

"They're fine, Ms. Barber," Jim assured her. "I was just checking if you were okay. I heard a loud thump and worried you had taken a fall."

The old woman smiled, blushing lightly as she looked over her shoulder into her apartment. "That wasn't me. I mean, it was me, but what you heard was a book. I needed to throw it, you see. I may have taken the effort a bit too far when I decided to climb my library ladder to do it. I'm so sorry it made you worry . . . umm, James, was it?"

"Everyone calls me Jim, ma'am. And I'm sorry; you climbed a ladder in your apartment to throw a book? Is that—"

Jim caught himself, thinking better of asking the older woman whether her actions were entirely safe. She was definitely up there in years, but she seemed spry enough.

Ms. Barber chuckled, clearly not offended. She signaled for Jim to wait a moment, then closed the door just enough to undo the chains and let him in. When Jim stepped in, his landlady was deftly entering a code in a security system panel that was bleeping at her, no doubt asking why the door had been opened unexpectedly.

"It's not one of those rickety ladders for painting," she said as her fingers flew over the buttons. "It's the rolling ladder in my library. It has handrails, and it's not steep, though I admit, carrying that book up to the top required more careful climbing than usual."

The panel stopped beeping, and Ms. Barber motioned for Jim to follow her. She led him down a hallway that opened at the far end onto a large space that had probably once been two bedrooms.

On the wall opposite the door was a series of woven tapestries—geometric, vaguely African, and at least a quarter of an inch thick. They evoked the 1970s, yet with their earthy tones, they blended right in with the classic wooden decor adorning the rest of the room. Sunshine poured in through the windows facing the walled courtyard, pooling around a plush reading chair and footstool. Near this reader's haven stood an ornate wooden desk that seemed to hold lofty expectation Jim's writing could surely never live up to.

The rest of the walls were covered floor to ceiling with shelves filled with books. As he scanned the impressive library, Jim's gaze landed on the ladder in question. Constructed of wood that practically glowed in the sunlight, the ladder was clearly designed to move along brass rails that spanned the length of the wall.

"Yes, I have," Ms. Barber said from behind him.

Jim turned to face her. "Pardon?"

"I've done the thing where you push off and ride the ladder from one end of the room to the other. It's every book lover's dream, isn't it? But I haven't done it lately, not since my hip replacement a few years back. Now, I'm a good girl, and I even put the brakes on when I climb it."

Jim smiled at the image of the woman in front of him riding the ladder around her library. He had to admit, he would have done the same if the library were his. However, since they had just met, he thought it would be too soon to ask if he could take it for a spin.

Turning away from the ladder, he gestured toward the books themselves. "May I?"

"Of course."

Ms. Barber accompanied Jim as he perused her collection. She pointed out her favorite volumes and showed him inscriptions made out to her.

That was how Jim found out his landlady had once been an editor for one of the major publishing houses in the city. He was stunned, but she only laughed and casually told him stories of how she'd personally acquired and overseen the production of numerous famous bestsellers, starting in the 1960s and spanning several decades.

By the end of the conversation, Jim was shaking his

head. "For someone who clearly loves books and has an incredible collection in her home and even more in a specially designed climate-controlled storage downstairs—why did you throw a book? What did that book do to you to deserve that kind of treatment?"

Lifting a heavy leather-bound volume from the edge of her desk, Ms. Barber offered it to Jim. "That book, my dear, is one of my favorite books in the world but also the one that frustrates me the most."

The corners of the book's spine were dented, perhaps from its flight from the top of the library ladder. When Jim flipped through it, he was surprised to find not the usual paper and print but full-sized, glossy-paged photos of typed sheets of paper, intermixed with what looked like vintage, amateur snapshots of locations all around the city.

"It was a gift upon my retirement from my dear friend Bobby," his landlady explained. "It's a collection of short stories we received over the years. They were each brilliant in their own way, but they also lacked two important things: an ending and a signature.

"I've read that book more times than I can count. Every time I do, I think to myself, 'This time, I'll figure it out. I'll get an inkling of who the author was—and why he never sent us an ending.' But then I get to the last page, and I'm no closer to the answer than I was fifty years ago. Today was not the first time I've thrown that book, and it probably won't be the last."

Jim studied the woman thoughtfully, latching on to one specific thing she'd said. "What do you mean, 'get an inkling of who the author was'? How would you do that simply by reading their work? Is that, like, some skill seasoned publishing folks acquire over time?"

Ms. Barber laughed and waved to the chair in the sunbeam. "Have a seat, Jim, and call me Dottie."

Jim readily hopped into the offered seat. It was every bit as comfy as it looked.

Dottie seated herself on the leather rolling chair behind the desk, legs crossed, back straight. Although she was dressed casually—loose linen pants, a light-gray cotton top, and a soft purple woolen shawl across her shoulders—she exuded a sense of quiet authority. It may have been the way she pointed her toes as she sat, perhaps a habit from years of wearing heels.

Jim squirreled the detail away, thinking he could include the posture as a stage direction for one of his plays.

"I'd offer you an afternoon cup of tea," Dottie said after a moment. "But my teapot is in the dishwasher, and I only own loose leaf—no bags. I swore to myself a few years ago that I would never spend time washing dishes again. I run that machine every day after my lunch, even if it only has four items in it. I have plenty of money to pay my bills, and I have never once regretted my prolonged dishwashing moratorium. It allows me more time to read."

"That's all right, Ms.—I mean, Dottie."

She pulled a silver case from the center drawer of her desk. "Do you mind if I smoke, Jim?"

"It's your house. You don't worry about the books, though?"

"They've spent more time in smoke-filled rooms and offices than you ever have." Dottie waved her hand as if to encompass the wall of books. "People only started stepping outside for their smoke breaks in the nineties. Still, I did buy this." She switched on a little device that sat next to a heavy glass ashtray.

"I promised Jorge, my building manager and a dear friend, that I would only smoke when I had a guest, and I always keep my promises. Of course, this came after he found two burns in the rug next to my reading chair when I had dozed off or just plain didn't notice I had dropped my embers. I don't have many guests, so I will take full advantage of your presence to indulge."

She took a long inhale and then blew the smoke from the side of her thin mouth toward the machine, which eagerly swallowed it up. When she set her cigarette down, the trail of smoke tried to reach up and away but was sucked into the hungry filtering device.

"Now, where were we? Oh yes, we were talking about reading, knowing the author through their writing, and how I do it."

Dottie tapped her fingertips against her lips, staring at Jim with squinted eyes and a furrowed brow, as if deciding something.

After a moment or two of silent deliberation, she finally said, "When I was younger, I didn't talk much about what happens when I read. I learned quickly that people thought it was weird—or worse, that I was delusional. But as I've gotten older, I no longer really give a damn about what people think of me. And you strike me as an open-minded young man."

Jim wasn't quite sure how she had come to that conclusion, since this was the first time they'd had a proper conversation, but he was intrigued.

"Thank you, Dottie." He leaned in, hoping to encourage her to continue.

Dottie picked up her cigarette, took a deep inhale, and then went on to explain herself. "It's not so much a skill as a gift, I think. I remember, starting back when I was just a child, that I would always get a sense of the person who wrote a book. It even happened when I read simple notes I found around the house or on my father's desk.

"At first, my mother wrote off the things I told her as the product of an overactive imagination, but then I received a birthday card from my favorite aunt. She was supposed to come see us for my seventh birthday, but my mother told me she hadn't been able to because she wasn't feeling well.

"My aunt sent me a lovely card with wishes for a happy birthday, along with a set of paper dolls to cut out and dress up. But when I read the message in her card, I started to cry. The words were happy, but I could tell my aunt was profoundly sad. I didn't know exactly why she was so sad, but I told my mother it was something to do with my aunt having lost something she loved."

Dottie stared past Jim out the window, took another drag, and then abruptly put out the cigarette.

"What my mother knew that I didn't was that my aunt had been around four months pregnant when she lost her baby. She couldn't attend my party because she was still recovering, physically and emotionally, from the loss."

"No way," Jim breathed, leaning forward with his elbows on his knees. After a moment, he cleared his throat and brushed his shaggy bangs out of his eyes as he thought about Dottie's story. "You don't think maybe you just overheard your mom talking about your aunt and her pregnancy, like when you were half asleep or something?"

Dottie waved a hand dismissively. "I don't blame your skepticism. What I glean from between the lines when I read a person's writing isn't specific enough for me to fact-check and prove things conclusively. I get impressions of what the author was feeling or bits about their personality.

"But I've always wondered what the next step in the evolution of the gift would be. If I can tell someone is in love or in pain or that they're missing their home, then can someone out there tell who they're in love with or what caused their pain or even where their home is?"

"Like a perfect reader? Someone who can read a story, and in doing so, read the mind of the person who wrote it?"

Dottie clapped her hands together. "I like that! Yes! A 'perfect reader'!"

Jim gestured to the book with the dented corners. "So, what do you get from the unfinished stories?"

"I get nothing from them. Bubkes!" Dottie threw her hands up in frustration. Then she took a deep breath and smoothed a wayward steel-gray hair behind her ear.

"Well, that's not true. I get a sense of New York. The person who wrote them feels like New York to me. And I get a sense of movement. The author doesn't like to sit still; they like to keep moving. But that's it. And not long before I retired, they stopped sending me stories.

"Sometimes, I lie in bed and think about how all these stories are frozen in time, dangling or maybe forever falling but never landing. And that's how the author is to me as well. I get vague impressions of them, but it's a version of them from twenty or more years ago. They could be a completely different person now. They could have grandchildren or might have moved to a farm in the country, or maybe they are paralyzed or in a coma."

"Or dead."

Dottie's breath escaped in a surprised exhale. Jim grimaced, regretting his offhand remark.

"The thought has occurred to me," Dottie said before he could apologize. "We are all getting older." She looked down at her hands and turned them slowly, examining the palms and then the backs.

"My friend Bobby passed away six years ago," she added in a small voice. "He made it through the HIV outbreak that took so many of his friends in the eighties. He met someone wonderful to spend his life with and lived past seventy, but he was struck down by lung cancer within three months of being diagnosed."

Dottie paused, then pointed at the book. "He wrote an inscription on the inside of the front cover when he gave that to me."

Jim opened the book and turned to the front as Dottie sniffed and discreetly dabbed at the corner of each eye with her shawl.

Dearest Dottie,

I miss our days rummaging through the slush piles! You've come a long way, baby! You made a name for yourself and opened lots of doors for others along the way. Enjoy your retirement. Here's a little light reading for all the free time you're going to have on your hands.

Love always,

Bobby

PS I still think we'll find 'em, kid!

"It was Bobby and me, Ted, and Gail, thick as thieves back in those early days." Dottie turned a picture frame on her desk so Jim could see it. Two women and two men smiled back from the black-and-white photo. One was clearly a younger Dottie.

"Bobby left Tandem Bike for agenting work, frustrated by traditional publishing, while I stayed on and tried to progress things from the inside. He got a lot of queer writers their breaks.

"Gail left just before Bobby did. Despite being a child of old money, she never let her family's wealth go to her head, wanting to be her own woman. She bounced between independent feminist lit magazines and publishers for years, and then used her trust fund to found her own publishing house. She put out some excellent books that the bigger imprints wouldn't touch. She met a lovely Japanese man at a Buddhist temple in California, had a few babies, and now they have a load of grandkids, two of which still run her publishing house. We email one another, talk on the phone sometimes, and of course, send each other books.

"Ted—he was always an odd one to pin down. He came off as a rough-and-tumble guy who looked like he belonged at a construction site rather than with his nose in a book. In fact, he did work construction to put himself through night courses at NYU. He told us he spent his lunches, hard hat and all, in the closest library to each job site. He used to joke that he only managed to get his job at Tandem Bike because he flirted with the receptionist and wrote her a sonnet inside a book of matches."

Dottie smiled wistfully, lost in memory.

"Ted adored poetry. He read it and studied it, but he also ate, slept, and drank it. He wrote some but was shy about sharing it. When it came to poetry, I sometimes wondered if Ted had a touch of the same gift I do. But I don't think that was the case. He was just a very open person, despite his strict Italian-Catholic Brooklyn upbringing.

"Then, well, he tried acid in the midsixties, and he really liked it. He bought an old van and set off on the road. We lost track of him after that, but I swear I saw him dancing naked in a documentary about Woodstock. And there were postcards sent to Gail from all over the world, never signed. We knew they were from Ted, though, because they always had poetry scribbled on the back. Haiku, monoku, and in recent years, he experimented with blackout poetry."

"She's still getting them? After all these years?"

"Less frequently." Dottie shrugged. "But still about one or two a year. If the poetry wasn't enough, Ted always had a distinctly boxy way of carefully printing with small letters." She pantomimed printing with an imaginary pen and deep concentration, then broke into a light chuckle. "And of course, I could tell.

"He loved her, you know. He never told her out loud, but it was there in every line. Even without my gift, Gail knew. They were each rebels in their own way, just different kinds of rebels. She needed roots and stillness; he needed to fly."

"And what about you, Ms. Bar—Dottie?" Jim quickly corrected. "What did you do after retirement?"

"Oh, I did well for myself at Tandem Bike; otherwise, I wouldn't have stayed as long as I did. When I retired, I bought this building for a song because the neighborhood was much rougher than it is now. I used to live in the penthouse, but it was just too much space for me; I only need room for me and my books. So I moved down here, where I have fewer stairs to climb and the back garden to enjoy on nice days.

"These days I read, and I'm part owner of Flights of Fancy."

"Oh! The bookstore next door!" Jim cast a glance over his shoulder at the wall covered in tapestries. "Flights of Fancy is really cool inside. That mobile in the back room is incredible. Certainly a good investment for a bibliophile."

"Indeed." Dottie smiled. "Philip, the main owner, calls me Aunt Dottie. Bobby and his sweetheart took Philip under their wing when he was a teenage runaway. They helped put him through school, and he followed in Bobby's bookish footsteps. He came to me with a business plan about ten years back, wanting to rent the space next door, but he didn't have quite enough revenue to get off the ground. So I invested, and Flights of Fancy Books was born.

"Now, I get new books for free, and I only assert my opinion when I want them to invite this author or that poet to come do a reading. I'm quite comfortable, and"—she gestured toward her walls of books—"I'm never lonely."

She returned her focus to Jim. "What about you? I assume the theater brought you to New York?"

Jim sat up straighter, suddenly feeling like he was being interviewed. "Yes, I moved here because of the theater, though I'd always wanted to live in New York. I never really felt like I belonged in Ohio. There was nothing traumatic about my childhood; my life in Ohio just always felt like an ill-fitting, scratchy sweater. I saved up to move by living with my parents and working two jobs, but I ended up coming here before I could bank as much as I'd hoped, because my play was chosen for a one-week run at the Cherry Lane Theatre."

"Oh, that's a lovely venue! I used to go there a lot in the seventies. The young man I was seeing at the time did their lighting, so I got to sit with him during shows. Saw Judd Hirsch, Olympia Dukakis—lots of big names came through that little converted-warehouse space. There was something else big I saw there . . . oh, damn it; I can't remember now." Looking frustrated, Dottie waved for Jim to continue. "Anyway, you were saying?"

"Well, I figured that break was a sign, and I made the move. The production went really well and got good reviews. I think that bit of press helped get one of my other pieces picked up for a festival of one-act plays at Playwrights Horizons in the spring. In the meantime, I'm making a little from writing freelance theater reviews, doing editing gigs, and publishing pieces in anthologies used for theater classes. It's not quite making a New York living, but I've got enough to finish my lease here, and hopefully something else will come my way before—"

"*Godspell!*" Dottie exclaimed. "How could I forget *Godspell?* My boyfriend hummed 'Day by Day' for weeks. I think it contributed to our breakup, actually."

"Ah, yes." Jim nodded. "Definitely one of the risks of working in theater. I'm sure *Godspell* took out many a relationship."

Dottie chuckled, then smiled wryly. "I liked your one about the funeral. It struck a good balance between bitter and sweet, and the humor was sharp and well-timed."

Jim's eyes widened. "You . . . you know *Cold Thursday for a Wake?*"

"Don't act so surprised, Junior." Dottie's lips pulled up in a satisfied smirk. "I know how to search the internet, and I looked up all the applicants for the basement studio. While I was doing that, I ordered a copy of each of your plays. They're why you got the place when several other folks offered me much more than the rate I listed. I didn't want the studio used as a short-term sublet for travelers; I wanted someone living there who had a desire to be part of New York."

"Wow." Jim couldn't help how low and stunned that one word came out. "Thank you, and thank you for reading my work.

"So, umm . . . what did you think of the other plays?"

"I think you're still finding your voice, but you have a good knack for dialogue and nuanced stage direction." Dottie nodded decisively.

"Thank you," Jim repeated. "I think good stage direction is sometimes as important as the dialogue itself. And did my writing tell you anything about me?"

Dottie's smile softened. "You had your heart broken around the time you wrote the play set on the boat. You have a good relationship with your parents, but you especially adore your mother. And you love hazelnut-flavored coffee."

Jim felt some of the color drain from his face, quickly followed by a fierce blush and possible heart palpitations. "How could you possibly know all that just from reading my plays?"

"I could feel it as I read your words. Also, you grind and brew your flavored beans every morning between seven and eight, and the smell wafts up through the wall vents. It's delightful. Where do you get your beans?"

Jim couldn't help but laugh. "You can't tell from reading the signature on my rent check every month?"

Dottie joined in Jim's laughter. "Ha! Oh, you are a cheeky one when you want to be!"

Once she caught her breath, Dottie crossed the room to where Jim sat and, her knees audibly crackling, carefully lowered herself to sit on the stepstool beside him. She lifted his hand in her cool, soft-fingered grasp and patted it. "I'm glad you moved in, and I'm glad you came to check on me and visit."

When she stood, Jim could tell their visit was at an end.

As they walked back to the door, he ventured, "How about I make you a deal? I'll bring you a bag of those hazelnut beans, and you promise me you won't climb the ladder just to throw a book again. If any books need a good roughing up, you bang on the floor three times, and I'll come up and throw them for you."

"Deal!" Dottie held out her hand. Her grip was firm and resolute, no doubt honed from decades of closing contracts with authors and their agents.

Just before closing the door, Dottie called out, "Oh! Next time you drop into Flights of Fancy, go find the plaque that explains the story of the mobile. It's a tribute to Bobby and his partner, Jeff, inspired by the book that brought them together. Their romance was like a fairy tale—definitely one for the books."

What's Your Favorite Book, Honey?

New York City, 1986

Bobby pulled up the hood of his raincoat and shouldered through the midsummer storm. Though heavy enough to require a hood, the rain brought the city no relief from the heat. As soon as the clouds cleared, steam rose from the asphalt, and the thick air filled with the scent of dumpster-stench tea.

That morning, Bobby had almost grabbed one of his bright floral-print shirts from those carefree summers on Fire Island, but he'd ultimately decided against it. His last memories of the island involved passing around the *Times* with his close friends and poring over a story about a new, rare cancer that had just been identified, inflicting forty-one homosexual men. The article had described the disease's telltale bruise-like lesions and the quick decline and death that followed.

By the end of that weekend, the relaxed air of Fire Island had changed. Questions like "Why don't you come back to my place tonight, handsome?" or "Who's up for moonlight skinny-dipping?" had been replaced with desperation: "Oh my god, what am I going to do? If I get sick and my family finds out I'm gay, I'll die alone."

"The doctors will get a handle on this in no time, right? Right?"

The terror might have felt premature on Fire Island, but it hadn't been misplaced. So many had already had the mark of death on them. It was hard to take in.

Not long ago, Bobby wouldn't have put much thought into what shirt he pulled from his closet, but that morning, he'd ended up returning the magenta hibiscus on turquoise background to its hanger. Wearing it now just seemed disrespectful, especially considering where he was going.

Shaking off the rain as he entered the lobby of St. Vincent's Hospital, Bobby nodded to the nun manning the visitor's desk and signed in. "How are you today, Sister?"

A black-and-white veil wreathed her face, but it didn't hide the pinched smile she gave Bobby in return. "The rain is making my knees ache, but this, too, shall pass."

They knew each other well by then, given how often he came to visit. When Bobby had first started coming to the hospital, the sister had given him the cold shoulder. With the Catholic attitude toward homosexuality, it was no surprise. But over time, the nuns had softened to their young male patients and the people who came to visit them.

Suffering has a way of tearing down walls between people. Nodding to the sister, Bobby moved forward.

Entering the elevator, he was relieved to be its sole passenger. It gave him space to collect his thoughts and muster a smile. He took a few deep, slow breaths, appreciating every one of them. Over the past few years, he'd seen so many men—painfully young, beautiful men—die of pneumonia, gasping for breath.

He pushed the images aside and fidgeted with the clasps on the little leather overnight bag he had strapped over his shoulder, silently reviewing its contents. There was a sachet of lilac flowers for Mickey, who said lilac was his favorite scent in the world; four pairs of warm wool socks for anyone who wanted them; two boxes of mixed truffles from the candy counter at Macy's to distribute all around; and an extra-large sleeve of candied pecans from a street cart he had passed on his way to the hospital.

They were still warm.

The pecans he would leave for the nurses. A thank-you for the ones who cared—and a subliminal bribe for those who hated getting stuck with a shift on the AIDS ward.

Please. Please give a damn about these dying men.

The bell dinged, the doors opened, and Bobby stepped through them with a smile firmly in place and a consciously forced spring in his step. Within seconds, though, his smile was genuine. Music drifted from the nurse's station, which meant Patricia was the duty nurse. She wore an aura of joy the way others wore perfume, and it trailed behind her, lingering on everything she touched.

Although her younger brother's death had brought her to the AIDS ward, his passing had been her rebirth, as she explained to anyone who wanted to know.

"My brother and me sang together in the church choir every Sunday since we was little," she would say, a hint of her inherited Southern drawl seeping in. "Freddy got all the solos, though; he had a gorgeous voice. So, imagine the family's surprise when their only son—their beautiful and blessed Freddy—died from AIDS."

Freddy had worked at a nice hotel in Manhattan, where he'd risen through the ranks from bellboy to overnight head concierge in the span of a few years. He would bring home stories of meeting rock stars and heads of state and about the tips and gifts he received.

What Freddy's family never knew was that he didn't work six nights a week, as he told them, but the standard five. On the sixth night, he transformed himself into Madame Freddi Fierce and graced the stages of all the best drag clubs in New York. On the weekends, while Freddy might say he was training staff in a new hotel opening out of town, Madame Freddi would put on shows in other cities or flee to beach towns and discos, where he could trade his church clothes for short shorts and silk shirts tied above his belly button.

He had led one life in the closet and another on the stage.

Patricia said she had wept twice at his passing: once for losing her brother and again for having never really known him.

So, she had gone searching for him.

Patricia went to all the clubs where Freddy had performed, met his friends, was gifted with polaroids of him in full drag regalia, as well as candid dressing-room shots, his work blazer draped over the back of a chair as he applied glittery false eyelashes. She soaked in the stories he hadn't been able to tell, and parts of her inner self were nourished in a way they had never been before.

In discovering her brother, Patricia had started to think about her place in the world and how she could make a difference. She attended rallies and wrote passionate letters to politicians. She made signs for protests on her days off and wrote Freddy's name on the back of every one of them.

As Bobby rounded the corner from the elevators, he

found Patricia blasting "It's Raining Men" by The Weather Girls from a big boom box at the nurse's station, singing at the top of her lungs in a voice honed over decades of hymn practices. Wearing a shiny bright-yellow raincoat, she waved a clear child-size, dome-shaped umbrella with one hand and spun a skinny young man in a wheelchair with the other.

Even though she almost ran Bobby over, he couldn't help but join in the singing. As the song ended, he gasped out, "You're going to hurt somebody with that driving of yours, lady!"

The man in the wheelchair waved the umbrella he'd commandeered Patricia at Bobby. "Sweetie, this is AIDS land! She can't hurt us; we're already dancing on death's door! But I'm going to meet the big guy with a wink, a smile, and my dancing shoes on!"

Patricia smiled affectionately as one of the other nurses wheeled the man away. Then she stole a quick look in her compact and produced a pick from her pocket to fix her hair.

When she was done, Bobby slid the paper cone of roasted nuts across the counter of the nurse's station. Patricia tsked but opened the gift. Closing her eyes, she took a long sniff and popped a pecan into her mouth.

"Mmm, just like Aunt June sends us from the tree in her backyard in Georgia. How you doing, baby?"

"All right."

Actually, Bobby had had a damn good week. He'd sold one of his client's manuscripts in an upper-five-figure deal, he was in negotiations with a major TV network for another client's book to be made into a miniseries, and he'd just made an offer of representation to a young writer whose manuscript was so gripping, Bobby had read it all in one go. But he never felt right bringing up such successes when he visited St. Vincent's. He was one of the lucky ones. He was healthy. Anything beyond that was bragging.

Patricia might have guessed some of what Bobby was feeling, because she didn't push. She nodded and waved him off to go make his rounds.

Bobby made his way around the ward, stopping in rooms where he knew the patients and others where he didn't, dropping off the little gifts he'd brought. The socks he gave to the quieter guys who didn't get many visitors. For one of them, who had his mottled feet propped up, Bobby put the socks on for him.

The guy started to cry. "I haven't been touched by a man in what seems like ages. The lady nurses are nice, but it isn't the same. It's silly, I know." He tried to wipe away his tears with the back of his hand, only to have to switch to the hand that didn't have IV tubes sticking out of it.

Bobby pulled a plastic chair to the end of the man's bed and, sitting, massaged his feet for about twenty minutes without saying a word. The man smiled, sighed, wept some more, and then finally fell comfortably asleep.

Once Bobby was sure the man wouldn't wake up, he gathered his things and slipped out of the room, making sure the door didn't close too loudly behind him. Satisfied, Bobby turned.

And ran straight into another man who was rounding the corner.

The rain-damaged brown-paper bag the man was carrying ripped and dropped its contents to the tiled floor. Books thumped and scattered. Apologizing simultaneously, Bobby and the man he'd just run into bent to retrieve the mix of used paperbacks and hardcovers, only to crack their skulls together good and hard. They both stood then, clutching their foreheads, halfway between laughing and cursing.

"You okay?" Bobby managed.

"Yeah, will probably get a goose egg outta the deal, but okay," replied the younger man, his Brooklyn accent coming through loud and clear.

They locked gazes, and the world of death, disease, and little cups of green gelatin fell away. They stood like that for several moments, until one last book fell from the bag the nameless man still held, slapping against the floor tiles.

Coming back to himself, the younger man held up a hand before Bobby could bend to retrieve the scattered books. "You stay; I'll go down first." He squinted, seeming to realize the possible innuendo of his statement, but shrugged it off and crouched to start picking up his books.

Bobby collected a few that had slid away from the rest in the commotion. There was neither rhyme nor reason to the titles, it seemed. They comprised poetry, pulpy sci-fi, a few classics, and even an ornate leather-bound edition of *Le Petit Prince* in the original French.

Bobby held out the stack of books. "You've got varied tastes."

"Oh, they aren't for me; these are for the boys." The younger man was trying to wrap the books in the ripped paper bag.

"I think that bag is done for. But I can help you with your deliveries, if you'd like. I'm Bobby."

The other man juggled the books to one side in an attempt to extend his hand. "Jeff," he supplied with a smile, just barely freeing one hand enough to hold out his fingers for a little shake.

Introductions made, Jeff led the way through several rooms, making deliveries to each. Some of the patients were sitting up and chatting with visitors: animated, happily sharing about improved T cell counts, talking hopefully about being back home in a few days. They expressed gratitude for Jeff's deliveries and how the books had kept them sane during the long hospital hours spent fighting infection. Other rooms were quieter, with no talk of leaving, but the books were still appreciated.

Jeff handed one man some paperbacks with various versions of spacemen and phallic-shaped rocket ships on the covers. "Is this the kind of thing you were looking for?"

"Perfect!" The man's voice sounded far too young and strong to be coming from his gaunt, gray face. "I've been having crazy, vivid dreams lately about traveling in space. These"—his eyes danced from cover to cover—"make great fuel for the fantasies. Don't tell the Sisters of Charity, but I've got a joint stashed in my shoe under the bed. After dinner, I think I'll smoke it out the window, settle in with a good read, play some Bowie on the Walkman, and traipse the galaxies for the rest of the evening. Not a bad way to spend the night!"

"Hell, I might do the same!" Bobby dug in his bag. "Want a champagne truffle for your flight, Captain Stardust?"

"Don't mind if I do!" With a skeletal hand, the man daintily picked a pink-paper-skirted chocolate from the box Bobby offered him.

From there, they made several more deliveries. Even after enough books had been handed out that it was no longer necessary for Jeff and Bobby to share the load, they still stuck together.

When they came to a room whose door was firmly shut, Jeff stopped Bobby with a gentle hand on his chest, blushing.

"I better do this one without you, friend. He's older than most here, and well, he's struggling. He's mad as hell—like, all the time. He even yells at Patricia, and she's an angel. But I noticed he always has on a Yankee's cap. And the gym bag in the closet has reddish dirt on the bottom and a baseball glove shoved in the side, as if someone packed the bag for him after he got admitted and they grabbed the first thing they could find.

"My bet is he was deep, deep in the closet, a real man's man type, and this is blowing his whole world apart. I could be imagining it, but I think there's a tan line on his finger from where a wedding ring used to be. Anyway, I brought him a book about DiMaggio, with lots of pictures and stats. Everyone likes DiMaggio, right? Even my Irish grandmother used to say, 'Oh my, that's a good-looking Italian boy!' So, I'm going to give this one more try."

"One more try?" Bobby asked. "Has he run you out of there before?"

"Last time I was here, he threw a pitcher of ice water at me," Jeff admitted. "For as sick as he is, he's got one hell of a throwing arm, and he's got a fire in his belly that may help him along the way. If he could just let some of us in, maybe he won't hate himself so much. Maybe he won't have to die alone."

Jeff took a deep breath, squared his shoulders, and entered the room.

Bobby leaned his head toward the door. He could hear Jeff's soft voice, like a mailman placating a chained guard dog. Then there was a bark and a grumbled question, followed by quiet. Just when Bobby's heart was beginning to beat faster with worry, he heard the low rumble of conversation. Maybe? There were definitely no projectile pitchers of water, at least.

A few minutes later, Jeff came out, smiling ear to ear as soon as he cleared the threshold. "Success!" he whispered, motioning Bobby around the next corner.

"So, he wasn't happy to see me, of course. I skipped the small talk and just held the book out to him, told him I hoped he liked it. He was skeptical, but he took the book. Then he actually started paging through it and asked me if I liked baseball. I told him I played Little League as a kid and still went to the occasional game.

"Without looking up, he asked, 'Yankees or Mets?' I told him Yankees, and I think maybe half his mouth smiled. He flipped through the pictures, then held one up to show me. It was of DiMaggio's streak in forty-one. He said his dad managed to get one ticket to a home game during it, when he was just five years old. Said his old man bribed the guy at the gate to let him bring his kid in too, told the guy he would sit his kid on his lap the whole time.

"It worked.

"He said it was one of the best days of his life, and his eyes started to get glossy. So I just told him I would look for some more baseball books for him and started to go. Didn't want to press my luck. He waved the book and nodded to me as I left. I think that's the closest I'll get to a thank you from him. But that's big progress, don't you think?"

Bobby had never wanted to kiss a man he'd just met so badly before. Jeff's triumph shone from him like a beam from a lighthouse, and Bobby was drawn to the brightness.

Then the reality of where they were and why caught up with him.

They were in the AIDS wing of St. Vincent's, and almost everyone around them was dying. The man with the DiMaggio book, Captain Stardust, even the guys who were lucky enough to go home for a while. And this beautiful man standing in front of Bobby—this man with the freckles, the books, and the brightest smile Bobby had ever seen—was he dying too?

Jeff reached up with one hand but stopped short of touching Bobby's cheek. "Hey, where'd you go? It's like the clouds just rolled in and stole the sunshine that was just here."

Bobby put his practiced smile back in place like the mask it was and shrugged off the question. He handed back the last few books he'd been holding, then looked at his watch and made an excuse to get going. He wasn't going to look back, but he couldn't help himself. "You're doing really good things, you and your little book-delivery service. It was nice meeting you, Jeff."

"Nice meeting you too, Bobby," came the reply as Bobby rounded a corner and made for the nearest exit.

Back out in the humid, post-rain heat, Bobby found himself walking away from the hospital as fast as possible, weaving through a throng of fellow New Yorkers. He had the urge to break into a run—shed his bag of gifts for the dying, shed his carefully chosen clothes—run right to the Hudson and plunge in. A cold, shocking cleansing.

He didn't fear infection; it wasn't that at all. He feared caring for new people. New people became names on the mental list of those Bobby would have to keep tabs on, asking himself such things as "When was the last time I saw him?" or "Was his name in the obits when I was out of town?" every time they came to mind.

Winded and sweating, Bobby dropped onto a bench

in a little patch of shade, still in sight of the hospital. He let his leather bag fall to the wet concrete between his feet and took slow, purposeful breaths. After a moment, he reached into the side pocket of his bag for a handkerchief to wipe his brow with, only for his fingers to encounter something else.

A small, ornate copy of *Le Petit Prince*.

Bobby paused, wondering how the book had even gotten into his bag. Had he slipped it in there earlier without thinking to make carrying the stack of books easier?

Shaking his head, as if that would shake the memory loose, Bobby opened the book and leafed through it. His high school French had never resulted in fluency, but he recognized a few words here and there, and the illustrations helped. A few pages in, the simple story of *Le Petit Prince* came back to him.

The first time Bobby had read *Le Petit Prince*, he'd thought he would always like to be able to pass the test of the narrator. The pilot asked all new acquaintances what they saw in the plain line drawing of what looked like a hat but which he declared to be a picture of a snake that had swallowed an elephant. Only those who saw the ill-fated elephant and stuffed snake did he deem worthy of talking to about wonderfully fanciful things. The little prince passed the test, and so their friendship was struck.

Although the prince didn't have freckles or the faint beginnings of smiling crow's-feet around his eyes, he reminded Bobby of Jeff. The comparison set off a hollow pang in Bobby's chest, and half unsure why he did it, Bobby continued to slowly peck his way through the French, reading what he could.

He lingered over the chapter about the mapmaker who never traveled and knew very little about the world he was recording. Although Bobby knew from literature and philosophy classes that the mapmaker was a symbolic warning about becoming too specialized in one area, he saw himself in the old man, hunched over his maps. Bobby celebrated and championed projects that took risks and made big leaps, yet here he was.

Sitting on a lonely bench, hiding from a new experience.

From the prince and the mapmaker, Bobby's mind raced back to a different story he'd first read some twenty-odd years before, one about a shy businessman in love with his milkman. Albert had never shared his feelings. The unfinished story left off with Albert still sadly loving his milkman from afar.

Bobby found himself looking back up Twelfth Street, to the white sides of St. Vincent's reflecting the sunlight. The next moment, he was on his feet, walking back to the hospital. Then jogging, then flat-out running. He kept running all the way in, through the doors, past the sister at the desk, to the elevator, where he slid in sideways through the closing doors just in time.

Patricia was leaning against the back wall of the elevator with two armfuls of cellophane-wrapped flowers that looked a wee bit past their prime—probably unsold items from the gift shop on the ground floor. "Ooh! Where are you running to, Bobby? Leave your wallet someplace up on the ward?"

"Nope. I, umm . . ." Bobby shifted his weight from one foot to the other. "I'm trying to be brave."

"Well, I'm sure I don't know what you mean by 'trying.' You come here every week, like clockwork, and you do what you can for these boys. You don't have to do that, but you do. I mean, at least I get a paycheck out of the deal!

Every one of the volunteers, those who do and don't have AIDS themselves, are the bravest people I know. It's the first time in history a community has banded together to take care of their own health like this. And don't get me started on the ones who put themselves on the front lines at protests, training on how to get arrested without hopefully getting beat in the process, all while still keeping their wits about them enough to get in sound bites to the press. Woo!"

Bobby smiled at Patricia.

"What? Is my hair sticking out funny?"

Still smiling, Bobby leaned in and gave her a big smack of a kiss on the cheek. The elevator dinged, and the doors opened. Bobby helped the blushing nurse carry the flowers to the sink of the ward's kitchenette and got two pitchers off the high shelf when she asked him to.

He tried his best to be nonchalant as Patricia filled the pitchers with water. "So, is that guy with the books, Jeff, still around?"

"Oh, Jeffy?" she asked, arranging flowers. "Bless his heart, he was looking pretty tired last I saw him. He must scour every secondhand bookstore and thrift shop in the Village looking for books the patients ask him for. He told me everyone should have their favorite book to comfort them when they're dying. Sometimes, he stays long hours, sitting vigil, reading to them. He's a good boy. Big heart on him. Not sure if he's still here; you could have a look."

Bobby helped Patricia carry the flowers back to the nurse's station, then carefully made his way around the floor, looking for Jeff. Every time he rounded a corner, his heart sped up a little at the possibility of catching sight of him.

Several minutes of searching later, Bobby was just

about ready to call it a day, disappointed but holding out hope that he would run into the regular visitor again, when he heard, "What's your favorite book, honey?" from a doorway to his left.

Bobby peeked through the gap where the door had been left partly open. There was Jeff, bent way over the bed of a patient to hear the faint, wheezing voice of the man on oxygen.

"Oh, that's a good one." Jeff reached out to smooth the man's thin, blond hair. "What? No, don't be silly. I'll find it for you. And if I don't get back in time, remember, the brain is an amazing thing. I firmly believe that everything we have ever read is still stored away up here." Jeff tapped his temple "Maybe not word for word, but the way it changed us, it's up here. So don't you worry."

Jeff spent another few moments holding the man's hand, then quietly exited the room. His expression transformed from tired to wide-eyed when he saw Bobby there. "Bobby! I thought you had an appointment to get to!"

"I lied," Bobby admitted around a lump in his throat. "I didn't have anywhere I had to be. But that's neither here nor there." He offered him the ornate leather-bound hardback. "Jeff, did you happen to slip this book into my bag by accident?"

"Oh! *Le Petit Prince*! I was wondering where that got off to! No, I haven't the foggiest how it got in your bag. It's, um, my book, actually. I found it at a little hole-in-the-wall used bookstore I hit on the way here. It's my favorite book. I must have at least a dozen copies of it at my place."

Smiling wider than he had in a long time, Bobby took a deep breath. "Jeff, do you like pot roast, by any chance? I know a diner that serves one hell of a pot roast."

All the Books

New York City, 2018

Jim wrote scenes, he went to see plays he could afford or could score comped tickets to, he submitted reviews to publications, and he tried to network with New York theater society. Sometimes he got paid; sometimes he didn't. He remained anxious about his dwindling savings and whether he would be able to afford to stay in New York. He ate cheap slices of pizza and cheap bowls of ramen, he grabbed discounted bags of bruised fruit from the corner grocer that boasted being there for more than sixty years, and he chastised himself for occasionally splurging on expensive coffee.

Every morning, when he brewed his fresh-ground hazelnut beans, Jim thought of Dottie. He hoped she was well, but he hesitated to go see her again. He felt more than a little exposed after his last visit, and he wasn't sure how to classify her "gift."

Was it something supernatural? Or some next step in the evolution of the communication portion of the human brain? Could it be a skill she'd developed from reading so much and getting to know the people who wrote throughout her lifetime?

The only other option was one Jim didn't even want to entertain. He didn't like to consider that his landlady might be in the beginning stages of dementia, her story of "knowing" things just a delusion.

Steaming mug in hand, he looked at the extra bag of coffee beans he'd bought on a whim a few days ago. A direct deposit for an article he'd written had hit his bank account, so Jim had been, relatively speaking, a little flush with pocket change. But once the bag was purchased, it just sat on his counter, slumped over and lonely, instead of being delivered to its intended recipient.

Making up his mind to go visit Dottie, Jim shook his head, drained his mug, and set it down.

He took a shower in his tiny stall and got dressed in something a little neater than a T-shirt. Then he popped across the road to the gift shop that boasted a lone bakery case featuring a rotating array of items from home bakers trying to make it in the big city. As the lady wrapped his box of blueberry crumb cake, Jim thought about how everyone in New York was looking for their big break.

Gifts in hand, Jim crossed back to his building and went right to Dottie's place, knocking on the door. It felt weirdly like picking up a girl for the first time, even though this was definitely not a date and he wasn't taking her anywhere.

It was odd. His previous visit with Dottie had felt almost familiar, as if they weren't meeting for the first time but rather getting reacquainted after a long absence. It was as if the friendship had already been there; they were just catching up on the details.

After some moments of no response, Jim knocked

again a little louder. He was just contemplating whether it would be rude to knock a third time—and if he should call the building manager to check on Dottie—when he heard slow footsteps. The door was unlocked and opened cautiously.

There was Dottie, peaking around the edge of the door. Her hair was disheveled, and she wore a giant sweater over plaid pajamas that were threadbare at the edges. She smiled but didn't make a motion to open the door wider.

"Oh, Jim! It's you! And you brought me coffee!" The words were followed by a chuckle that turned into a light cough.

Jim's apology for bothering her was already on his lips when she cut him off.

"I'm sorry; I'm not dressed. Some days, I feel like a million bucks, and others, I don't. Today,"—she smoothed down her wispy gray hair—"I'm a bit of a mess, aren't I?"

"I can come back another time," Jim offered.

"No, no, you come in." Spying the box in Jim's other hand, Dottie craned her neck to get a glimpse of the confections inside through the clear plastic window. "Oh, you brought cake too! I've never met a cake I didn't like."

Closing the door, she undid the chains and was already walking toward the kitchen as Jim let himself the rest of the way in. She wore moccasins, he noted, lined with real fur.

"I'll get out the plates and things; you get a pot of coffee going," Dottie directed when Jim caught up to her.

There was an old manual cast-iron grinder next to a shiny new coffee maker, all chrome with a digital control display. Setting down the coffee and package of crumb cake, Jim fiddled with the grinder. To his credit, he managed to figure it out without help, only spilling a small smattering of coffee beans on the counter in the process.

While the coffee brewed, Dottie put out a spread of the cake, coffee condiments, and cut fruit, which she transferred from a plastic container into a nicer bowl. Sitting down, she cut a generous slice of the blueberry cake for herself and one for Jim, then took a few pieces of fruit.

Only as Dottie tucked into her breakfast did a tightness Jim hadn't recognized unwind within him, an unnamed worry he'd had for Dottie's well-being.

"So, how are you today?" he asked before taking his first bite. "And sorry, again, for waking you."

"Oh, I was up," Dottie said dismissively. "I was reading. It's just been one of those mornings where the reality of my own mortality weighs on me. You know, the usual morning for someone over eighty."

"You don't look a day over—"

Dottie raised an eyebrow so sharply, Jim paused, and now that he'd hesitated, there was no right way to end the sentence. Instead, he ran his fork though the side of his cake, shoved an impolite—and irresponsibly sized—portion into his mouth, and mumbled around it.

"You say the sweetest things!" Dottie responded sarcastically, even as she laughed.

Jim smiled, still working on the forkful of coffee cake, and Dottie had another laugh. Watching her, Jim thought he caught a glimpse of her younger self.

The coffee gurgled to its completion, and Dottie got up to fill two mugs, breaking the moment.

Jim finally managed to swallow. "Nice moccasins."

"Thanks." Dottie handed Jim a mug. "They're Alaskan moose hide trimmed with beaver fur, from a friend whose book I published."

She drank her coffee black, nodded approvingly at the flavor, and didn't give Jim a judgmental look when he put two sugar cubes and a big splash of cream in his.

After another appreciative sip, Dottie lowered her mug to the table. "So, are you going to renew your lease in two months? Has New York been kind enough to you?"

Jim offered her a weary half smile. "To be honest, even with the very reasonable rent here—which I am extremely grateful for—my bank account is dwindling faster than I'd planned. I'll probably have to move outside the city. And by outside the city, I mean Jersey."

Gasping, Dottie clutched invisible pearls. "Jersey? Oh no, that won't do. Once you've lived in the city, you can't become part of the bridge-and-tunnel crowd. Maybe you can find work at one of the theaters or somewhere else—something part-time that will still leave you with time to write?"

"I don't know, Dottie," he said wistfully. "If I picked up a job as a waiter or something, it still wouldn't be enough for me to stay. I need a decent, reliable wage, supplemented by my royalties, to make a go of it. My dad has a college friend who runs a building management business in Jersey and owns a few of his own apartment buildings. Dad swears he's not a slumlord, and he's willing to give me a job in the office and set me up with a little place in one of his buildings. The rent will be reduced even more if I cover for the super sometimes."

Jim hated saying it all out loud. He wanted to make it in New York. Moving, even if it was just over the river to Jersey, felt like a failure.

Dottie took it all in, her face fixed with an intensely focused frown. "There are jobs other than waiter in this city, you know. Have you thought about working for the city in some capacity? Good wages, union support, and a full benefits plan."

"Like a sanitation worker? I hear the waiting list for those jobs is huge. Besides, I was a BFA English and drama major. I'm not qualified for anything in a municipal office."

"I've heard it said that New York is the biggest little town in the world. You always need to know somebody to get in anywhere." Dottie took another sip of her coffee. "Luckily, you know someone who has connections and who is fond enough of you to want to keep you living in her basement."

"That makes you sound like a serial killer, Dottie. And you know people at the sanitation department?"

She chuckled, eyes sparkling. "Oh goodness, no; I'm not *that* well connected. But I do know book people. Library book people, to be more precise, and you happen to have the fact you worked at your college library on your LinkedIn profile."

He flushed, and Dottie chuckled again, even as she waved away anything he might have said in response or protest. Then she went and retrieved her address book, a pen, and a thick piece of monogrammed paper. Jim hadn't seen an address book with alphabetical tabs since the one that had sat next to his grandmother's landline on the little table she'd dedicated solely for phone usage. He couldn't help staring at it as Dottie wrote down the name, phone number, and email of someone working at the main branch of the New York Public Library.

When she handed him the paper, Jim thanked her several times in succession. The expensive letterhead felt so good in his hand, he didn't have the heart to fold it and stick it in his pocket, so he carefully laid it to the side while he finished his cake and coffee.

After a moment, he pointed at the book with his fork. "You have a working knowledge of online professional social networking platforms, but you still use a hard copy address book?"

"There's something lovely about writing out the names of your friends and colleagues, in your own hand, on actual paper, and then flipping through and remembering all the characters, both major and minor, who play a part in the story of your own life."

Jim nodded, setting his fork down on his plate. "Thank you again, Dottie. If you don't mind my asking, what had you feeling so existentially sad earlier?"

Eyes on her plate, Dottie used her fingers to collect the remaining crumbs of her blueberry cake and licked them clean. "So, I didn't distract you from that episode with my cute furry moccasins and my offer to help you get a job?"

"Nope!" Jim slurped the last of his coffee loudly, then hopped up to get the pot and give them both a refill.

"It's silly, really, to get upset and despondent over something so . . . laughably unrealistic yet so mundane all at the same time. Every book lover says it at one time or another, don't they? That they want to read 'all the books'? Yet no one ever entertains the notion that they'll have time to. For that matter, think of all the written words lost to decay and fire and time before I ever even learned how to read! The tragedy of the burning of Alexandria alone! And then all the books that were burned by the Nazis and the Fascists, *yimach shemam ve-zichram!*"

Jim tipped his head, confused by her passionate turn of phrase.

"It's a Hebrew curse used only on the worst enemies. It means 'may their names and memories be obliterated.'"

"Mmm, very fitting, considering how many lives and how much knowledge they erased." He held back the urge to ask about Dottie's family history, whether she'd lost anyone in the Holocaust. From the vehemence she spoke the phrase with, he felt he knew the answer.

Dottie grew quiet, a faraway look on her face. After a few moments, she said, "You always think you'll have time, but anyone can be taken at any point. You could have gotten hit by the bus when you walked over to pick up this lovely cake today! And I know now, with a sad clarity, that there are books in my possession, and books on the shelves of Flights of Fancy, that I will never have the time to read. Even if I were to read two or three hundred books a year for the rest of my life, I wouldn't." Dottie bit her lip as tears fell freely. "I know I won't get to read all the books.

"And the one that mocks me the most is one I've read hundreds of times!" Dottie motioned toward her library with her fork. "That damn author who wrote those beautiful stories and never ended them! Why would someone do such a thing? And now here I am, with my ending looming, and . . ."

Although Jim didn't feel the same about reading, Dottie's emotion held such raw ferocity that he had no choice but to cry for her and with her. He didn't know what to say, so he reached out and took her hand in his, giving it a little squeeze. Dottie squeezed back hard and smiled at him through her tears.

After a few quiet moments, she sniffed and let go of Jim's hand, before pointing to the paper she'd given him. "You promise me you're going to call her, all right? I rather like you. Besides, working in some office in Jersey and being the standby super? There's no inspiration in that setting for a talented young playwright. But the New York

Public Library? You'll get more character ideas than you'll know what to do with."

Jim shook his head. "I wish I could do something for you in return."

"Oh! You can!" Dottie assured with a wink. "I wasn't sure it was quite the right time when you first visited, but now seems perfect. I'll be right back."

Dottie stood, went to her library, and returned quickly, this time carrying a few slim books. She handed them to Jim, along with the pen from the table. Flipping through the books, Jim realized two were his scripts, published by his university press back in Ohio. The third book in the stack was the anthology he had a piece in.

"Make them out to your friend, Dottie."

Jim signed them as he was told. He had the clear realization that this was one of the proudest moments in his life and that Dottie was quickly becoming one of the main characters in his own life story.

When he was done signing, he reached for her address book. "May I make an entry in here as well?"

Dottie's eyes shone. "I would like that very much, Jim."

As he printed his name and contact information, Jim tried to imbue his words with his fondness for Dottie and how much he valued their new friendship, hoping she would feel it every time she opened to his page.

The Main Branch

New York City, 2018

Jim's job at the Main Branch of the New York Public Library was deep in the bowels of the Stephen A. Schwarzman Building. All day long, he packed sturdy plastic boxes full of books to be shuffled between sites due to patron requests and holds. It was not unlike the fast-food job he'd held in high school or working in an online fulfillment center. However, instead of dealing in cholesterol-laden food stuffs or cheap imported goods, Jim was dealing in knowledge, personal betterment, and escapism.

He loved seeing the variety of books contained in each shipping bin. One person was getting into smoking meats, while another was looking for vegan recipes to cook in their pressure cooker. One reader was studying nihilism, while someone else investigated forest bathing.

There was even the possibility they were all for the same person. Jim liked to think so.

Jim enjoyed a lot of things about his new job, and he was continually grateful to Dottie for opening the way. Following the phone call he'd made to Dottie's connection, the hiring and onboarding process had taken less than a month. Jim had soon become the proud owner of a New York Public Library system employee badge, with *Circulation Associate* emblazoned under his smiling headshot.

The pay was steady and not too shabby, and he received health insurance and even a pension plan. He also had access to free Wi-Fi and a quiet, warm place to work before and after his shift.

Dottie had also been correct: there were a lot of characters. Though Jim only saw the most interesting folks—the patrons and librarians—when he was off duty.

What Jim liked most about his job was that it gave him time to think. He could fill a bin with books, double-check them against the order slip, carry them to the loading dock, and grab the next empty box, all while running dialogue in his head.

He was toying with the idea of basing a play in the library, with scenes moving from one department to the next, but only using two actors and minimal set changes to indicate transitions. Maybe he could even stage it with a single actor. That would be interesting.

If he fleshed the idea out, Jim knew his opening scene would be a real one from his first day on the job.

Lenore had been the first person Jim had met who wasn't from HR or management. The others had told him how to dress, how to properly pick up boxes so he wouldn't blow out his back, how to read the order slips, how to scan the books, and how to load them. They had also told him what paperwork to fill out if he ever got a serious paper cut. He wasn't sure whether the last part was a joke, but he took it seriously, just to be safe.

On the other hand, Lenore had taught him to roll his shoulders and swing his arms at least once every hour, "like in PE in second grade," so he wouldn't get neck cramps or headaches. She'd taught him how to arrange books to get as many as possible in the shipping boxes. She told him not to be afraid of flagging books that smelled funny as in need of repair and tossing them into the rolling cart against the wall.

"People leave nasty things in books sometimes. If you smell something, don't open the book to find out what's in there. You don't get paid enough to see those things! And don't ask me what I've seen that taught me the lesson! Don't make me relive that shit!"

She'd laughed loudly at her own joke, then repeated it a few more times, even though Jim didn't argue with her.

Lenore hummed to herself all day long. She had hands and arms so sinewy, any MMA fighter would have been envious, and she didn't mind being hot and sweaty, though she didn't like being cold.

One day, due to plumbing work being done on pipes in the ceiling above her usual station, Lenore had to work much closer to the open bay of the loading area than she preferred. She wore her coat all day and pulled her skull-cap down as far as it would go, the ends of her thick corn-rows just peeking out from underneath. That day, she hummed louder than normal and rocked her whole body, though not to the beat. She flapped her hands whenever she didn't have a book in them.

Despite the disturbance to her usual routine and all the stimming it triggered, Lenore still put out more bins of books than anyone else in the room. Thousands of patrons a week received books that had passed through Lenore's hands.

If he did run with this library play idea, Jim wanted to give Lenore the spotlight and the respect she deserved. Yet he hesitated to write characters based on people he admired most. He didn't want to fail to do them justice.

And with Lenore, Jim didn't want her to be seen as the "token neurodivergent character." He liked her for her generous personality, her sense of humor, and her amazing focus. Casting the right person for the role would be a challenge. He wouldn't want her to be played by someone who would aim for comedy or misguided pity, instead of seeing that Lenore was a whole, wonderful person, who loved her job and did it damn well.

During his mandated breaks, Jim would walk the stacks to do some subtle people watching on rainy days, and he stepped out to get some air when the weather was fine. When his mind was lost in words, scenes, one-liners, and character quirks, he would find a place to sit and just zone out, gazing at this mural or that statue. He accidentally ran over his allotted time more than once when he was preoccupied like that, so he had to get in the habit of setting an alarm on his phone that gave him enough time to jog back down the stairs to rejoin Lenore and the others.

Lenore never wanted to take a break except to go to the bathroom. One of the floor managers had decided not to argue with her about it anymore, letting her work through the whole day, but they did insist she stop to eat lunch. Lenore did, though she stood at her usual spot, commenting to those around her how they could fit more books in their bins.

It took longer for Jim to get to know the librarians, IT people, pages, and those squirreled away in offices, doing things like perpetual fundraising and grant writing. Slowly but surely, though, he learned some names.

He shared lunchtime with an archivist named Kate, and as they both liked to eat outside, they eventually made a habit of chatting over sandwiches and thermoses of tea or coffee or bottles of water. Jim would sit on a low wall, and Kate would pull her wheelchair up next to him.

They became friendly enough that Kate commented on it one day. "I like our daily lunches, Jim. It's hard to make friends as an adult. I know you probably have cool theater friends and do amazing Off-Broadway stuff, but I'm glad I get you for lunch."

Jim almost spit out his water midsip. "You make it sound like breaking into the theater scene is easy. I only moved here from Ohio a few months ago, while so many others have been auditioning and walking the boards together since they were teenagers or kids. Playwrights think they're all in competition with one another, and they come and go as fast as the reviews roll in. I don't have anything staged right now, so no one has any reason to get to know me. I just kind of keep showing up and lurking, and I try not to be too obvious or creepy about it."

He took another sip of water. "To be honest, I'm in this weird in-between place. I had a play that got good reviews, and I have one small project on the horizon, but besides that, I'm kind of just writing ideas here and there and treading water. I haven't been able to build any momentum. And I like my job here a lot—it's paying the bills and allowing me to stay in New York—but it's like I have half a foot in each world, without truly being part of either."

Kate nodded along. "Well, that may not be unique to your situation, though. I mean, I'm doing what I want to be doing, but I often get the feeling I'm not doing everything I need to. It's like I should be more involved in activism for the causes I'm passionate about, and I should be there for my family more, and I should write research articles for library and museum publications. But at the end of the day, I'm tired and I only peck away at each of those other things. It never seems like I'm giving any of them my all, but maybe that's just adulting."

"Well, I'm not a fan!"

Kate laughed. "As for it being hard to make friends, that's every workplace. The library branches, especially the big ones, are full of cliques. I mean, even when we all head to the Circulation Desk, people sit at tables according to their floors and departments." Sighing, she took a bite of her chickpea-salad sandwich.

Jim quietly chewed for a moment. "The Circulation Desk? What, is there some secret-society librarian speakeasy tucked away in a back alley somewhere? Do you need to whisper the Dewey Decimal number for bartending through a slot in the door to get in or something?"

"Not so secret, and not in a back alley." Covering her mouth, Kate snickered. "It's on West Thirty-Third, near Koreatown. And you don't need to technically be a library employee to go there, but you do need your library card to sign out a book."

Jim's bite of apple almost fell out of his mouth as he stared at his purple-haired friend, slack-jawed with disbelief.

"What?" Kate asked after a moment.

"You're just screwing with me," Jim mumbled around his bite of apple.

Kate put her sandwich down on the beeswax cloth wrapper and pivoted her wheelchair to face him fully. "I most certainly am not. The Circulation Desk has been around for decades. It's a normal bar with booze, beer, fried foods, billiards, darts, and a jukebox. There's even a stage for live shows on the weekends.

"The place just also happens to be filled with books

you can check out. And it's almost exclusively patronized by NYPL employees. Oh, staff from the Brooklyn and Queens library systems would be welcome, but they don't come by as much. Maybe they have their own bars we don't know about. I mean, think about it; there are cop bars and sports bars and bars for firefighters, so why not a librarian bar?"

Her point made, Kate went back to her sandwich.

"You're taking me there," Jim declared. "I need to see this place. How does the world not know about this?"

"Us library people—we know how to keep things quiet."

Psychic Becky

New York City, 2017

Becky didn't think about money until her card was declined at a bakery. That same day, she returned to her crummy apartment to find what remained of her things on the curb. Most of her clothes and all her good shoes were gone. She only still had her running shoes because she had been wearing them.

She had been reading as she walked home, and it was a herculean task to pull herself from the beautiful fugue of words to figure out what to do next. She gathered what was left of her scattered belongings and wandered until she found a relic of a pay phone. She called her sister collect.

She was greeted by a surprising amount of weeping. "Becky? Oh my god, is it really you? Becky, where are you? Are you still in New York? Are you okay? I haven't heard from you in two months!"

Becky started to protest all the fuss but stopped short when she caught sight of the digital display of a bank across the street. According to the date it showed, it had actually been two months and three days since she went to the amazing conference in New York that had changed the trajectory of her life. It had given her so much to think about, opened so many doors in her perception of reading.

One presentation had been on the evolutionary jump humans had made as they transitioned—culture by culture, language by language—from oral history to written history. There had been a panel that tackled the chicken-and-egg conundrum of how repeated tropes of various religious texts played themselves out over and over again. And there had been an eye-opening discussion about the history of fiction billed as "The Art of Lying and Dreaming."

Becky had felt high the entire weekend. She'd ended up pacing in her hotel room at night, reading the presenters' books she'd bought. She understood each of their separate, yet not terribly disparate, views on how literary works altered and enhanced life, society, and history, and Becky had folded them into one another in a dough of new understanding about the world.

When the conference ended and it was time to go home, Becky simply hadn't. She had changed hotels in a daze of swiping a credit card and signing her name, and then she had gone to library after library. She had taken books off the shelves and started reading, then dropping, one after another, letting it all in without any filter. Later, she had moved from the hotel to a cheap week-by-week apartment, until she was left standing on the street with her possessions stuffed in a bag, listening to her sister cry on the other end of the line, surprised it had been two months.

"Yeah, Mo, it's me. I'm okay. No, really, I'm okay. I just . . ." Becky couldn't think of a coherent way to tell her sister she had been, well, reading.

"Why didn't you call or email me, at least? You sent me one email—only one!—asking me to bring your cat to my house 'because I'm going to stay for a little while longer.' And that was it! Then you disappeared off the face of the earth! You know, you're probably in trouble at the university, tenure or no tenure. But at least you sent them a request for an emergency sabbatical and gave them a list of names of people who could cover your classes. You know how I know this? Because I had to play detective because *my sister disappeared!*"

Mo's voice was nearing the fevered pitch that meant she was truly freaking out. Wanting to head her off before then, Becky broke in.

"You contacted the university, and they told you about my email? Did they say who covered my classes?"

"They didn't mention it. I did get a message over social media from one of the people on your list, someone named Elise? I forget her last name. I don't know how she found me, but she expressed concern about you and asked if you were okay. She said the university had forwarded her your sabbatical request when they inquired about her taking over. It was actually kind of spooky. I mean, how could she have known there was something wrong from a short, professional email?"

Becky smiled. She had always suspected Elise was a little bit like her, with a special gift for reading. Becky wanted to ask more about her colleague's message, but Mo exhaled loudly, the way she always did when she was losing her patience. Becky formulated a cover story.

"Maureen, I didn't call or anything because I had a job offer—a really great one—but it fell through, and I was embarrassed. I spent a bunch of money setting up shop here, and then I didn't have anything to show for it. My bank card is frozen because my spending looked like suspicious activity. I just need a few hundred to get me through. Could you cover me? Wire me some money?" Becky bit her lip, hoping her ruse worked.

"You're lying," Maureen said, her tone flat. "You only ever call me Maureen, instead of Mo, when you're lying. Listen, if you're in some kind of trouble, I will absolutely help you. I just want to know you're safe and for you to tell me how I can keep in touch with you, okay?"

"I'm okay, Mo, really," she assured. "It's a little complicated to explain, but I'm having the time of my life. I feel like I'm doing what I was born to do. My phone broke, and I haven't had time to get a new one, but I have email access, and I'll email you weekly, okay? Can you send the money, please? I'm in a bind."

Maureen agreed, and Becky picked up the cash. It was enough to pay for a few nights in a motel, but she knew she would still need to figure something else out and fast.

Cash in hand, Becky went to a coffee shop filled with art. Art wasn't loud, and she needed to think.

Until that point, when those pesky base layers of Maslow's hierarchy of needs began asserting themselves, Becky hadn't thought about how she could use her gift to benefit herself. Sure, she had used it during her years in academia, but that had also benefited the understanding of young scholars. She could read the flaws in their thinking, or where they were less confident in certain points of their theses, and nudge them in the right direction. A paycheck just happened to come with the professor gig. But now, Becky had to figure out how she could use her gift on a daily basis to house, feed, and clothe herself.

A day job was out of the question. After sliding fully into her life's work, she couldn't imagine ever going back to how her life had been before. Back then, she had had to worry about deadlines, what people thought of her curriculum, and how she was doing on Rate My Professor. She'd had to wear clothes that made others take her seriously. She'd had to remember when she was due for a mammogram, when her car was due for its annual inspection, when people's birthdays were, and so many other inane distractions. All of it had kept her from consuming more written words and all the understanding, intention, and emotion behind them.

When people spoke, it was like a pixelated, black-and-white photocopy of what they really felt and meant. But when they wrote words, their communication was rich with so much more. Their writing was technicolor with a full orchestral soundtrack. It was the truth. Even when the words themselves were lies or entertaining fiction, what bled through the words was always truth.

Just sitting in the café, Becky had to turn to face the wall because the day's featured roast, written on a chalkboard above the counter, was broadcasting the barista's longing to be on the stage after months of no callbacks.

To keep herself focused, Becky wrote down her ideas.

I can:
Figure out what restaurants are willing to feed people for free by reading their signs
Figure out where I can get away with sleeping (safe place) for little or no money
Impress people with my knowledge and maybe they will give me money

Becky dwelled on that last sentence for some time. In the days that followed, she worked out the fine details of her "act," then set up shop on a busy street corner. Her sign read: *$5 for a quick handwriting reading. $10 for a reading, plus a question answered. Tips welcome!*

After several people dawdled, trying to think of something to write, she added: *Suggestions: Write three sentences about your day. Tell me what you think of my hat! Write about your last meal.*

She even bought a stack of index cards and some mini clipboards, to which she attached pencils with string, to arm her customers. That settled her "act," and her living arrangements fell into place shortly after.

Perusing the community bulletin board at one of the libraries she frequented, Becky found a handwritten flyer advertising a room for rent, and she immediately called the number at the bottom. Reading the carefully penned ink on college-rule paper, Becky could tell the woman who authored it was trusting and naive. The room she had for rent used to belong to her disabled son who had, until his death, been the center of her life.

The flyer said none of this, of course, but Becky knew it all the same. She could read the grief and loneliness and all the details underneath in the woman's elegant penmanship.

That evening, when Becky met Ruth, her new landlady, she might have fabricated a little of her own history, throwing in some loss for good measure, but in the end, she secured for herself a clean bed in a clean home, not too far from the closest train line, for not much more than a song.

The only drawback was that Ruth often wanted Becky to have conversations with her and, occasionally, to eat with her. Ruth loved to cook and wanted someone to cook for. During these meals, she would share every detail of her latest phone calls with her younger son, who lived on the other side of the country. He never called; Ruth always had to call him, but she never indicated that she minded.

Becky would smile and nod, then make excuses to go back to her room with her latest bag of books, telling Ruth she was working on research for a big project.

Which wasn't too far from the truth, after all.

What Becky was doing was reading everything she could get her hands on. She let herself move from topic to topic as each new read nudged her in this direction or that. A *Don Quixote* reference led her to reread that classic, plus some of Cervantes's lesser-known works, a collection of the kinds of chivalrous tales that were said to have driven the gentle knight to his ecstatic madness, and some books about the history of windmills. The windmill content was fascinating and led to a whole other reading tangent about the history of simple machines up to modern theoretical physics.

Some days, Becky swore she could feel the synapses in her brain reaching and stretching, creating a denser and denser neural net with every connection and leap of understanding. The project Becky was working on was an understanding of the whole of human knowledge, to be contained, in its entirety, in her head.

Besides quick money, Becky's street act provided her with other perks. She got to dig into her bag of books and read whenever there wasn't someone holding one of her clipboards. Also, like a search engine on the internet that gathered data from every benign, embarrassing, or dirty search request, Becky gained more connections.

She thought it was brilliant, really. Most of these folks would never write anything she would pick up off a shelf, but here they were, letting her have little glimpses of their inner lives. It was like being allowed to look over someone's shoulder while they wrote in their diary. And the information she got from handwritten material had always been louder and clearer than content that had passed through the hands of editors or translators.

Her new profession was not without its risks, though. One day, a group of businessmen were killing time, not wanting to return to the office, so they each threw a ten in her bucket. When she got to the third one, Becky started to feel sick as soon as she began reading what he had written about the double cheeseburger with bacon he'd had for lunch. She saw flashes of what he was looking at on his phone every two seconds. He had a huge store of pictures he shared with other men like himself. He got off on looking at them while he sat talking with friends over beers, pretending he was texting his wife. He'd pulled that little trick even as he wrote on her clipboard.

She wanted to scrub the images from her mind, but they were there, already weaving into her quilt of human knowledge. "Think you're clever with your phone and those horrible pictures?" she screamed at him. "They're kids! They're just little kids, you bastard!"

Becky lunged off the box she sat on and punched him right in the nuts with all the strength she could muster. Then she had to grab her bucket of money and make a run for it. Her old running shoes served her well that day, as did the muscle memory from running marathons before her life in New York.

By the time her lungs gave out, the suits had given up blocks earlier, and Becky doubted the man she'd hit would try pressing charges. Being punched by a crazy busker in her fifties didn't fit with the image of himself she'd seen in his words.

There was one other time a customer lashed out at her, but that event was worth the trouble. It was a young couple, holding hands and enjoying their weekend in the big city. When they stopped in front of her box, he wrote about their day of sightseeing. Through his lighthearted words, Becky could feel the weight of the ring box in his pocket clearly enough she almost reached into the pocket of her sweater, thinking she would find the box there.

But Becky also saw the times that day that he'd held himself back from yelling at his pretty companion because they were in a crowd. She heard the disparaging remarks he made under his breath to her about what she chose to wear and how he thought she was a little too friendly with the attractive waiter at lunch.

His written question asked if the girl was going to say yes. The inquisitive words sparked and cracked inside Becky with a prowling possessiveness he interpreted as love and devotion. Becky had to shake her head to clear her mind of his warped perception of relationships, but he got impatient when she didn't answer fast enough.

The girlfriend stepped in, defusing his tirade. "Maybe you could do mine while you're thinking about his question."

Becky nodded, and the woman wrote about how she liked Becky's hat and wondered what kind of wool it was made of. Faint and small at the bottom of the card, she wrote, *Will he change?*

Through her words, Becky felt every bruise, every arm jerk, every slap, every harsh and demeaning insult that had been hurled at the younger woman before her.

Standing up, Becky looked her in the eye. Though she didn't worry about her appearance much those days, at that moment, Becky longed for one of her power suits, tailored just so, with her university-issued ID and lanyard around her neck. She wanted the girl to see her as more than a crazy woman on the sidewalk; Becky wanted to be seen as someone who understood and who possessed a certain wisdom about life and the world.

"No," she stated firmly, "he won't. Get out. Don't say yes, no matter how afraid you are to say no."

Becky saw it coming in her peripheral vision but made no move to stop the irate man. He flipped her makeshift table, kicked her bucket of money down the sidewalk, and got up in her face, scream-whispering obscenities through clenched teeth. Then he grabbed the girl's wrist and pulled her away into the crowd.

Before the younger woman disappeared into the sea of humanity, she looked back and mouthed, "Thank you."

A few people had noticed what had happened and stopped to help Becky pick up her money and see if she was okay. New York wasn't all bad.

She offered her helpers free readings, only realizing afterward that she was actively seeking reassurance of human decency. If Becky's literary pilgrimage was to be a proper scientific venture, then choosing the people whose words she read specifically because they made her feel good would render the information a biased sample. Yet these few were only one drop in the ocean of information she would ultimately gather, so Becky figured it would be okay.

As it turned out, they were all . . . normal.

One of them was internally patting herself on the back because she'd stopped her run to help Becky. She was planning to take Becky's picture from a distance and post it to her social media, along with a story.

The older man in the bad suit had vividly remembered his father's anger when he'd seen the young man lash out. He still fought those same urges in himself every day.

The young skateboarder in the kilt didn't really think much of the situation at all, but they felt the reading was cool. Growing up in the city as they had, they were used to such moments of violence and had determined that they needed to do their part to help sometimes. It was as natural to them as breathing. They were more focused on choosing between two possible designs to have painted on their board later that day.

Becky told them, "You're going to go with the geometric dragon. You know you love that one best."

That earned a smile that made Becky remember, in a rare flash, her sister's response the first time Becky bought Maureen a Christmas present with her own money. Maureen had slept with the Raggedy Ann doll for years afterward. It might have been halfway down her Christmas list, but Becky had been able to tell it was what Maureen had wanted most.

Once Becky had studied all her helpers' reactions to her attack, she was able to find some objective stillness within herself. She understood there would always be great anger and pain alongside ecstasy, relief, and revelation. They all had their place in the web in her mind.

Then came the day that made Becky retire from the psychic business.

It was gray and rainy, so she was down in the subway. Dirty puddles were scattered over the tiles, but Becky had found a relatively dry patch of floor on which to set up shop, and business wasn't bad. Whenever she set up near Broadway, Becky was able to cash in on tourists, who carried spending money and were willing to get a reading just for the sake of the New York-ness of it. She left folks astounded or, at the very least, amused as they waited for their trains to take them to their dinner reservations.

On touristy days, Becky altered her writing prompts to include, *Write three sentences about your hometown.* The variety of memories and nostalgia that swept over her with those scrawled descriptions of farmlands, tight-knit neighborhoods, or military family housing were better than anything Google Earth could ever pull off.

Reading a book on ancient libraries of Mesopotamia, Becky munched on a stale soft pretzel from a vendor she knew would give it to her for only a dollar if she asked nicely. Riding the soft waves of new data she had collected from her out-of-town customers so far, she didn't even look up from her book, at first, when a woman approached and slowly picked up one of her clipboards. The author of her book was so genuinely passionate about the topic, it was hard for Becky to tear herself away and attend to her new customer.

It wasn't until the woman placed the clipboard back down on the box with a soggy twenty clipped to it that Becky finally looked up.

The woman was soaked.

If Becky had provided pens instead of pencils for her customers' writing samples, the ink would have run all over the page from how much the woman's hair had dripped on it. She looked as if she had been wandering around in the downpour, making no attempt to shield herself from it. The woman shivered but kept her arms by her sides, rather than wrapped around herself, and her suede shoes squished as she shifted her weight.

"Need any change for this twenty?" Becky asked. "The reading with a question is only ten."

"You keep the change." The woman's eyes never met Becky's, instead staying focused on the note card she had written on.

Becky closed her eyes and took a deep, cleansing breath. Yes, this was partly theatrics, but it also gave Becky a minute to clear her mind and put aside her exuberant feelings about ancient libraries.

Then she read the card.

The woman hadn't used any of Becky's suggested prompts. She had simply written, *I miss his warmth next to me at night. I miss cooking dinner together. I'm not even mad; I just miss him. Will he ever come back to me?*

Becky had had a few long-term relationships in her life, but she'd never built a life together with any of her partners. She'd read about loss and love before; there were plenty of associations in her evolving network of knowledge that were colored with those themes. But the rawness of what this woman had imbued in her writing . . .

Becky was never one for hyperbole, but she gained a better understanding of the word *heartbreak* from that note card.

Closing her eyes and running her fingers over the indentations of the words she's already memorized, Becky felt the heat of the woman's husband's sleeping body and the security and contentment that heat carried with it. She could hear and feel the banter, music, and rhythmic clink of utensils as they danced around one another, making years of dinners in the different homes they'd shared.

Then Becky felt, like a cold, heavy cannonball to the sternum, his words to the woman in their last kitchen.

"Carol, I'm so sorry. I don't think I can do this anymore. You must have felt it, that something's changed between us. I've met someone, and I didn't mean to, but we fell in love. When I picture the future now, I picture it with her, even when I try to make it you in that picture. I respect and love you too much to go on lying to you. My feelings have changed. You are my best friend, but I think she's the love of my life."

Becky threw her eyes open in time to see Carol, her eyes still downcast, mouthing the words Becky had just heard ringing in her head. When Carol got to the end, her lips started forming the short speech from the beginning all over again, playing it on repeat.

Becky felt the love Carol still had for her estranged husband. She was telling the truth when she said she wasn't angry. Carol understood her husband. She knew he loved people wholly and completely and that he still loved Carol, just in a different way than he used to. He was an honest man and meant what he said. Carol even admitted to herself that she'd seen the signs leading up to the talk and that she'd made herself ignore them.

And Carol knew, just as Becky did, that he wasn't going to come back. Asking Becky was Carol's last-ditch effort to hold out hope. The romantic in her felt that happening on Becky had been a sign; she was going to get an answer, one way or the other, that would allow her to move on from the limbo she was in.

Becky was tempted to lie, to help Carol feel less crushingly sad. She could have easily done so; she wasn't a member of any professional consortium of sidewalk psychics; she hadn't taken an oath to always tell the truth. In fact, she mostly responded to questions about the future in vague and reassuring terms, pulling in nuggets from what she read from her customers' writings, and folks were satisfied.

But Becky couldn't predict the future. She only saw a person's experiences up until the moment they scratched their question down with a dull pencil and handed it to her. So Becky answered truthfully. She reported to Carol what the shivering woman already knew but was hiding from.

"You know he won't come back. I'm so very sorry, Carol."

Carol's breath left her in a great sigh, but she finally looked Becky in the eye. "Thank you."

Becky felt those words as clearly as if Carol had written them with a sharp-tipped fountain pen on Becky's palm, a painful blend of blood and ink, grief and relief.

Straightening her back, Carol smoothed her hands down her blouse, wiped her wet glasses with a tissue from her purse, and tucked her wet locks behind her ears. Carol then threw the tissue into the nearest garbage can, placed her handbag on the lid, walked with resolve toward the edge of the platform, and stepped off, right into the path of an oncoming train.

The unfortunate driver didn't even have time to throw on the brakes or make any other attempt to save the fragile life of the woman who fell in front of tons of barreling steel. The brakes came after, screeching in futility, as did the screams from onlookers, followed by a flurry of activity from the transit police and other subway personnel.

For the first time in a long while, Becky was pulled completely and totally into the moment. She was ripped from every bit of the constant background noise her brain made as it cataloged and knit in new information.

She still held Carol's note card in her hand.

Carol had been there. And then she wasn't anymore. Becky had witnessed the end of her story.

On autopilot, Becky picked up her few belongings and hightailed it out of there. She didn't want to be asked any questions by the police. She didn't want to answer more questions from customers.

She had no answers for them, anyway.

There was only the void where Carol had once been.

Becky made her way back to her little room. Thankfully, Ruth was out at a church function that night. Becky just climbed into bed fully clothed. She didn't bring any books with her. She only held Carol's note card, which she read over and over.

The Carol who had written the card was desperately sad, but there had been a spark of disbelieving hope inside her. The Carol who had written the note and the question remained alive, frozen in time. While writing those sentences, she had not been thinking about committing suicide. If she had been, Becky would have read it.

When Becky had answered Carol's question, when she'd thought she was being kind by creating the opportunity for Carol to get unstuck and start moving on, Carol became a person she hadn't been a moment before. That happened to everyone hundreds of thousands of times per day, Becky knew. But it was usually incremental. People changed their minds slowly. They gradually came to trust or distrust their assumptions and beliefs. Occasionally, there was an "Ah-ha!" moment, but these were rare.

The thought of the train was not there for Carol until it was. It manifested and was acted upon all within the space of thanking Becky and taking a few short steps. That was why Becky hadn't seen it.

Wanting to keep Carol in the moment "before" for as long as she could, Becky read the note card again and again. Finally, many hours later, when Becky's eyes and head ached from the effort, she put the note card face down on her nightstand.

Becky longed to pick up a book and fall back into the work of building the intricate map in her mind, adding to the connections and understandings forming within her. But something kept her from the work.

It was . . . herself.

She had spent so much time in the role of observer and information reaper, Becky had almost forgotten she was still a character in the story of it all. Even when she interacted with her sidewalk customers, she never saw herself as part of their neural web.

Becky thought on it now. How many people walked around with an image of her held in their brains? Maybe it was fuzzy around the edges, maybe barely accurate, yet there she was.

Maureen came to mind, and Becky thought about her sister missing her for the first time in a long while. Next, there were images of the girl with the thin wrists and the abusive boyfriend. Had she left him? Had she thought of Becky as part of her escape story?

What about other people? Ruth often asked Becky if she had eaten and offered to make her a sandwich or some eggs. Was that concern for Becky one of the reasons Ruth got up each morning? Did hearing Becky move around in her son's old room help her feel less alone in the world?

There were also the librarians that Becky saw so often, and the other library patrons. Was she someone the librarians talked about when they got together after work? Did any of the mothers with toddlers commit her to their mental "odd people" file and avoid her because of it? Were there any children who made up stories about her?

The realness of herself made Becky weep.

She dug out one of her old journals that had survived the eviction from her seedy apartment and been discarded in the gutter because it was made of words, not money. She read her old words, from months before she decided not to return to her university faculty apartment, her teaching job, and the cat she'd left with her sister for safekeeping.

A sudden, visceral memory made itself known: the sensation of little claws kneading into either side of her sternum, her cat "making biscuits" on her chest before settling down for a nap.

Becky hadn't thought about her cat in so long. His name was Mac, short for Macavity, because Becky loved T. S. Eliot's quirky mind. She'd loved that cat once, the feel of him heavy and warm in her lap as she read. Becky realized she probably took up so much room in that cat's brain, even after so long apart.

The Becky in her journal liked to dream about reading everything and anything. Sometimes, she would even start to plan trips to big cities, booking a vacation rental near a library so she could immerse herself for days in all the words. But then she'd never finish making the reservation, because it was the realm of fantasy, not a thing normal people did.

That Becky, the one captured within her journal as if inside a snow globe, knew she held a place in the world by handing out grades, paying bills, and meeting friends for brunch on the weekends.

As her previous self rang in her ears, Becky looked around. The little bedroom was a mess of clothes and books. Taking a few tentative steps, she looked into the dresser mirror, which still bore football stickers from the boy who used to live there. She barely recognized the old woman staring back, face thin from skipping meals and lined from sitting for hours in the wind and sun. Removing her knit hat, she found her hair was matted to her head.

Becky was too shocked to even cry. She searched the floor for a towel, thinking she would go shower. She didn't find one, but she remembered Ruth had told her she could use the ones in the linen closet anytime.

Grabbing a soft, fluffy brown towel, Becky took a long shower, staying in until the water went cold. She felt some guilt for sneaking some of Ruth's shampoo and soap because she didn't have any of her own, but Becky didn't think Ruth would really mind. She worked the knots out of her hair as best she could and put on the cleanest clothes she could find. Then she wrapped the rest of her clothes in her stale-smelling sheets and carried the bundle to the laundry room in the basement.

Ruth met Becky at the bottom of the stairs, beaming from ear to ear, and offered to do the laundry for her. Then she made Becky a can of chicken noodle soup. The gesture brought up a memory from Becky's youth, of making her sister condensed soup when Maureen was home sick from school and their mother hadn't been able to skip work at the factory.

It was so odd, to have an image filling her head that was entirely real and entirely hers, not one harvested from the words and minds of others, all while the same steaming soft-noodled soup filled her mouth, one slow spoonful after another.

Ruth treated Becky like an injured bird in a shoebox lined with tissues, afraid Becky would flail and flop away if Ruth did something to scare her. When she went to switch over Becky's laundry, she sighed heavily and smiled when she found Becky at the table still. She spoke in a near whisper as the clothes tumbled in the basement.

"You've been working yourself too hard, all that research you do. You read but don't eat, hauling your books around and not taking care of yourself. Whatever you're writing, it's not as important as your health and well-being. You're a good person; I've always known that. You need to treat yourself better. I'm glad you're coming around."

Becky nodded along, unsure how else to respond. Ruth pressed her luck a little further by making Becky cocoa with marshmallows on top.

Hugging the mug with both hands, Becky saw that the skin on her knuckles was split from the cold and her nails were ragged. She had another memory then, of she and her sister listening to records in their shared room as they painted each other's nails.

"Do you have some stationary and an envelope I could use?" Becky whispered. "I'd like to write my sister a letter."

Hopping up, Ruth brought Becky several sheets of paper and a heavy ballpoint pen. The weighty implement, she explained, had been a fifteen-year anniversary gift from the electric company she'd worked for until her retirement.

"It's . . . it's a nice pen."

She only had a vague memory of Ruth talking before about her job at the electric company. What people told her out loud never stuck as well as the things she learned from reading their written words.

Becky stared at the blank pages in front of her, unsure where to begin. Thankfully, Maureen didn't have a gift like her own and could only know what Becky chose to reveal.

Intending to keep it simple, Becky wrote that she was safe and that she was sorry. She gave Maureen the phone number for Ruth's house and then asked about Mac. Before Becky was even aware she was going to do it, she wrote down the memories of canned soup and painted nails. Then she started telling Maureen what she'd been up to all these months, but she found that writing about it was hard now that she wasn't in that headspace.

Anxiety rose within Becky. She felt like the net she'd

been building in her mind was slipping away, even though she'd only spent a few hours in her own life instead of in the world of words. Her hands started to shake, and her writing devolved into illegible scribbles.

Picking up the pen, Becky read over the last few lines, but doing so only created a feedback loop of panic.

Ruth had been quietly lingering, washing the dishes far more slowly than she needed to. Now, she put a hand on Becky's shoulder; Becky nearly jumped out of her seat.

"Oh! I didn't mean to startle you," Ruth said apologetically. "You just looked, well, real tired. Would you like me to put this letter aside for you to finish later?"

Becky knew she wouldn't be able to finish it and shook her head. She was able to sign her name, just barely, and muster the focus to ask Ruth to make out the envelope for her, then ask if Ruth had a stamp. But that was all.

As Becky watched Ruth address the envelope, she read Ruth's concern for her and Ruth's pity but also Ruth's feeling of renewed purpose because she had someone to take care of again. Becky saw what she had wondered about earlier: just how big a part of Ruth's life she had become. Ruth did hope Becky's sister would be in touch, but she also guiltily wished that maybe Maureen wouldn't so Ruth could hold on to Becky for a while longer.

When the letter was ready to be sent, Becky insisted on mailing it herself, somewhat afraid Ruth would pocket it and later use the tarnished tea kettle that always sat on the stove to steam open the envelope and read what she'd written. Not that Ruth would get the same level of information from it that Becky did, but still.

Becky also wondered if, like Carol, Ruth would do something unexpected. Maybe tear the letter up or slip it into the slots of the sewer drain instead of the mailbox.

What if Ruth just had the thought and then did it? Easy as stepping off a subway platform.

With no recollection of where the nearest mailbox was, Becky wandered down the block until she found one to drop her letter into. Task complete, she made her way back to her room, ignored Ruth's polite invitation to have some cookies before bed, and collapsed into sleep. She slept for almost a whole day.

Becky spent the next several days tidying up her room, locating her ID, her old bank card, and some other important documents that had ended up scattered among the debris of the life she'd abandoned right under her own feet. She stacked all her books in one corner of the room and put a blanket over them. Becky also ate three meals a day, showered daily, folded her clean clothes, made her bed, and spent evenings sitting on the front porch with a blanket wrapped around herself. She even dutifully came in when Ruth fussed at her about getting too cold.

On the fourth day of this new routine of realness, Becky received a call from her sister. She laughed nervously at the sound of Maureen's voice and happy tears. Ruth stood across the room, hiding her smile behind her hands, her own eyes swimming with tears.

After a while, Becky took the cordless phone up to her room, and the sisters caught up. Maureen said Macavity had slowed down some and might be going deaf, but he was still eating well and was as cuddly as ever.

Choosing her words with care, Becky slowly told Maureen about her reading habits and the mind project she'd been working on all this time. She felt the pull of the work as she told Maureen how brilliantly all-encompassing it was and found herself looking over at the blanket-covered pile in the corner of her room.

During a long pause, Becky could hear Maureen sniffle. She knew her sister well enough to know that Maureen was hesitating to say something that was on her mind.

"What is it, Mo?" she finally asked, tearing her eyes away from the mound of books.

"When you talk about reading like that, and all the extra information you're able to read and all the connections and the understanding . . . You probably don't remember her as well as I do, but do you recall Aunt Jeanie?"

Maureen was right. Becky had very few memories of their mom's sister, Jeanie. Their aunt had been in and out of mental hospitals from the time she was a teenager. Becky remembered her as funny and smart and that Jeanie gave the kinds of gifts little kids loved: dolls made out of handkerchiefs and crowns made out of bottle caps and other odd but delightful things. Jeanie was the kind of person who talked a little too loudly and sometimes broke into song in the middle of conversations.

Becky recalled that the family had been upset one Easter when Becky was still very little, because Jeanie had wandered off during the egg hunt. Accusations were thrown back and forth among the adults about who was supposed to have been watching her. Becky had found her aunt in her closet. Jeanie had had Becky's mother's good fabric scissors and had cut up her own pretty dress before moving on to Becky's clothes. She'd said she was making nesting material for the baby bunnies. Jeanie had been smiling but crying, both upset and overjoyed about the "multitudes" of bunnies hiding in the yard.

Multitudes became one of Becky's favorite big words to use as a child.

In the present, Maureen spoke of a few "episodes"

she remembered Jeanie having. She recalled the Easter incident as well, but with more concerning details.

"Aunt Jeanie was insistent about the bunnies being everywhere. She was covered in little nicks from when she'd cut up her own dress, and she had already started to hack away at the pretty frilly dress you had on when Mom came in and found you both. She had to wrestle Jeanie away from your dress, and she ended up with a few bad cuts from getting the scissors out of Jeanie's grip after Uncle Joe carried you out of the room. Becky, Jeanie didn't mean to be dangerous, but sometimes she was."

Becky thought of Carol and the train. She didn't mean for her words to be dangerous, but sometimes they were.

As Maureen continued to talk about Aunt Jeanie, Becky realize she was likening Jeanie's delusions about bunnies in the yard, reptiles in the walls, and Russian spies in her doctor's offices to Becky's reading experiences. Then Maureen carefully waded into using terms such as *psychiatric evaluation* and *psychosis*. These were topics Becky had read about and, therefore, understood as well as the experts who'd written them. She didn't think they applied to her.

Her experiences were real.

Carol had been real.

The businessman with the child porn on his phone had been real. He'd certainly felt real when she punched him.

But Becky knew enough about the symptoms of psychiatric disorders to also know the people experiencing them perceived their experiences as very real.

Of course, if her experiences weren't real, then how had she been able to understand the text about schizophrenia so well? Or was she just an astute reader and her mind was making up the extra abilities?

Becky was extraordinarily confused. She didn't understand how she fit into the story of her own life, and she wished she could step out of it for a short while, maybe read it in a book instead. Then perhaps she would understand it better and know which details were fact and which were fiction.

Maureen was still talking, though, and Becky made an effort to listen.

"I mean, I felt for Jeanie. You know how Uncle Bill and I cleaned out Momma's house after she passed? Well, we found some of Jeanie's journals that the last hospital she was in had given Momma. The stuff Jeanie wrote about, bless her heart! It was normal, everyday things, like complaints about the hospital food or another patient stealing her slippers, or nice little notes about the pictures of us Momma sent her. Then other times, it was just off-the-wall ramblings about creatures only she could see and how they told her to do things or told her that if she didn't do certain things, bad stuff would happen to us or the whole world. Being in her mind must have been exhausting!"

"Could you send them to me?" Becky asked.

If she were to understand Jeanie's afflictions, Becky needed to hear everything straight from her aunt. Hopefully, she could objectively compare what Jeanie had experienced to her own mental inclinations and see if they matched. Then she would know if she needed help.

Becky had always felt that more information was better than less.

Maureen begrudgingly agreed, adding that she would try to make a trip out to see Becky when fall break rolled around, right after she submitted the high-school math grades for all her students. Maureen even offered to book a return ticket for Becky, if she liked.

Becky didn't give her an answer.

While waiting for the journals to arrive in the mail, Becky used a composition book she found at the bottom of a drawer in Ruth's son's old desk to help organize her thoughts. On the top of each page, she wrote down an event from her life that involved reading. Then she made two columns underneath. One column held evidence that supported Becky's experience actually happening the way she remembered it. In the other column, she played devil's advocate, exploring how what she remembered could have been a delusion, a leap her mind took that had more to do with faulty brain chemistry than any abilities or perceptions she thought she had.

Besides the more recent events and her days as a "sidewalk psychic", Becky looked at other life experiences. She thought of Elise, the student she'd mentored for a few years and who she'd recommended to take over her classes. Elise was a brilliant, young woman who had gone on to do great things in her field.

Though they'd talked around it, like two gangsters trying to suss each other out, Becky had suspected that the younger woman was like her. She'd sensed that Elise saw behind and in between the words, gleaning more than the average reader.

Even Elise's areas of study supported the theory. She'd double majored in archeology and literature, with minors in sociology and biology. Elise had wanted to dig into historical manuscripts and find out the who, the where, the why, and the how of them.

Becky felt bad about losing touch with Elise. The

younger woman had always seemed to have it all together. Whenever Becky read what Elise wrote, she felt the structure and discipline Elise set up for herself, almost like the other woman had the ability to turn her gift off and on to manage it. Although their relationship had started with Becky being Elise's teacher, Becky wondered if she should have spoken up about the ability they had in common. If she had, maybe Becky could have learned that kind of control for herself.

This thought wouldn't leave her mind, and Becky resolved to get back in touch with Elise. But first, Becky had to figure out more about her own mental status. She had to be sure she wasn't just crazy.

She also had to talk to Ruth.

Becky apologized for not having all of next month's rent ready to go and for not being able to buy groceries to make up for how much Ruth was feeding her. Ruth waved her off, but Becky suspected Ruth had called Maureen back, using the number from the house phone's caller ID, and made some financial arrangements with her sister.

Then one day, a package arrived. It was thick and heavy with paper and thoughts. Becky tried not to alarm Ruth with her excitement.

"It's a package from my sister, Maureen," she said, with what she hoped was a small, unassuming smile.

Becky made herself walk slowly up the steps to her room and not run up them as she wanted to. Then she fluffed her pillows, threw back the covers on her clean-sheeted, nicely made bed, climbed in, and ripped open the package.

At first, she was taken aback. On top of the stack of diaries was a composition book that looked damn near identical to the one she'd been doing her recent journaling in. Becky glanced at the desk, half expecting to find the notebook she'd left there missing, having performed a strange leap in time and possession via the postal service.

But no, hers was still where she'd left it, just across the room.

When Becky got over the initial shock of the similarity, she saw that Aunt Jeanie's journal had an old coffee or tea ring on the upper-right corner of the front cover. Her own journal did not. And the fine print about the manufacturer was different on Jeanie's composition book.

Becky took a few slow breaths. "We are not the same," she whispered.

Then she opened the notebook and started to read.

Sometime later, Becky was walking the streets of New York. Or was it her hometown? Or Jeanie's hometown? She couldn't tell, but there were connections dancing everywhere around her. Strange animals, people who were also animals, songs, magazine covers—all of them held messages that were just for her.

Or for Jeanie.

Or for her.

Sometimes the songs were angry, and sometimes they congratulated her on being the only one who saw things for what they really were. Other times, they blamed her for things that went wrong in the world, or that would certainly go wrong because she failed to act, or acted with too much or not enough caution.

There were colors she'd never known existed. And when Becky read the billboards advertising beer, the graffiti, the discarded newspapers, and the handwritten paper sign in the window of the takeout place—*Delivery drivers wanted! Mileage reimbursed!*—all of them spoke to her on levels beyond what they ever had before. They all held . . . multitudes.

When Becky returned to Ruth's house, her feet were sore, as was her left arm, in which she'd clutched Jeannie's journal collection as she walked the city. Becky wasn't sure how long she'd been out. She seemed to remember night falling twice.

Ruth wasn't home, which was just as well. Becky went up to her room, removed the blanket from the stack of books in the corner, sat down on the floor, and started to read. Eventually, she made it to her bed. She fell asleep, woke up, read more, fell asleep, woke up, brought a book with her to the bathroom, drank from the faucet in gulps, and went back to her room to read.

Only then did Becky notice that her sheets were muddy. Probably because she hadn't removed her shoes when she came back from her walkabout.

Caught up in muddy sheets and the words printed on pages, Becky didn't look up, even when someone called from the bottom of the stairs. It wasn't Ruth. The voice was masculine, not terribly young but also not old. Becky frowned at her book, annoyed. She was making up for lost time. Jeanie's passion for connections and her openness to the world, both outside herself and inside the confines of her skull, coursed through Becky.

Becky was so engrossed in reading, she didn't hear the footsteps ascending the stairs or notice that the owner of the voice was there until the door flew open, hitting the wall.

"Who the fuck are you, and what are you doing in my dead brother's room?"

It was Ruth's other son, the second of the two boys in

the pictures scattered around the house. Becky recognized the spoiled air of privilege and hostility she'd read in the sparsely worded, obligatory Mother's Day cards hanging on Ruth's refrigerator. The ones that always arrived late.

"Jesus!" He moved around the room, picking up Becky's few belongings and flinging them back down with a look of disgust. "Are you some bum? Some squatter?"

"I'm Becky, your mother's renter." Then, belatedly, "Where is Ruth?"

"Mom's been dead for three days! You've just been living here in her house after she dropped dead at church from a heart attack? Fucking hell! All right, get your shit together and let's go, lady."

"But I pay rent. Or my sister, I think, is paying—*was* paying Ruth."

Becky could practically hear the pathways in her head, the ones borrowed from Jeanie's journals, screaming out. They were calling him filthy names. They were telling Becky he was a giant, but one made of insects. They were telling her to run, and not stop running, from him.

A quiet part of Becky wanted to cry for Ruth, cry because her story had ended, but there wasn't time. Ruth's son snatched up Becky's clothes, books, and other meager belongings and started shoving them into a garbage bag, not caring how the paperbacks were getting mangled in the process. Becky lunged for Jeanie's stack of journals. She stuffed them up her sweater and tucked the hem into her old jeans.

Within the space of a few minutes, Becky was out on another curb, holding a trash bag and struggling to put on the coat that had been thrown at her, all while making sure the journals didn't slip out from under her sweater. Ruth's son stood on the stoop, looking back and forth along the street. Perhaps afraid that someone behind a window would judge his actions, he opened his wallet and threw two twenties at Becky, then turned and went back into the house. He turned off the porch light.

After that, Becky spent her days in libraries. She didn't want to answer people's questions for money any longer, knowing she didn't have the answers. When she wanted knowledge that wasn't in books, Becky read over people's shoulders. She could usually grab a few sentences of insight before someone shooed her away due to her impolite proximity or her offensive smell.

At night, Becky slept on the subway—or on her blanket in the park when it was warm enough. She would lie on her back and read until she could no longer hold the book up and it fell to her chest. If the night was just right, she could use the stars as pushpins in the map of connections she was weaving out of what she read.

If the night was just right, Becky could see multitudes.

The Circulation Desk

New York City, 2018

Jim and Kate pulled up to a row of ground-floor storefronts in an older five-story building. Kate verified the payment with the rideshare driver while Jim pulled her wheelchair from the trunk and popped it open on the curb. He then stared down the obviously impatient driver as Kate slowly got out with the help of her forearm crutches.

Free of the car and its rude driver, Kate pointed to a dimly lit thin, vertical sign that hung over an unassuming door tucked between two cell phone stores. The arrows on the bottom of the sign indicated their destination, the Circulation Desk, was upstairs.

"If we go into the foyer, there's an elevator," Kate noted. "Some days, I can do the stairs, but I just don't think today's one of those days. C'mon, it's this way."

She stuck her tie-dye crutches in the long bag on the back of her chair, sat down, and started wheeling her way to the door. The speed and proficiency Kate demonstrated was enough that Jim had to jog the last few steps to open the door for her. Kate could have managed on her own, but Jim felt it was the least he could do after she'd taken the time to bring him here and paid for their ride. The two closest subway stations had stairs, so Kate had suggested the rideshare and insisted on paying, even though Jim had tried to get her to split the bill with him.

As soon as the elevator doors closed for the short ride up to the second floor, Kate's eyes flicked sideways to Jim. "So, you know this is just a friendly outing, right? It's not a date."

Jim had been so excited that this niche bar even existed that he hadn't given much thought to the implications of going there with Kate. He shrugged. "That's cool."

"Cool," Kate echoed with a relieved sigh.

The doors dinged and slid open with a bit of a grumble, and the yellow lights in the hallway beyond flickered. Across from the elevator, a black bulletin board named the offices on the floor in white letters: two accountants and a "professional medium."

Kate led Jim to a thick black door labeled *Private*, through which music and voices drifted. Reaching back, she grabbed one of her crutches and banged it against the door. Nothing happened for a moment, and she was in the middle of banging a second time when the door flew open. The aproned person who let them in didn't even look to see who was there before heading through a nearby swinging door, presumably into the kitchen.

As Kate had described, the Circulation Desk was like any other bar except there were books crammed into every inch of wall space. Upon closer inspection, Jim realized there were also smaller bookshelves used as end tables next to old velvet sofas, bookshelves built into the bases of high, round tables that people stood at, and even crates of books under the pool tables.

None of it was disorganized, not even a little. All the books stood tall, with their spines facing out, and bookends of every shape and size held the volumes in place. Vintage black elephants with what could have been real-ivory tusks, creepy ceramic clowns, even some X-rated hula girls with shiny pink nipples—kitschy items supported the books everywhere Jim looked. Labels at the top of each shelf and stack stated the alphabetical range of authors' last names or the range of call numbers, leaving no room for chaos.

Jim took it all in as Kate found them a table, moving a chair out of the way so she could slide hers into the space it had occupied.

"This place is incredible!" Jim burst out at last. "And it's so well organized! You said you can actually check books out? Is there a desk with an old lady wearing horn-rimmed glasses and wielding a date stamper instead of a bouncer?"

Kate chuckled. "No old lady, no bouncer. But there is an old-fashioned stamper at a desk by the front door, right next to the card catalog."

Jim snapped his head back around to stare at Kate. "There's a freaking card catalog? No way!"

"Go see for yourself." She waved her hand in the direction of the entrance. "I'm getting a hard cider when the server comes by. You want anything?"

"I'll take whatever you're having and some fries," Jim replied, already moving toward the entrance.

And there it was, in all its little-drawered, brass-label-holdered, finger-hook-handled glory—the card catalog. Jim was young enough that even in his earliest years, the public libraries had already switched to computerized catalogs. His tiny Catholic grade school's single-room library had still boasted a card catalog during his first few years there, but he had been too young to understand how to properly navigate it, lending it an air of magic and mystery in his memory.

Hesitantly, feeling oddly like an intruder—or possibly Indiana Jones trying to pick the right iteration of the Holy Grail—Jim approached the drawers. The Templar's warning of "Choose wisely" rang in his head.

"They don't bite, you know."

Jim jumped and may have uttered an embarrassing squeal. He turned to see a tall, blonde woman stripping off her leather jacket, which she hung on one of a series of hooks on the wall. Smirking, she swept her hair into a quick, messy bun.

If Jim hadn't already been blushing from being found fanboying over the card catalog by a beautiful woman with tattooed, muscular arms, that simple act would have had him red anyway. He considered himself an everyday kind of guy who was more into a woman's personality and attitude than her looks. But man was he a sucker for that effortless up-do maneuver. And oh goodness, the back of her head was shaved!

"Uh," he stammered, wanting to say something cool or witty or, at the very least, coherent. "This place is incredible, right? The books! The freaking card catalog!" he finally managed.

"First time, huh?" Smiling broadly, the woman pulled an apron from her jacket pocket and wrapped it around her waist. "Well, welcome! Be sure you meet Samara while you're here." She winked, then turned and entered the bar.

Jim stared after her with a starstruck smile for longer than necessary before he moaned and smacked himself on the forehead. "'This place is incredible! The books!' Way to go, Jim. You can write hours of stage dialogue, but then when you meet a pretty girl, all you can think to say is, 'The books, amirite?' Way to go, champ."

Letting out a long sigh, he pulled open a drawer at random. Headings indicating topics, authors, and book titles greeted him. He closed the drawer, deciding to look up the first book that popped into his mind: *Playwrights on Playwriting* by Toby Cole, a favorite of his.

There was indeed a card for it! Not only did the Circulation Desk have it, they had a first edition from 1960. The card was a combination of typewritten text, each letter clearly pressed into the card stock by a real typewriter, and carefully handwritten printing. The penciled-in bit indicated that the book resided in the "brick wall shelves."

With care, Jim slid the card back into its designated spot, then went in search of the book. The wall that ran behind the bar was the only one made of brick, and Jim followed the labels fixedly. He looked away as he got close, only to realize he was about to walk in front of an active dartboard. Stopping, he waited politely until one of the players saw him and waved him through to grab his book. Jim guessed they were used to such interruptions.

He was already leafing through *Playwrights on Playwriting* when he got back to the table where Kate waited.

"Ordered your fries, and I got you one of the seasonal flavors of Woodchuck, since it was on draft. That okay?" Kate spotted the book Jim held. "Oh! What did you get?"

Jim smiled. He loved how library people never tired of books. It was an excellent personality trait of the profession. "It's a first edition of *Playwrights on Playwriting*. I'm surprised it isn't listed on eBay, instead of hanging out on a shelf in a bar."

Kate shrugged. "I hear book theft happens here sometimes, but rarely. It can get you banned from the bar and socially shunned on the job. Most of the books here have been bequeathed from the private collections of dead librarians. Check the bookplate in the front."

Turning to the inside of the front cover, Jim found a bookplate that depicted the sign hanging above the stairway entrance. Under the illustration, the bookplate listed the name of the woman who had donated the book to the Circulation Desk, as well as her dates of birth and death, and the dates of her employment in the New York Public Library system.

"Oh!" Kate exclaimed. "I bet you got that from the shelves by the dartboard."

"How did you know?"

Another shrug. "Look at the spine."

Jim glanced down. Sure enough, small holes peppered the entirety of the book's spine.

The bar was fairly busy, so it took a while for them to get Jim's fries and Kate's battered mushrooms. Just as the food finally arrived, a booming, full-belly laugh rang out from the direction of the bar. The infectious sound turned several heads, including Jim's. When he realized it was the blonde woman from the card catalog, Jim wished the bar had handicap-accessible seating so he could have a shot at earning one of those laughs for himself. And perhaps getting the woman's number in the process.

Oh, well. The night is still young.

Kate and Jim had discussed hometowns and the theater and were moving on to the archives when a group of at least two dozen people entered, adding to the noise of the already busy bar.

"Oh, shoot!" Kate nearly shouted over the din. "I forgot the Kips Bay branch had an after-hours event tonight. They always come here afterward since they're located close by. Hey, Jim, go grab us another round from the bar before they all start ordering drinks, okay?"

Jim hopped up, happy for the chance to be closer to the bartender. He ended up getting caught in the fray of the rush but managed to reach the bar. Everyone around him was recapping their day at the library, and Jim soaked up the conversation as he tried to catch the eye of the bartender to place his and Kate's order. From this vantage point, Jim was close enough to see that the blonde had a damn-good tattoo of Oscar Wilde on her forearm.

"So, I almost had to break up a fight today. I'll give you two guesses as to who the culprits were," the woman to Jim's left said to the man next to her.

"Hmm, well, one of them has to be Stinky-Mink-Stole Molly, because I know you worked in biographies today and that's where her favorite computer is."

"Yep!" The woman quickly leaned across the bar and ordered a vodka and soda with a lime twist.

"Ha! Knew it!" the man celebrated. "Now, who would she fight with? It would be over the computer, obviously. Big Bill? He's nuts enough to think he could cross Molly and get away with it."

"Nope!" The woman smirked. "Good try, but he wasn't in today. You have one more guess!" Then, to the bartender, "Thanks, Jessie! How's your nephew? Did he like the book?"

"My sister said he loved it!" returned the bartender, Jessie. "I'll have to get more of those chewable toddler books for him. What can I get for you, stranger?"

It took Jim a moment to figure out she was talking to him. "Oh! Two draft ciders, please."

"Sure thi—shit! Out of pint glasses! The dishwasher called off last minute tonight, and I haven't been able to keep up with the glass washing out here. Umm . . ." She looked around for an alternative.

Jim saw his chance and went for it, yelling over the building noise. "Well, want me to come around and wash some until you catch up? I worked at a diner in high school that had a glass washer for all the milkshake glasses we went through."

"Liquor laws say you can't come behind the bar, but"—she raised her voice—"anybody going to tell on us if my new friend—ugh, what was your name, brown eyes?"

"Jim, ma'am," he said, before immediately cursing himself. Ma'am? Why had he said ma'am? Smooth, real smooth.

"Anybody care if Jim here washes glasses for me?" Jessie called out, as if she hadn't even noticed the *ma'am* debacle. A resounding chorus of good-natured noes answered her, and Jim made his way around the corner of the bar and got to work.

"Thanks for volunteering, Jim," Jessie said. "What branch are you from?"

"I work in the distribution area at the Main Branch," he replied as he finished his first batch of glasses, having run them through the glass brushes, the sanitizing wash, and the rinse sink.

"The Schwarzman Building, huh? Oh! Do you work with Lenore? She never comes here, but I hear she's a fucking legend!" Jessie said with genuine awe.

Right then and there, Jim knew he and Jessie would get along splendidly. Unfortunately, there were thirsty librarians who needed drinks lined up at the bar, and Jessie swept away to fill their orders, leaving Jim to listen to the rest of the conversation continuing on the other side of the bar.

"Crazy Becky, with the pigtails?" asked the friend of Vodka-and-Soda.

"Oh! You were so close! It was Psychic Becky, who always reads over people's shoulders!" Vodka-and-Soda shot back.

"Gah! I almost guessed her! Besides getting too into people's personal bubbles, though, she never really does anything worth fighting about. What happened?"

"Well, Molly was cruising Craigslist, as she normally does, scribbling in one of her chicken-scratch-filled note-books, when here comes Becky walking behind Molly and peering over her shoulder. Becky got really upset over something Molly supposedly wrote. I mean, like, she was genuinely bothered. I've never seen her like that. She started saying something along the lines of 'I know what you do to those poor animals!' and telling Molly how the archbishop isn't going to sleep with her no matter how many kittens she sacrifices. Well, Molly didn't like that at all. I've never seen her so angry. I had to maneuver a rolling rack between them and try to talk them both down until security arrived."

"That is so weird!" Vodka-and-Soda's friend replied. "Not for Molly—Molly will throw hands with anybody—but Psychic Becky usually leaves well enough alone. Did you catch sight of what Molly wrote?"

Vodka-and-Soda waved a hand. "Yeah, like I said, the usual chicken scratch. Couldn't read a word of it."

Continuing to listen to the surrounding conversations, Jim made good progress in getting the glasses caught up while Jessie pushed past the rush. He even grabbed one of the bus tubs and did a sweep of the room.

When Jim was through, Jessie thanked him several times over and gave him a free round for him and Kate.

Then she slid a cocktail napkin and a felt-tipped pen across the bar. "Hey, if you're ever looking to pick up a shift here and there, like when someone calls off or we know we're going to be busy, leave me your cell phone number or email or whatever."

Jim happily gave her the info, hoping that maybe she'd call him for another reason too.

He spent the rest of the night relaxing with Kate in their quiet corner of the room. She regaled Jim with stories of the weird things people had donated, or tried to donate, to the library for their "historic value."

"Just last summer, some old lady came in and handed us a file box full of carefully organized handwritten reviews of diner lunches her husband had written. He ate at some diner or other in the city every workday for thirty-five years and wrote a detailed description and evaluation of every one of them. The powers that be said we couldn't keep what was basically decades' worth of descriptions of tepid meatloaf and mediocre coleslaw, with the occasional outstanding Monte Cristo or pot roast thrown in.

"But the woman was so earnest about wanting to do something with it, you know? 'It's his life's work,' she told me over and over, so I contacted the New York State Restaurant Association. I bounced around their phone system until I found someone willing to take the collection. It might end up in a basement or bound as a book or framed and displayed. Who knows! But it made her happy."

"You're a good person, Kate." Jim raised his glass in a toast to his friend, feeling warm and at peace—probably because he didn't drink often and it was his third round.

Kate clinked her glass against Jim's. "I try, but I draw the line at teeth!"

"I'm sorry, wha—"

"I said, no teeth! I don't care who they belonged to! I. Don't. Take. Teeth!" She drained the rest of her cider, banged her pint glass down on the table hard enough to tell Jim *that* was a story she didn't want to elaborate on, and then excused herself to the restroom.

Jim stood to look at the books some more but swayed a little when he got to his feet. He figured he should get some water first. Jessie was just busy enough that she let him get his own water from the soda tap and didn't make conversation, but Jim thought he caught her throwing him a wink.

That wink made his heart do something funny in his chest. But Jessie was cool and way out of his league. Jim wasn't the type of guy tall, quick-witted women with tattoos and leather jackets went for. Hell, he didn't even know if she was into guys.

Still, she had his number, even if it was due to his glass-washing skills, and he'd take that as a win for the night.

His browsing turned up a volume on the New York Public Library system, which he figured would come in handy as research for his play. In that moment, he realized it had gone from just an idea for a possible next project to something he was definitely going to write.

Before he and Kate left, Jim went to the checkout desk next to the card catalog. There was no scanner, just a long box to hold cards and an antique date stamper that was already set up for exactly four weeks from the current date. Jim looked in the back of both books, and sure enough, there was a lined card in a pocket at the back of each. Jim dutifully wrote his name and library card number on each card, then stamped the date on the cards and on the pockets in the books.

On the curb, Jim and Kate bid each other good night.

Kate called herself another rideshare, and Jim hit the subway. Finding a seat in a car full of other folks heading home from their nights out, Jim reflected on his own. He had enjoyed a good night, and he had two excellent books with him as a result of the evening's escapades.

Actually, he had two books and a burgeoning crush on a bartender with literary tattoos.

Thinking of Jessie winking at him, Jim blushed, then laughed at himself under his breath.

Focusing on the books, he opened the library history book. Instantly, his face broke into a huge smile. Almost every page had notes in the margins, adding details to the original text. Some were funny stories, some offered gentle corrections, but every entry was initialed and dated by the person who'd written it.

Maybe it was the three hard ciders, but Jim felt his eyes well up. Up until that moment, he had considered himself a playwright working at the library just to make ends meet. After visiting the Circulation Desk, though, Jim felt like he was part of the New York Public Library.

Flights of Fancy

New York City, 2018

It was Jim's day off. He slept a luxurious extra hour, then made himself a larger-than-average cup of coffee. Humming show tunes, he broke open a fresh set of felt-tipped pens, his favorite to use when color-coding notes, and plotted out the first several mini-scenes for his new play on note cards.

Around midmorning, just as Jim finished pinning the cards to his bulletin board, three loud thumps sounded above him. Smiling, he took the steps up to Dottie's two at a time. The door to her apartment was already unlocked and ajar. When he called out, Dottie responded from the library, as he had suspected she would. Entering the room, he found her nicely dressed and at the ready, leaning regally against her desk and holding a book out to him.

Jim took the book and bowed low. "How many rungs shall I ascend to cast forth this volume to the ground, milady?"

"Take it all the way to the top and let her fly!" Dottie declared.

Trying to channel the grave seriousness of an executioner leading a prisoner to the guillotine, Jim climbed the ladder. At the top, he took the book firmly in both hands and flung it to the ground, doing his best to make sure it landed flat, creating a noise heavy enough to satisfy his lady liege's disdain.

Closing her eyes, Dottie nodded, granting her approval of his efforts, and Jim came down and picked the offending book up off the floor. Only then did he realize the cover was familiar, and it took him a minute longer to recognize why.

"Wait, isn't this the book that's on the flyer posted in the window of the bookstore next door—the bookstore you're part owner of?"

"Yes, it is." Retrieving a compact mirror from a desk drawer, Dottie applied her lipstick.

"Isn't the author coming to read his book, like, today?" Jim asked.

"Yes, he is."

"Dottie, did you have Flights of Fancy invite him to do the reading just so you could tell him how much you don't like his book?"

"Yes. Yes, I did."

"What did he do that was so wrong?"

Dottie closed the compact. "My dear boy, it would take much less time for me to tell you what he did right."

"Okay, then, what did he do right?"

"He spelled the names right. That's it. That's all he got right in the so-called comprehensive analysis he titled *Leading Ladies of Twentieth-Century Literature.*"

"Dottie, you're going to make that poor man cry, aren't you?"

She smiled from ear to ear. "You should come, Jim.

You can be my date. It will make people talk. Oh! And I ordered some delicious cake for them to put out. I may make the author cry, but I will compliment his spelling, and he can eat the cake."

Jim hummed thoughtfully. "It is traditional to serve cake at a funeral. When is this offender sentenced to die by humiliation?"

Dottie crossed her ankles. "In about an hour."

"That gives me time to shower, shave, and press my good shirt. I'll see you in about forty-five minutes!"

True to his word, Jim returned to Dottie's looking dashing, if slightly self-conscious about how his button-down stretched over his belly more than it used to. It wasn't time to worry about his waistline, though; it was time to be Dottie's escort. Jim held out his elbow, and Dottie looped her arm through his.

The walk to the retrofitted storefront of the bookstore was barely twenty steps from Dottie's front door, but Jim noticed that Dottie seemed to stand taller, and he didn't think it was entirely due to the low heels she was wearing.

Dottie was in her element.

When they arrived, Dottie introduced Jim to Philip, the other owner of Flights of Fancy. Philip greeted her with enthusiasm and kisses to both cheeks, then led her to an armchair that appeared to be reserved for her. The rest of those present for the reading would get folding chairs.

"And who is your handsome young friend?" Philip asked, pulling a folding chair over for Jim and setting it up next to Dottie's throne.

"This is James Lowry, an up-and-coming playwright. You may have heard of his play *Anytime*, which the Cherry Lane put on a few months back. It got excellent reviews in the *Times*. I expect big things from Jim in the future."

Jim blush and gave the hand that still rested in the crook of his elbow a gentle squeeze. Dottie squeezed back.

"We have a few minutes before the reading, don't we?" Dottie asked. "Philip, why don't you give Jim a quick tour of Flights of Fancy. I'll be fine here; you two boys go." Her wave of encouragement was not to be ignored.

Philip winked. "Yes, Auntie."

Philip was a gracious host. As he showed Jim around Flights of Fancy, he explained that the space the bookstore occupied had originally been part of the first-floor apartment but had been converted into a storefront about ten years before Dottie bought the building. It had started as a men's haberdashery, then became a discount clothing store when the neighborhood fell a bit into ruin. After that, the space changed hands several times before sitting vacant for a while in the early two thousands.

"I'd just graduated from SUNY Cortland with a bachelor's in business, a minor in marketing, and a dream of opening my own bookstore. Bobby and Jeff would have helped, but I refused to let them lift a finger. They basically saved my life when I was a fifteen-year-old runaway and supported me all through college; I just couldn't let them do more. Did Dottie tell you about that? How Bobby and Jeff found me?"

Jim shook his head and eagerly accepted the framed photo Philip took down from a shelf behind the sales desk. There was Bobby, looking much as he had in Dottie's picture from their Tandem Bike days, except in color and with a few extra wrinkles around his eyes. He had his arm around Philip, who was dressed in a graduation gown. On Philip's other side stood a man with freckles and a bright smile—Jeff, Jim assumed.

"I was on my own in the city because, well, the usual."

Philip gestured vaguely at nothing. "My family found out I was gay and disowned me, so I was going to a lot of parties and couch surfing around the Village with whoever would have me for a night or two. I somehow ended up at a party that Bobby and Jeff were at; I probably crashed it, to be honest. Jeff came right up to me and asked what I was doing there. I thought he was coming on to me at first, like a lot of older guys did, but then I saw the worry in his eyes.

"Do you know how long it'd been at that point since anyone had shown an ounce of actual concern for me? I think I almost started crying on the spot, I was so tired. When Jeff asked me how old I was, I told him the truth. He called Bobby over, and they offered me their spare room on the spot. They didn't know me from Adam, but they invited me into their home, no strings attached. I grabbed my bag so fast, all my worldly possessions tumbled out in front of everyone—my dirty laundry, literally, as well as my collection of paperbacks, which I'd stuffed in my bag before leaving home. Jeff picked up my high-school French-class copy of *Le Petit Prince*, with all my bad translations scrawled in between the lines. His jaw dropped open, and he showed it to Bobby.

"Bobby looked at the book and said, 'Well, then, this is just meant to be, isn't it?'

"From that moment on, Jeff and Bobby took care of me, and there were always lots of books to read. When I graduated, I wanted to do something with my life that would bring books into the lives of others but that would also allow me to be independent and on my own. I mentioned it to Aunt Dottie at my graduation party, actually, and she invited me to come see this space in her building.

"I remember walking into this old showroom with her for the first time and seeing all the built-in shelves. Even though they were painted horrible colors by whoever was here last, I could just picture these shelves cleaned up and lined with books. I told Dottie that, and by her smile, I knew it was all going to come together. Flights of Fancy was born!"

From there, Philip showed Jim the store's different sections, including the permanent display dedicated to LGBTQ authors and literature. In the back room, the most modern space, Philip explained how they had renovated the former storeroom into a bright showroom and gushed about the artist, a friend of his, who'd created the mobile that spun above the shelves. Each dangling ornament depicted scenes from *Le Petit Prince*. Jim admired it all and commented on the mirrors lining the interior wall, how it made the space feel much bigger.

"Yes, doesn't it?" His eyes still cast upward, Philip tilted his head. "Oh dear, the rose is stuck again. She's supposed to rotate, but she always gets stuck."

Jim looked up. The rose was the one still element in the otherwise-moving tableau. Philip stood on his tiptoes and tried to nudge the red bloom back into motion but caught sight of his watch.

"Oh, and look at the time. We should head up front for the reading."

As they made their way back, Philip touched Jim's arm and dropped his voice from tour guide to a more intimate tone. "Jim, thank you for being Dottie's friend. She's a special lady."

"I feel honored she considers me a friend."

As Jim took his spot next to Dottie, Philip walked to the podium and introduced the author. The unfortunate man who was unknowingly there for his own funeral looked like a younger, thinner Ernest Hemingway. Dottie smiled and politely golf clapped, not letting on that she was about to verbally eviscerate him in front of a bookstore full of onlookers.

The man did his reading. Whenever he said something Dottie didn't like, she shifted in her seat or fiddled with her handbag. When it came time for him to take questions, Dottie let several others go first.

A few agreed with his take on things; others didn't. Then Dottie raised her hand up, up, up—an eager gesture that made Jim picture her in her school days, trying to get the attention of the professor in a mostly male setting, refusing to be overlooked.

The flared sleeve of her dress fell away, revealing her thin, softly wrinkled arm and an angry purple bruise near the elbow. Jim stared at it, wondering if he had missed a thump on his ceiling, an unintentional one that had left Dottie with that bruise instead of a dented book.

Yet when she spoke, all sense of fragility disappeared behind steel wit, backed up by an arsenal of knowledge.

The public event became a two-person conversation. Dottie and the author volleyed back and forth for at least twenty minutes, each defending their opinions with memorized passages from various books and interpretations of scholarly writings on the topic. No one in the audience seemed to mind in the least. They followed the discussion like spectators at Wimbledon, knowing they could never participate on that level but happy to witness it play out.

Finally, Philip stood up and glanced pointedly at his watch, twice. Then he politely interjected himself into the conversation, before the author could speak again, mentioning that he knew the man had another engagement that day, and he thanked everyone for coming out. He reminded the audience that Flights of Fancy was well stocked with copies of the author's book and that the author had graciously agreed to sign them.

"Well," the author said, his voice laced with relief, "I guess we will need to agree to disagree and save the rest until we meet again someday."

Dottie smiled but lifted her chin an extra inch. "I don't recall agreeing to any such thing."

Jim was proud to be sitting next to Dottie and to be her friend. He didn't like the author one bit, not even a little. The dislike wasn't even related to the man's literary opinions; it had more to do with the last thing he'd said to Dottie.

"*. . . until we meet again someday.*"

Maybe he hadn't meant anything by it, or maybe it was just a turn of phrase, but to Jim, he seemed to be saying, "*Well, you may be right, but you're also going to be dead soon, so who really wins here?*"

If Dottie harbored similar feelings, she didn't show any sign of it. She was too busy, as she'd attracted a circle of bookstore patrons who'd flocked to her to ask her thoughts on various literary topics.

"Do you lecture anywhere? I'd love to take any class you teach," one stated, probably assuming Dottie had been a professor of English lit or women's studies.

Dottie laughed but reached into her purse and pulled out a few business cards with her name and email. Once her admirers had dispersed, she gestured for Jim to join her at the refreshments table. Dottie cut a nicely sized slice of cake and carried it to the queue of patrons waiting to get their books signed. She didn't push ahead in line, even though she could have parted it like the Red Sea after winning the room's admiration. When it was her turn, she placed the cake on the table and slid it over to the author.

He leaned back and crossed his arms. "A peace of-fering?"

"Sometimes a piece of cake is just a piece of cake." Dottie reached into her purse and pulled out the copy of the author's book that Jim had thrown from the ladder for her earlier that day. She placed it on the table before the man.

The author took a bite of cake, perhaps to gird him-self. Then he stared down at the dessert, surprised, his face melting into sheer delight.

"This is delicious!" He went in for another forkful. "Oh my God, did you make this? Do you bake in addition to . . ." He wagged his crumb-laden fork toward the area where they had sparred not long before.

"Oh no, I don't bake. No time for it. Too much read-ing to do. You can make the book out to Dorothy Barber."

He grabbed one more bite of cake before pushing the plate aside and taking up his fine-tipped Sharpie. "To Dor-othy Barber, who most certainly never agreed to disagree with me."

Dottie smiled, thanked him, and picked up a small box tied with string that Philip produced from behind the register. She then made for the exit, and Jim opened the door for her so they could return to her apartment.

Dottie kicked off her heels as soon as they were through the door. She made for the kitchen, telling Jim over her shoulder to make them some coffee to go with their cake. The box she carried held a smaller version of the cake at the reading, just big enough for the two of them. Cutting it right down the middle, Dottie placed one half on each of their plates and licked the icing from her fingers, smiling to herself.

Once they were settled at the table and had each had

their first few bites of cake, humming their appreciation, Jim said, "I didn't know you had business cards."

"They're not business cards. They're acquaintance cards. I give them to new acquaintances."

"How come you never gave me one?"

"Because we are friends, not just acquaintances, don't you think?"

Smiling, Jim held up his coffee cup to clink with hers.

About halfway through his cake, Jim added, "You never did compliment his spelling."

Dottie wrinkled her nose, shrugged, and went back to her cake without comment. In that moment, Jim was sure she had caught and taken offense at the author's quip that had bothered Jim so much.

Before he could say anything about the matter, Jim's phone buzzed in his pocket. It was a text from Jessie at the Circulation Desk, asking him if he could come help out. Apparently, the head librarian of the 53rd Street branch was having a birthday, and Jessie expected a crowd. Jim quickly texted back, agreeing to come in.

"Who's that?" Dottie inquired. "An acquaintance? One who makes you smile when they message you?"

"It's probably all the sugar from this cake," Jim said, trying and failing not to blush. "As for acquaintance or something else, we'll see."

When they were done, Jim loaded their plates in the dishwasher. He was about to pour out the last of the coffee when Dottie told him to leave it. She wanted a second cup. Instead of her usual midday nap, Dottie explained, she was going to call Gail on the West Coast.

"I can't wait to tell her about today. Gail's very well connected out that way. I bet she could get that author invited to read somewhere and give him one hell of a round two! And her grandchild Shion runs an imprint of Gail's small press, as well as a podcast. Assuming the feminist theme doesn't scare the author away, I'm sure Shion will have him on. Then Gail can give him hell, and they can broadcast it to the ends of the earth!"

Jim poured the rest of the coffee into Dottie's cup. "You evil minx, you!"

Dottie shrugged. "I've been called much worse, and so has Gail. Working in what was once a male-dominated profession, you get used to that kind of thing." She paused thoughtfully. "Actually, no, you don't get used to it. You just get used to being angry about it on a regular basis. I decided to stay in the thick of the fray and work on things from inside the industry. Gail struck out on her own and created new space and opportunities for women writers. Same goal, different paths.

"That author today—I've met a few thousand like him. He thought he had it all figured out, to the point where it barely occurred to him that anyone would question his opinions on the topic." Dottie jabbed her thick-knuckled index finger at his book before opening it and pointing to the message he'd written to her. "But when he wrote this, he'd started to consider that he'd got some things not quite right. He was worried others would figure it out too but hoped the outspoken old lady in front of him was just a fluke."

"Dottie, you are many things, but I'm pretty sure a fluke is not one of them."

Dottie winked. "You have fun with your 'acquaintance or something else.'"

Cake at a Funeral

New York City, 2018

As Jim emerged from the subway and headed toward the Circulation Desk, he fussed with his shirt—a navy-blue short-sleeve button-down with a subtle print of TARDISes and Daleks. This shirt, too, had gotten tight around his belly, the result of too many slices of cheap pizza and no money for a gym membership.

Taking a deep breath, he gave himself a silent pep talk. *You're the only one who cares about your midsection. Just be grateful you have a body that lets you get around the city easily. Besides, your stomach may have gotten soft, but your arms are coming along nicely.*

Just before mounting the steps up to the Circulation Desk, Jim remembered something he'd put in his pocket to add to his outfit: an enamel pin depicting a bust of Shakespeare wearing a ruffled collar in the bisexual pride colors: pink, purple, and blue. The pin had been a graduation gift from his high-school drama coach, a reference to how vehemently Jim had argued that there was no way Shakespeare had been completely straight.

Attaching Willy to his breast pocket, Jim wondered if it would help kick off a conversation with Jessie. He hoped the place wasn't already slammed so he'd have some time to get to know her better before the birthday party rush.

When he got inside, Jessie was hustling around the mostly empty bar, taking down birthday decorations. "Hi, Jim! Hey, take down that piñata over in the biography section, would you?"

"Yeah, sure." He carried the multicolored donkey over to Jessie. "Did I miss something? Did the party already happen?"

"Nope." She glanced around the room. "I think I got it all. Anyway, someone died, so the birthday party's off."

"Was it the birthday guy?"

"Oh, no! That would have sucked, huh?" Jessie shook her head. "No, Galang is fine, as far as I know. Rat-Friend Fred died. He was the 53rd Street branch's favorite homeless patron; he was there almost every day. He died on the toilet. Security found him during their final sweep at closing time. I got the call that the birthday party has turned into an impromptu wake about fifteen minutes ago."

"So, you still need me to stay?"

"Hell, yeah! Same-size crowd expected, just more subdued and no piñata." Jessie's eyes swept over him. "You look nice, by the way. Love the pin! Wish I had worn something other than a concert T-shirt tonight."

Jim turned away so Jessie wouldn't see him blush. He didn't have time to build on the opening, though, because the crowd began to arrive.

Someone had blown up a blurry but smiling picture of Fred on the library's printer and set it up on the small stage. Fred had one of those faces that made it hard to tell his age; he looked youthful and ancient all at once. Or maybe that was just the result of the photo being hastily enlarged from what was probably a cell phone pic. Jim didn't know.

Galang, still wearing a big, shiny button declaring *It's My Birthday*, started off the evening.

"We're here to celebrate the life of Fred, a.k.a. Rat-Friend Fred. For those of you who didn't have the pleasure of knowing him, Fred earned his name by not-so-secretly having at least one rat on his person at all times. He treated those alley rats like kings. In his hands, they were tame and content. I think all of us, at some point or another, made the decision to look the other way when we saw beady eyes peeking out of Fred's pockets as he read or snoozed."

A ripple of knowing giggles rolled through the somber crowd.

"But Fred's kindness didn't extend just to rats. He also made it his responsibility to take care of us librarians. He may have been one of our patrons, but I think Fred took on the role of steward, always trying to make our days brighter.

"I'd like to open the floor now to anyone who'd like to share some memories of Fred."

There was the expected awkward silence, everyone a little hesitant to go first; then a Black woman wearing a bright dashiki stood up in the crowd, not bothering to go up on the stage for the mic.

"Ya'll can hear me all right, yeah? Well, I loved Fred because he spoke my love language, which is food. Whenever Fred had a little bit of money, he would go get Hershey bars at the bodega and leave them on the return carts for us librarians to find.

"When we had cookies in the break room, I know we all slipped some to Fred, and I brought him leftovers from home a few times. I was confused when he would politely ask about the ingredients and then say, 'Thank you so much! I have a hungry friend who would love this!' Now, I have to admit, after the third time or so I brought him food and he said that, I was feeling some kind of a way, so I asked him about it. I said, 'Fred, why don't you eat the food I bring you? I'm a good cook, and you won't even give it a try!' He said, in that sweet way of his, 'I'm sure it's delicious, Sandra, but I'm a vegan.'"

Sandra laughed, and everyone in attendance joined in.

Once the mirth died down, she added, "So the next day, I brought him peas and rice and a big helping of fried plantains. No animal products used! We sat on the steps, and he ate every bite and said it was one of the best meals he ever had. I think it was the proudest moment of my cooking life! But that was Fred, you know? It was a simple act—a simple meal—but his joy was contagious. He had a generous heart, and I will miss him. Tomorrow, I'm bringing in enough peas and rice and plantains for the branch, so bring your appetites!"

A woman who could have been casually cosplaying Ms. Frizzle from *The Magic School Bus* stood up next. "We do story time and kids yoga every other week. Fred came to every session. Some of the parents gave him a bit of side-eye, but he'd just stay in the back and do all the moves along with the group.

"One time, Fred let out a staggeringly loud fart. I mean, there was no pretending it didn't happen. He proclaimed, 'Everybody toots, kids!' and just went on to the next Downward Dog. The kids absolutely lost it, as did most of the parents. All but one, who complained to the instructor about how Fred didn't belong there. The instructor informed the parent that everyone was welcome, and judging by Fred's form and breath control, he was probably experienced enough to teach an advanced class.

"The next time the yoga teacher came, the parent who'd complained and their child weren't there, but Fred was in his usual spot at the back of the group. The instructor read the book *Everyone Toots* and explained how sometimes that happens during yoga. The kids *loved* it, but the class did become a bit of a fart competition that day."

Again, fond laughter filled the room, and Ms. Frizzle added, "I know the kids are going to ask why Fred isn't there anymore. It won't be the same without him. We'll all miss him."

A young man with tattoos covering his forearms and climbing up his neck from under the collar of his plaid shirt stood. "Fred was also a stone-cold badass. He somehow figured out the city exterminators' schedules, and on those days, he'd be there when I unlocked the library doors and make a beeline for every place the exterminators dropped their glue traps for the mice. He'd pick up each one and trash it.

"And then, of course, there was the day with the dog out front when we all covered for him. Earmuffs, Galang!"

The library director dutifully put his hands over his ears, closed his eyes, and said in a singsong, "I hear nothing; I know nothing."

"Well, anyway," the man with the tattoos carried on, "some big dude was on his phone just outside the front doors. He had a little dog on a leash that he was being real rough with. I was working security that day, so I got to see the whole thing. The dog started to pee on the corner of the wall, and dude walked right into it midstream. He hauled off and kicked that poor dog so hard, it yelped and cowered.

"I was about to go out there, but quick as a flash—much quicker than you would think for a guy his age, Fred came barreling down the sidewalk and threw his shoulder into the big dude, linebacker style. That asshole fell over the low wall around the shrubbery and into the thorny bushes. Fred grabbed the dog and ran. Dude couldn't recover in time to see where Fred went, so he came inside and had Judy call the cops. Told me and everybody else we were witnesses.

"Funny thing, though, none of us saw a damn thing. Old dude in a knit cap and an army surplus jacket? Never saw him before in our lives. Security tape? IT said that camera was malfunctioning.

"Fred didn't come around for a few days after that. When he did return, I quietly asked him about an alleged dognapping. Said, 'I wonder where the dog is now?' Fred smiled. 'With someone who needed a furry friend to love and keep them company, I'd imagine.'"

There was a lull in the sharing after the tattooed man sat down. Then a short, middle-aged woman with glasses stood, took a deep breath, and keeping her head bowed, started to talk. Her words were so quiet, it was hard for anyone to hear her, though, so Galang grabbed the mic and brought it to her, saving her the walk up to the stage.

The microphone let out a squawk of feedback, but when it stopped, the woman began speaking again. "Fred brought us flowers almost every day, even in the winter. Sometimes they were just a handful of dandelions or dogwood blossoms from the street or park. Other days, he must have gone dumpster diving behind a floral shop, because his bouquets were bruised roses and birds of paradise with crooked stems."

She dabbed at her eyes with an already crumpled tissue. "He's the only one who ever brought me flowers in my whole life, and I'll never, ever forget him."

When the woman sat back down, there was barely a dry eye in the bar.

Taking the mic back, Galang addressed the room. "Fred saw all of you, caring day in and day out, and he loved each and every one of you for that and tried to return the favor whenever he could." He raised his glass. "To Fred! We are so glad you called our library home. You will be missed."

"Hear, hear!" the crowd cried in agreement.

Later, as Jim was collecting empties, he overheard the director tell one of the librarians, "You know, it turns out his name wasn't even Fred. It was Ted something-or-other. The EMS guys who came found an old, expired New York driver's license in his pocket. He also had a list of names and addresses for emergency contacts from all over the US and abroad."

"Well," the librarian remarked, "it's good he had that. Maybe the coroner can use the list to get in touch with any family he may have left."

The director shook his head and returned to his flower-adorned slice of birthday cake. "We were his family."

Rat-Friend Fred

New York City, 2018

Ted returned to New York City, the place of his birth, because he was dying. He understood his body, how it functioned, and the many nuances of sensation it experienced. Years of yoga, as well as the communication he maintained with the bacteria in his gut, pointed to something growing in his liver and pancreas. When the pain started, Ted knew his time was near, so he went home.

He liked to stay close to Central Park. It was a green heart in the middle of a steel-and-glass city. Ted slept on the ground in the fancy sleeping bag a sweet couple he'd met in Ithaca had given him the previous summer, when he'd taken up residence at Buttermilk Falls State Park. But even on cold nights, Ted left one hand out so he could dig his fingertips into the grass and feel the earth.

His days were spent foraging in the park's underbrush and garbage cans, doing yoga, reading in the nearby library, and writing poetry. Ted had a long walking stick he'd tied a floppy paint brush to. He would dunk the brush in water and write his poetry on the sidewalks. Some days, when it was sunny, the first words he'd written would be gone by the time he finished the last line, but that was all right. Ted just let the words flow until the brush was dry.

Sometimes, there would be bills and coins in the take-out cup he anchored against the wind with a rock in the bottom. Other times, it would remain empty, but that was all right. Whenever Ted used the money to buy his next meal, he'd think of the old children's tale of stone soup. He'd turned water, words, and a rock into a meal for himself. It was the same kind of magic as in the story.

At the library, Ted washed up in the bathroom, filled his water bottle, rested his feet, read to his heart's content, and left notes, poems, and goodies for the librarians. He also used the public computers to email friends around the world. He checked in with the daughter of his Yogi in Delhi and received the latest news from the studio she ran. He got notes from his former lovers in Canada and asked after their son—whom they'd named after Ted—and how he was doing with his art.

Sometimes, when the librarians didn't look terribly busy, Ted indulged his ego and asked about certain books. How many copies did the library system own? What kind of circulation did they get? He'd smile and nod, not letting on that he asked because he'd helped bring those books into the world. He'd found them floating amid the slush pile that it had been his job to wade through, looking for possible treasure. Ted was happy to have played a role in the life of those words.

Mostly, Ted just needed to remember to keep his little friends tucked away when in the library. Ted had a habit of forming companionships with small animals, and rats were prolific throughout New York. They made their way in the world with great adaptability and cleverness. People hated them, even though people themselves were also just trying to make their way in the world, learning to adapt, striving to be clever. People could learn from the lowliest of their neighbors.

The librarians knew about the rats he occasionally had in his pockets. The rodents peeked their noses out or quietly climbed up to the crook of his neck to nap when he was too engrossed in reading to notice and encourage them to hide. The librarians didn't know about the baby pigeons in his inside coat pocket, tucked against his heart, though.

Mostly, the librarians were kind to Ted. They shared their lunches with him when other patrons weren't looking and gifted him with new clothes and little bottles of shampoo or body wash from the hotels they visited when they left the city on weekends. The ones who weren't kind to him, Ted knew, were just trying to do a good job, attempting to make their way in the world.

He'd write them poems, too, because they needed them the most.

Sitting in a sunbeam, Ted leaned against the trunk of a young tree, facing the glass front of the library, and he watched others come and go. He felt the life concealed in his coat, alongside the cancer growing inside him, and his own heart beating. He sensed the people teeming around him, each their own universe of thoughts, loves, fears, hopes, and dreams.

Around Ted was the enormity of the city; below him, the depths of the roots of the tree he rested against, as well as those of the older trees in Central Park. There were man-made depths as well: the subway tunnels and sewer system. And of course, there was the water surrounding the island they were all on.

Higher up, Ted's awareness flowed with the tension

of cables on bridges connecting the island to the mainland. Pigeons and seagulls broke free of the pull of gravity and rose up and over the traffic on those bridges.

Everywhere, there was the music of the city, the stories that played out on the stages, and the stories that played out in the alleyways. All the players in the universal drama sought to make their way in the world, put food in their stomachs, be clever, and be remembered.

Ted didn't mind if no one remembered him. Some would. He had friends. But they, too, were temporary on this planet. Others would see him and forget him the next moment. To many, he was as fleeting as poems made of water that evaporated from the pavement.

Recently, he'd met a woman who had seen him writing his poetry and stopped in her tracks. She looked rough and hungry, but her eyes were sharp and alert with just a trace of wildness. The woman sat right down in the middle of foot traffic and watched him, swaying to the motion of his writing.

While Ted wrote, he often fell into *ujjayi* breathing, or ocean breathing. A slight constriction at the back of his throat produced an internal sound resembling waves crashing and receding. As the woman moved to his words, her breath synced with his, an echo to his tide.

Just as Ted noticed that his bucket of water was almost empty, the woman seemed to as well. She stood and approached him, and Ted saw that one of her old running shoes was held together with duct tape, the sole having long since given up its relationship with the rest of the shoe. The question in her eyes came out in a few whispered words, as if her voice were rusty from disuse.

"Can I hold your hand while you write?"

"Of course." Ted dipped his brush into the bucket,

sopped up the last bit of water, and wrote his last line of the day. He felt his words drop into her mind. She looked into his eyes and smiled, and he knew she had experienced the world as he did in that moment.

"What's your name, young lady?"

She laughed, a sound as light as air. He had the feeling she hadn't laughed like that in a while. "I don't know about the young part, but my name's Becky. I used to be known as Professor Rebecca Steadwell, once upon a time."

"People around here call me Fred, but I used to be called Ted. What's in a name, anyway?"

"Everything and nothing."

Ted considered this and nodded. "A friend of mine at the library gave me some muffins today; would you like some?"

They found a spot to sit together and eat. Well, Becky ate. Ted picked at his muffin. He generally had very little appetite as of late, and eating too much at a time gave him stabbing gas pains.

As people often did around Ted, his new friend began to talk.

"What you wrote back there was beautiful. I saw the connected associations in the world but in a different way than I usually do. I went from looking at a forest through a million different microscopes, trying to keep it all straight in my head, to looking at the same forest through my own human eyes from a high, gorgeous vantage point. There are no rose-colored glasses involved, and there don't need to be. From that viewpoint, there's still death and deception and evil intentions, but overall, there's life and time, which are bigger than everything else."

"Yeah," Ted said after a moment's consideration, "that's about it. Right on."

"I also like that what you wrote disappeared." Becky broke off a piece of the muffin and chewed it slowly. "It's still in me, I still hold that understanding, but it's nice that the words from that moment in time have disappeared instead of lasting forever. If they were there forever, there would be a point when they no longer matched reality. I know things evolve and people change, but sometimes it leaves me feeling dizzy and all turned around when they change so much."

"Yeah, linear time is a bitch to wrap your head around, man. It's as my mom used to say: a sticky wicket. She learned that little line from a British lady she worked with in the garment factory."

Becky smiled. She'd eaten her muffin with great gusto, as if she'd realized after the first bite or two just how hungry she'd been. Ted reached into his bag and offered her another, which she took from him and started devouring immediately. She took big bites, speaking in between swallows.

"I started out looking at the world from that high vantage point when I was a little girl, I think. I would read and read, but all the wonderful new things I learned would swirl together in a natural and comfortable way. Like, no matter how many colors I added to the paint I was mixing, it was still lovely. But then I started to think about things too closely, especially as I studied literature and went on to teach it.

"At that point, it was like I was zooming in and out, seeing the overall color but also all the little particles making it up. Sometimes, the color was neutral. Other times, it was . . . harsh. But I could look away from it and live my life. I could be in the moment."

Becky licked her fingers clean of the last crumbs,

brushed off her hands, and only then noticed that her hands were filthy and cracked, having clearly been neglected. She self-consciously wiped them on her equally dirty hoodie.

Ted held up one finger and started tapping the pockets of his army surplus jacket, listing the contents as he searched for the right one. "That one has green tea bags. Nice but not what I'm looking for. Multi-tool, baby pigeons . . . oh! Success!" He reached into the pocket he'd identified, pulled out a handful of individually packaged hand wipes, and passed the whole lot of them to Becky. She shyly nodded her thanks, ripped one open, and started removing the grime from her hands.

As she worked on her tattered cuticles, Becky continued her tale. "After that, I let myself dive into the paint of words, and I could only see the particles in a whirlpool around me. I couldn't see that I was drowning. I was able to climb out every once in a while, but those times got to be fewer and farther between, until I convinced myself that drowning was inevitable and exciting. I just let it happen.

"Then I read something that became a part of me in a different way. The person who wrote it was smart, kind, and creative, but they had difficulty discerning reality from hallucinations and delusions. It was like my mind borrowed those misfiring pathways and made me question whether there was anything outside the whirlpool at all.

"Those words made me think that those who thought they were on dry land, or that they were swimming, were just fooling themselves. I felt I was the only one who could see that we were all drowning together, but I also questioned if the opposite were true. Maybe I was drowning by myself, or rather dissolving, and there was no noble intellectual exercise to it at all. There was just water in my lungs and the melting of my skin. I welcomed it, even though it was killing me."

They sat in silence for a while after she finished.

"How did you get so clear?" Becky tapped her temple. "Up here?"

Ted smiled. He had a feeling that asking something out loud and trusting the answer was something new—or perhaps some old, forgotten skill—for his new friend. Ted thought back over his life's journey.

He'd started out not unlike Becky, wanting to learn so many things about the world. His mode for doing so had been poetry. Ted liked how poets took simple words that could be found in any dictionary and arranged them in a way that made them mean so much more than their definitions. It was like poets blasted those words through the prism each person had inside them, whether or not they knew they had one, and the words became something entirely different.

Ted had met other people like Becky throughout his life. Some loved words the way he and his old friends from Tandem Bike Publishing had. Dottie especially—she'd always sought something behind the words. He'd also met musicians, artists, and dancers who had done the same thing. Then there were chemists and biologists who wanted to examine and understand the makeup of each person's prisms. Ted had tried some prism-enhancers that chemists had made. Some were enlightening, while others made the colors run in ways that didn't feel right. The colors had remained true, but their texture and taste had been off. The experiences were similar to what Becky had described as the whirlpool of paint.

But then had come meditation, yoga, long walks in forests, floating in warm lakes, and plunging into holes in the ice. They'd all worked in reverse by taking the haphazard colors and simplifying them into pure light again. When he kept the balance between being in his body, feeling the earth around him, and understanding through poetry, it all made sense and no sense at the same time. There was self and no self.

Ted tried to find the words to tell Becky. He started reciting them as if he were writing them on the street in poetic form and watched as she tried to understand. Perhaps she wished he would write it down instead, but they both knew she would then just absorb his understanding of things instead of reaching her own place of understanding.

Afterward, they sat there a bit longer.

Ted took a few pinches of suet cake and fed it to the pigeons in his breast pocket. Ted knew of a place—a ledge under a bridge—that was home to two pigeon nests. People sat on benches nearby and fed the birds. He planned to put the babies there to learn to fly with the others preparing to make the big jump. The rats, on the other hand, would make their own way in the world. They were clever, and they would know when it was time to leave him.

As he thought of these things, Ted held Becky's hand. He looked down at their entwined fingers. He knew others had difficulty deciphering his age by looking at his face, but his hands showed his age. He had led a good, long life.

"What are you going to do next?" he asked Becky.

"I'm going to call my sister, and I think I'm going to ask her to send me a bus ticket to her place. She lives not far from our hometown. I'm going to go swimming at the park next summer, like I did when I was little. I'm going to swing on the swings too, and I'm going to read children's books to kids at the library. Maybe I'll volunteer at a literacy center or teach again someday, if they'll have me. I think I'll get in touch with a younger woman I know, Elise. She's also a special reader, and I think she can help me learn how to move forward in a safer way. I won't stop reading completely, but I will stop sometimes, when I need to. I'm going to find my own colors and see how they fit into the world. It might work; it might not."

Ted raised his fist like the old hippie he was. "Right on."

"What are you going to do?" she asked in return.

"I'm going to let these pigeons learn to fly and sleep in my usual spot. It's a good spot. I'm going to eat some good food, read a little, write some poetry, and then I'm going to die."

"Right on." Becky smiled at him, tears rolling down her cheeks. "Thank you." She gripped his arm before getting up from the bench and going on her way.

Ted watched her go, then moved to the ground in front of the bench to sit in meditation. The pain in his gut had been making itself known. He let it wash over him, faced his feelings about it, and then allowed himself to detach from it. When he was able to walk again, he took the pigeons to their flight deck. He was looking forward to seeing them fly.

A few days later, a bit sooner than he'd anticipated, Ted was dying. Life was always full of surprises, so he supposed it was fitting.

He was at the library because he had a few poems he wanted to deliver to some friends there. Just before he went in, Ted sat under the little tree just outside to catch his breath, to breathe through the pain. His two rat friends came out of his pocket and ran under his hands repeatedly, wanting to be petted. Then they licked his hands and left, running into the gutter and down the sewer drain.

That's when Ted knew it was his day.

Getting up, he went inside and walked slowly through the library. He said hi to some of the people he knew from the streets, handed his poems to the librarians, and gifted one of them a smooth rock he thought she would like. The rest of his gifts Ted left at the information desk, to be given later to those not working that day.

"Are you okay, Fred?" one young lady asked. "Your color isn't good, and you're sweating. Do you need to go to the clinic down the street? I can take you on my break, if you need someone to walk with you."

Patting her hand, he assured her everything was fine and as it should be. He told her he would go splash some water on his face and rest for a while.

None of it was a lie.

Ted wanted to die someplace comfortable, among things he loved. It was attachment, but he allowed himself the indulgence. He'd thought about dying in the park, but he worried a child would find him and be traumatized. Floating down the river had been his next idea, but if he were honest, he'd never liked being cold. It would distract him from enjoying his death, and Ted wanted a good death.

So he'd decided to die among books but knew he needed some privacy. If someone caught him in the process, they might call him an ambulance, which would result in a loud ride to a hospital, lots of wasted resources, and his dying among strangers with tubes inside him.

Unfortunately, now that the time had come, all the private study rooms were already signed out. Ted had been hurting too much to get there sooner that morning, and the study rooms were always reserved quickly. And even in a study room, he would have run the risk of discovery, as they all had windows, allowing the librarians to keep an eye on those using the spaces and make sure no one was having sex or shooting up. It was a mostly effective measure.

With no other option, Ted went to the men's room off the adult nonfiction section. Most likely, there would be no unattended children to find him. He washed his face and hands with great care in wonderfully warm water, then patted his breast pocket out of habit before remembering the pigeons were gone. He'd seen one flutter and fly the first day he put them on the ledge with the others. Now his pocket contained his ID and a list of those to contact about his death, a handful of names from around the world.

Ted went into a stall and shut the door. Folding his coat carefully, he laid it over the toilet, covering the hole, and then straddled it, facing the wall with his arms folded over the tank. The toilet flushed once, which made Ted giggle and then wince. Resting his head on his arms, he breathed through the pain.

The bathroom wasn't a bad place to die, not really. It was a place people went to take care of their most basic bodily needs, and there was no shame in those functions.

And Ted's body needed to die.

He willed his breathing to slow, something he had been practicing for some time. He took only the smallest of breaths until oxygen deprivation euphoria began to set in, then allowed himself to daydream about his ideal death.

In his mind, he was in the library of his youth. Ted would have liked to lie down on one of the ancient wooden tables in the middle of the stacks and gazed up at the ceiling mural of blue skies with fluffy clouds. The librarians would have stood around him, along with his friends from around the world: all the poets, yogis, hikers, artists, and musicians he'd met on his travels. There would be people from his past as well: his childhood friends, his teammates and fellow students from high school, and his comrades from Tandem Bike Publishing.

Picturing their faces, Ted thought of Gail for the space of several breaths. He was glad he'd dropped that last postcard in the mail to her. It would reach the West Coast today or tomorrow.

He let the thought fade from his mind and be replaced again by all those wonderful folks from over the course of his life. They would all be holding hands and just smiling at him as he died. There would be no fear, no uncomfortable shuffling of feet, no averted eyes.

No one would be declaring, "We should do something!"

They would all know Ted had done all the things he'd wanted to do and everything was fine. His friends would just be happy for him and his good life, and they would witness his good death. And maybe, just as his last breath escaped his lips, they would applaud him.

The space between Ted's breaths became longer. He didn't even need to consciously control it anymore. His body was tired, and it knew the way; it knew how to put itself to rest.

Even with his eyes closed and his face pillowed against the sleeve of the old sweater he wore, Ted's vision was filled with a beautiful expanse of light. The light was green and joyous and infinite.

He swore he heard applause.

What's in a Name?

New York City, 2018

Once the memorial was over and everyone had left, Jim helped Jessie get the Circulation Desk cleaned up for the night. Once all the clean glasses were put away, the chairs put up, and the floor mopped, Jim and Jessie stood at the end of the bar, deciding what to do with the leftover cake. It was a grocery-store sheet cake and not nearly as good as the one Dottie had ordered earlier that day.

"Well, everything's all spick-and-span," Jessie said. "Want to go up on the roof and sit around the ole oil barrel, start a campfire, smoke a joint, and eat some cake?"

"Sounds like a plan," Jim agreed. "But afterward, I think we should leave the rest of the cake in the back alley for rat friends."

"Deal. You cut the cake, I'll grab my stash and some boxes to burn. Oh, and open the chest under the stuffed raven. Grab us each a blanket."

Jim got the cake, then located the bird. It was up high in a corner. Someone had attached a note card that read *Nevermore* to the bird's beak. The wooden base the raven was perched on bore a tarnished-brass nameplate, but it was too high up for Jim to make out more than an *S* at the beginning. Curiosity getting the better of him, he pulled a chair over and stepped up on it to get a closer look. Wiping his thumb across the metal plate, he was able to read the name *Samara.*

Jim smiled, remembering what Jessie had told him when they first met by the card catalog. *"Be sure you meet Samara while you're here."*

"Nice to meet you, Samara," he whispered.

Putting the chair back, Jim opened the chest below the bird. It held several quilts and woolen blankets. They looked old but smelled of the cedar trunk.

With the blankets over his shoulder and a slice of cake in each hand, Jim followed Jessie out the kitchen window and onto a large fire escape, then up a few flights to the roof. He wasn't fond of the height and how the metal stairs rocked with every step they took, but he liked the company, so he kept climbing.

Jessie carried a box of crushed cardboard and a few broken planks of pallet wood. She quickly got the fire going as Jim arranged folding chairs with a blanket on each.

"Wow! Nice fire!" Jim exclaimed. "You must have been a scout or something."

Jessie glanced at Jim out of the corner of her eye, gave him a perfectly executed scout salute, and then took her chair, expertly wrapping herself in a blanket. Reaching one arm out from among the warm folds of blanket, she pulled a half-full bottle of wine from the box, uncorked it with her teeth, and handed it to Jim so he could take the first swig. She then lit the end of a joint and took the green hit. After a moment, she blew the smoke up into the sky, where it mixed with the smoke from the barrel.

She took one more hit before passing the joint to Jim. As he accepted it, she beckoned with her outstretched hand. "Cake me, baby!"

Holding the joint between his lips, Jim handed Jessie a plate from the overturned box serving as a table. Once she had her cake, he inhaled. The old familiar taste was gorgeous, but out of practice, Jim coughed it back out.

"Take it easy, chief," Jessie mumbled.

Jim followed her expert directions for the next two drags, then handed the smoldering joint back to her and tasted his dessert.

"This is okay cake," he said around a bite. "It's moist, and the icing is decent, but it's nothing like the one I had earlier today. That one was lemon, with some kind of berry jam and cream filling in the layers and real buttercream on the outside."

"Oooooh!" Jessie cooed, blowing out smoke. "That sounds amazing. How about this: next time we come up to the roof together for a smoke, you bring the cake. We can't count on there being another birthday-slash-funeral to provide for us, anyway."

"Will do!" Jim wondered if bringing cake would make their next excursion a date.

Jessie smirked. "Cool, then it's a date." She passed him back the joint.

Their fingers brushed, and Jim felt pleasantly warm inside in a way that had nothing to do with the weed.

They were silent for a while after that, allowing the weed, wine, fire, and sugar to blend into an incense of comfort and camaraderie. Eventually, Jim started telling Jessie about the play he was writing about library life. He had told people he was thinking about it, but he hadn't mentioned he'd started outlining it, not even to Dottie or

Kate. Jim was excited, and he hoped Jessie understood that his trusting her with this dream-in-progress was something special.

Well, actually, Lenore knew he was writing the play, because he'd asked her permission to base a character on her. She'd grown uncharacteristically quiet and thoughtful when Jim made the request.

"Will you write me nice?" she'd finally asked.

"Absolutely, Lenore," he'd assured her. "You have my word. You're amazing, and I'd love for people to see that. And I promise, I'll teach any actor who plays you how to pack the books the right way."

That had earned Jim a huge smile and a repeated pat on the back that had almost knocked him over.

Telling Jessie about the conversation with Lenore made Jessie smile as well.

"You did good, Jim. My one cousin—my *favorite* cousin—is on the spectrum. She's an incredible artist. Found out one of her art teachers wrote an anecdote about her for an article in a teaching journal. Never asked my cousin for her permission or input. It never even occurred to the teacher to ask."

Jim nodded. When he asked Jessie how she'd come to work at the Circulation Desk, she said she'd worked as a page at one of the libraries after dropping out of her master's program.

"I was a double major during undergrad, psych and English lit. Went on to get my MS in psych, but my advisors didn't like the premise of my thesis. I wanted to explore the power of stories to shape our brain chemistry and anatomy. Because stories can change our beliefs, our world views. Stories tell us when and what to fear and, conversely, what is safe."

"But that sounds amazing," Jim protested. "Why didn't they let you roll with it?"

"Well, there was the part where I challenged one of the department heads in the middle of a lecture over how male-centric, misogynistic histories have run wild and literally damaged the brains of generations by limiting their full emotional experiences, and how Freud's entire theory was just a big dick joke that was accepted because men love to think about their penises as being the most important things in the entire goddamn world, so of course they deserve to have an entire fucking, all-encompassing theory of human interactions built around them."

Jim stared at Jessie with his mouth hanging open, then burst into a gigantic smile. "Freud's whole theory *is* just a big dick joke! Why have I never seen that before?"

They both had a good laugh. Jessie's made her whole body shake and filled the air around them. Jim wished he could bottle that laughter and keep it for a day when he needed it. The world could use more laughter like that. He also wished he could lay his head on Jessie's chest and feel the sound inside her.

Remembering this was only their first time hanging out, he realized that putting his head on her chest would probably be out of line.

Luckily, Jessie distracted Jim from the urge when she started talking about how, as a page, she'd cursed out her boss for making some really inappropriate remarks to her. Unfortunately, it had been a branch where employees from the old guard outnumbered the younger employees. The manager in question was close to retirement, and his friends protected him by lying. Jessie ended up being the one disciplined and slated to be transferred to a different branch.

"But I was working for the Circulation Desk part-time anyway, so I fell backward into it, kind of like you did tonight. The owner, Kodiak Jane, had been trying to cut back her hours for a while. She's an older lady and couldn't be on her feet for long, the way she used to. But Jane didn't trust any of the other staff, who'd never worked at a library, to oversee her bar and, more importantly, her collection. So she took me on full-time. The pay's good, and I get tips on top of it. And of course, there are the books."

Jim turned to Jessie and squinted at her hard.

"What?" She giggled more than was probably called for.

"You can't just drop a name like 'Kodiak Jane' on me and not tell me her story! I am an artist!" He threw up his blanketed arm dramatically. "Stories are my lifeblood! Speak, woman!"

It took Jessie and Jim a few minutes to compose themselves from the laughing fit that followed. They started out laughing at Jim, but then they were laughing just because laughing was lovely.

"Okay, okay. Whew! Okay, I'm good. What was the question?" Jessie asked.

"I don't know. I forget. Did I ask it, or did you ask it?"

"I'm not sure. But oh! Oh! I can ask you my favorite question! But first, let's lie down." Jessie started gathering up her blanket. "The sky looks amazing."

They somehow managed to get one blanket down on the rooftop and the other stretched out on top of them both. They kicked their shoes off somewhere into the darkness beyond the glow of the dying fire and propped their socked feet up on a box. Their elbows touched under the blanket, and Jim found that simple point of contact to be terribly intimate in that moment.

Jim felt a little more sober but no less warm and content. "You were going to ask me a question."

Jessie turned toward him. From that angle, Jessie wore the night sky like a half crown of infinite stars. "First, I'm going to answer yours: Kodiak Jane is a wonderful woman from Alaska. She's a writer and a former librarian who lost an eye during a bear attack."

Jim blinked hard several times. "That really just leaves me with so many more questions, but you go first."

"Okay! Here's my question. When did monsters stop being monsters and started being just animals? Like, when did a giant squid become a giant squid instead of being a kraken? When did vampire bats start being just bats that consumed blood as food, as opposed to winged monsters that silently descend from the sky and steal blood? When did these creatures become known things instead of otherworldly fears?"

"Wow," Jim whispered after a moment or several too long. He was in awe of the question and the woman next to him.

Jessie graced him with a million-dollar smile—and may have looked at his lips. Then she flipped onto her stomach, kicking her feet up behind her like a little kid. One pant leg slid down, and light from the fire's embers danced reflections on the fine hairs on her ankle.

"C'mon." She nudged him with her shoulder. "I really want to hear your answer."

"Okay, okay! Umm . . . I guess it was probably when humans realized we could kill them. I mean—oh! Oh, no! Was that the wrong answer? You look really upset."

Jessie's face had fallen the minute Jim mentioned death as a simple answer to a much more complex question. She flopped back down on her back. "Yeah, I am.

Guys always answer it that way. I only know one person who ever answered it correctly the first time."

"Well, hey, can I get another chance? Everybody should get a second chance, right?" Jim turned on his side so she could see him better and see how important it was to him to give her question more thought.

"Okay. The stars are bright, we've had okay wine, good weed, and mediocre cake. So yes, Jim, I grant you another chance."

"Yes! All right. So, when did monsters stop being monsters to us? It's not when we could kill them. What would make them less scary and more understandable? Because monsters are unknown. We don't know why they exist or where they come from or what they want or how they live, so we've filled in the gaps with magic and fear and wonder. I guess we stopped calling them monsters when we told enough stories about them that they became normal. They became normal—still dangerous but ultimately normal—things like us when we named them and talked about them and—Mph!"

Jessie had unexpectedly rolled over and kissed him. She did it with her mouth closed, but her lips were warm, firm, and soft all at the same time. Jim smiled against them, knowing he'd gotten the right answer.

But even through the joy of her kissing him, Jim's mind was still going. Jessie had set something moving down a track in his thoughts, and Jim wanted to see where the tracks went. He pulled away. "Diseases!"

Jessie's face twisted in confusion, and she touched her lips before looking at her fingers with concern.

"No!" Jim waved her worry away. "I don't have diseases! And I'm not saying you do, either. You can kiss me whenever you like. What I mean is, the same thing went for diseases. We called the horrible diseases we couldn't understand plagues. But then we learned enough about them to know how they traveled and what caused them and, yes, how to kill them. But the killing was part of the knowledge of how to cure the diseases, not just for the sake of power over them. And can I kiss you again?"

Jessie answered by leaning in slowly. This time, the kiss was more relaxed. She tasted like smoke, warm wine, and flowers made of icing.

"Anything else?" she asked at last, her lips moving against his.

"I think there's some link to religion to be made in there somewhere, but I can't knit it all together right this minute. I'm, mm . . . distracted. Ask me again tomorrow."

"I look forward to it."

They kissed slowly and then kissed some more. Later, as they carefully carried blankets, plates, and an empty wine bottle down the stairs of the fire escape, Jim asked, "So, who was the one person who got your question right the first time?"

"My ex-girlfriend Elise. But she, well . . . she kind of had an unfair advantage."

"How so?" Jim asked.

"She's got a knack for this kind of thing. And it's her profession. Elise is what she describes as a book archaeologist. She's part historian, part sociologist, part linguist, and part literary scholar. And she's read, like, every topic imaginable. She reads about art, music, psychology, physics, and biology. She told me that when she read about the science behind evolution and all the theory and thought that went into taxonomy and classification, she felt when the monsters became real things to those who were naming and discussing them."

Jim stopped dead in the middle of the last stretch of stairs despite his shaking knees and the fact he could see right through the bars to the alleyway two and a half stories below. A memory from the day he'd first met Dottie leaped to the front of his mind.

"Like a perfect reader? Someone who can read a story, and in doing so, read the mind of the person who wrote it?"

"I like that! Yes! A 'perfect reader'!"

He turned to face Jessie, who was right behind him. "Are you saying Elise feels things about an author when she reads their work?"

Surprised, Jessie fumbled the blanket she was carrying. "Well, I didn't say that exactly, no. But yes, she does. Elise talked about it a lot with me, and well, she was able to tell things about me when she read the love letters and birthday cards I gave her. Sometimes, she even knew how I was feeling just from reading my grocery lists. How did you know that, Jim?"

"I know someone like that too. A little like that, anyway. And she's been looking for other readers like her for years. You need to tell more about your ex. Like, how specific and accurate was she with the stuff she knew about you from reading your writing?"

Jessie hugged the blanket she'd almost dropped more tightly. "Can we talk about this inside?" she asked more quietly than she had spoken all night.

"Yeah, sure." Jim's knees felt shaky again, but it wasn't from the height anymore. He was afraid he'd made some sort of misstep with Jessie. She had such a big, boisterous personality, yet she'd suddenly become small when he'd pushed for more details about her ex.

Jim was already apologizing before they got back in

the bar. "Hey, I'm sorry if asking about your relationship with your ex has brought up some bad memories for you or anything. I don't mean to pry. It's just that what you said about her reading matched up with something my friend talked about, and it's the only other time I've ever heard about this before."

"No, it's fine," Jessie assured him. "Elise and I have no bad blood. Nothing traumatic happened between us. She just started traveling more because her expertise was in high demand, and we drifted apart. We still email sometimes, and we keep up with one another's lives on Instagram. It's just . . ."

Jessie moved behind the bar and got herself a drink of water. She didn't come back around afterward, keeping the expanse of polished wood and the brass rail between her and Jim.

"I asked Elise to move in with me by writing her a letter I left on her pillow. I'm a pretty straightforward person these days, but I was kind of shy at that point in my life. You see, I wasn't always honest with others, or myself, about who I was inside. And that made any vulnerability scary.

"I think that letter was the first time Elise got anything from me besides a text. When I saw her later that day, she hugged me tight, agreed to move in, and then just kept holding me. When I asked her why, she pulled back, looked me hard in the eyes, and told me I didn't need to hide who I was from her, or myself, and that I could be myself in the home we'd share together."

Jessie took another drink of water, her eyes shiny around the edges. "Then Elise told me that if I ever wanted to go by a different name, one that fit me better, she'd love to know that name. So Elise became the first one to call me Jessie. Before that . . ." Jessie's voice got quiet again, dropping to almost a whisper. "People always called me John.

"But you see, I never came right out and told Elise in the letter that I was trans. She read my words and she just . . . knew."

Jessie's eyes flicked from Jim to the bar, to the stuffed raven in the corner, then back to Jim.

"Well." Jim cleared his throat. "I have some more questions for you, then."

Jessie's face twisted, just for a moment, and she crossed her arms, jutting out her chin.

"How did your boss, Kodiak Jane, lose an eye in a bear attack? Did the bear invade the library she worked at in Alaska? You never did get around to telling me about it, and I absolutely must know before I agree to a second date. If you don't tell me, I won't bring the good cake."

Jessie's laughter burst out, and her eyes shone bright. She threw a bar towel at Jim, then came around the bar to kiss him again.

Jim felt like he was floating as he walked from the subway back to his apartment, and it had nothing—or almost nothing—to do with the joint he'd shared with Jessie. It was far more about the time he'd spent with her. She was smart, funny, gorgeous, and she actually liked him back.

The fact she could introduce Jim and Dottie to someone who read like Dottie, maybe even with more detail than Dottie—well, that was icing on the proverbial very good cake. The introduction would have to wait until morning, though, as it was long past Dottie's bedtime.

But as Jim neared his building, he noticed a light on

in Dottie's front window—her bedroom. That was unusual. He guessed she was up late reading. Letting himself in the main door, he took a few steps toward Dottie's apartment, contemplating knocking.

Ultimately, Jim decided against intruding and possibly getting his octogenarian best friend out of bed. He chuckled at the thought as he went down the stairs to his studio, passing the purring of the humidity control devices in Dottie's book depository. Jim had gotten used to that sound. It was like a white-noise machine helping to drown out some of the noise from the street.

Jim was putting his key into the lock when he saw the folded piece of paper taped to his door. On Flights of Fancy letterhead was a handwritten note. Taking it inside, he switched on the light to read the hastily scrawled words.

Jim,

Dottie was taken to the hospital. We think it's a stroke. I'm going to follow. Call me on my cell phone when you get in.

Philip

Jim reeled. His back hit the wall, and he slid down until he sat sprawled on the floor. His breath caught in his throat, and the hum from the book room roared in his ears.

"But she still needs to read all the books."

One Last Postcard

San Francisco, 2018

The morning mist had left the stairs up to the porch slippery. Despite knowing every curve and dent in the stone like the back of her hand, Gail wasn't one to tempt fate, so she took her time. When she reached the door, she had to give it an extra push unlocking it; the hinges always stuck on humid mornings.

"Riku!" she called out as she entered. "Sadie was sold out of the baby bok choy, but she did have some nice mizuna, which I think will work in the recipe as long as we don't overcook it." When her husband didn't respond, she added, "Riku? Did you hear me?"

Peeking around the door into their study, Gail found Riku playing air *biwa*, eyes closed as he swayed to the music playing through the fancy new headphones Shion had given him for his birthday. She giggled under her breath and nearly tripped over the mail that had dropped on the floor from the mail slot.

Setting down her net bag of produce from the farmer's market on a nearby table, Gail bent to retrieve the mail, holding the tetchy tight spot on her lower back as she stood.

There was the water bill, some political flyers, a literary journal, a padded envelope from Fukuoka for Riku, and—

"Oh! A postcard!"

It had been well over a year since her last postcard from Ted, and Gail had begun to worry about her old friend, as she always did when time went a bit long in between postcards. The last one had depicted beautiful waterfalls from somewhere in upstate New York. This one was a run-of-the-mill New York, New York, souvenir card.

"Oh, you made your way home," Gail whispered, turning the card over.

The first thing that struck her was Ted's signature at the bottom of the card, the cursive a sharp contrast to his usual small, careful printing. That was odd. Ted had never signed any of his cards before. She'd always known they were from him of course, but why start signing them now?

Her eyes scanned back to the top.

Dear Gail,

I know I've written you a lot of poems over the last fifty years or so. I hope you've liked them, even my monoku phase. Here's one last one.

I always loved ~~sending~~ you ~~poems~~

Yours,

Ted

"Oh, Ted." Gail's tears dripped onto the postcard, streaking the ink of the postmark.

A Slow Reader

New York City, 2018

Jim dialed the number at the bottom of Philip's note with shaking hands. When he got the other man on the phone, Philip assured him that Dottie was stable.

"They gave her a clot-busting medication right away, and the doctors are optimistic about having caught it early. They admitted her for observation, but she could be home as early as tomorrow if all goes well."

"Which hospital is it? Is she awake? Is she scared?" Jim demanded rapidly. "I should come; I want to come."

"She's sleeping right now, Jim," Philip told him gently. "They said it's normal to be really fatigued after a stroke and that it's good for her to get some rest. I'm actually heading home in a few given I've been here since eight. Why don't I pick you up in the morning, and we can both go see her? We may even be able to take her home then."

Gratitude for the older man swelled within Jim's tight chest. In his midtwenties, Jim was still getting the hang of adulting, so he was glad there was an adultier adult taking the lead. He agreed to Philip's plan, and they arranged to meet up in front of Dottie's building at nine, which would get them to the hospital in time for the beginning of visiting hours.

Despite the assurance that Dottie was as well as she could be, Jim didn't sleep well. He hadn't realized until that night how much he'd gotten used to the sounds of Dottie living above him. He knew the creaking of her floorboards, the flushing of her toilet, the squawk of the hot-water tap when it first turned on, and the sounds of her dishwasher kicking into gear. The absence of those common noises was deafening.

Come morning, Jim was on the curb early, pacing as he waited for Philip's orange compact SUV with the Flights of Fancy logo emblazoned on the doors. When Philip pulled up and double-parked to let Jim hop in, he immediately started apologizing for the mess.

The mess in question? Boxes and boxes of books.

"I'd say it doesn't always look like this, but I'd be lying. Such is the life of a bookshop owner. And don't get me started on my office. There's barely enough space for me to wedge myself in front of the computer."

Philip went on to explain how he'd been in that over-stuffed office after closing when there'd been an odd rap on the door leading into the building.

"No one ever knocks on that door. Hell, no one has a key to the building besides Dottie, you, me, the building manager, and the quiet couple who live upstairs—and I think they're overseas this month. So I called out, 'Who is it?' I recognized Dottie's voice, but I couldn't make out what she was saying. I had to slide two boxes of books out of the way just to open the door.

"Dottie was horribly pale, holding her head with one hand and leaning her shoulder against the doorframe. She kept mumbling something, though. Right away, I knew something wasn't right, and I helped her to my chair. She promptly turned to the wastepaper basket and threw up. That made me think she had the flu or something, but when she looked up at me, I saw that half her face was drooping. That's when I finally made out what she was trying to say: 'I'm having a stroke.'"

Philip explained that he'd called 911, then grabbed Dottie's "hospital bag" from under her bed because she'd insistently slurred directions about getting it. Then the paramedics arrived, loaded Dottie up, and told Philip what hospital to meet them at.

"By the time I found Dottie at the ER, she'd been able to communicate well enough to tell the doctors that her symptoms had started just minutes before she knocked on my door and that it was okay for me to be with her and get updates. The staff were all wonderful and professional. Dottie was already talking better before I left."

They made small talk after that, but Jim couldn't focus on it. Despite Philip's positive report, too many possible scenarios ran through Jim's head. Would she be the same? Would she still be safe living on her own? Would she retain that confidence she'd had when facing off with that author? The book reading had only been the day before, yet it seemed so long ago.

The thoughts lasted all the way to the hospital, right up until they were directed to Dottie's room.

"Knock, knock, beautiful!" Philip called out. "Are you decent? I brought company!"

Dottie was sitting up in bed, wearing a robe that was clearly her own. A cup of hospital coffee sat untouched on the rolling table next to her. She was scowling at the remote clutched in her hand, but she immediately brightened as

Philip and Jim walked in. She put down the remote to receive Philip's hug and a kiss on her cheek.

"Philip, I told you, you didn't have to come back so early today after being here so long with me last evening. But I am glad to see you, dear. Now I can stop wrestling with this archaic remote control. I was going to watch Book TV on C-Span, but I couldn't even get the damn thing to turn on. Oh, and you brought Jim!"

Although they had never hugged before, Jim couldn't keep from reaching out to hold his friend. He wanted to know she was okay.

She returned the embrace with strength and warmth, but he couldn't help noticing how small she felt in his arms. When he pulled back, Jim immediately started scanning Dottie's face for the signs of drooping that Philip had described. He thought he detected the slightest difference in her left eye and brow, but her speech was practically perfect, though perhaps a little slower and more careful than usual. Breathing out, Jim forced his shoulders down from around his ears.

Dottie confirmed that they would be releasing her later that day, after she was seen by her doctor and cleared by the occupational therapist.

"Then I'll be on some new medication and will have to get a physical therapist to come to the house and help me build up my strength. I need to exercise more, so I'm thinking of ordering one of those recumbent bikes. I wonder if I can read while peddling . . ." She considered that for a moment before adding, "Really, the only sad thing is that I've been strictly ordered to stop smoking even the occasional cigarette."

Shrugging away the regret, Dottie recounted the onset of her symptoms for her guests. "I couldn't get through to

Gail by phone, so after a light dinner, I sat down at my desk to email her. I had the slightest headache, but I didn't pay it any mind until I realized I was typing nonsense. Now, I took typing way back in high school, and I've always prided myself on making extraordinarily few typos, but what I was typing just then was absolute gibberish!

"I watched my hands as I typed. One of them was doing fine; the other was not. I shook my hands out, and the one just felt heavy and slow, as if moving through water. When I stood up, I felt dizzy, and that little headache turned into a head-splitting pain. I tried to stomp my foot on the floor to get you, Jim, but then I remembered that you were out.

"That's when I started to panic. I don't know why I didn't reach for my phone, but I didn't. Instead, I stumbled out to the hallway, hoping Philip was still around after closing."

"And thank the gods I was!" Philip interjected.

Dottie reached for the cup of coffee she'd previously left sitting and held it with two hands as she brought it to her lips. She made a face after taking a sip. "Ugh, this hospital coffee reminds me of the weak drivel they served us back in the basement of Tandem Bike while we picked through manuscripts."

Philip offered to go get Dottie some real coffee from the shop on the corner, an offer Dottie eagerly took him up on. "Pick one up for Jim too, dear. He likes the flavored kind. And see if they have any nice baked goods."

As soon as Philip was out the door, Dottie slumped a bit, her smile faltering. Jim instinctually moved to her bedside.

"I feel bad," Dottie said. "I gave him such a scare."

"You scared me too, but who's counting?"

Dottie picked at the sheets. "Jim, I don't suppose you have a book or anything else to read on you, do you?" Her tone was almost nonchalant, but Jim quickly understood.

"Oh! Oh, Dottie, are you worried about being able to read and . . ." Glancing at the closed door, he lowered his voice. "*Everything?*"

"The thought has crossed my mind. I didn't want to ask the nurses; they're all so busy, and they wouldn't understand what it means to me." Dottie's lip quivered, betraying her anxiety.

Jim stood up. "I'll be right back. I'll track something down. I'm sure it'll be fine. I'll just . . ." He ducked out of the room in search of a book or magazine, repeating "I'm sure it will be fine" under his breath.

Jim probably looked a touch frantic as he started down the hallway, only to double back within a few steps as he realized the hall was a dead end. Steadying himself, Jim set off looking for a waiting or visitation room. There at least had to be an outdated golf magazine or a *Chicken Soup for the "Fill-in-the-Blank" Soul* hanging around.

All the while, Jim thought about how it would crush Dottie if her reading was affected, or if her *reading* was affected. Her ability was what she lived for. It was literally what got her out of bed in the morning. Dottie without reading would be . . .

He didn't want to think about it.

Finally, Jim spied a frayed paperback legal drama sitting on a table next to a fake potted palm. Snagging it, he hurried back to Dottie's room, waving the book as he entered like a prize he'd won at the fair. He stopped short when he found a doctor with Dottie.

Dottie assured the doctor that Jim could stay while she asked Dottie to do things like squeeze her hands, follow a pen light with her eyes, and name the year, what hospital they were in, and the name of the president. The doctor told Dottie she was fine for discharge as long as the OT agreed and wished her well.

"And no more smoking, Mrs. Barber!" the doctor said as she exited the room.

"It's *Ms.* Barber!" Dottie called after her. "Honestly," she grumbled to Jim, "with all the talk of using people's proper pronouns, you would think young folks would stop assuming that every little old lady they meet is a missus."

Reaching for the book in Jim's hand, she donned her reading glasses and took a quick breath. "Well, here goes nothing."

Sitting on the edge of the plastic hospital chair, Jim stared at Dottie as she read page one. That got awkward fast, so he crossed the room to look out the window. He didn't know exactly how long it usually took for Dottie to get a read on anything from an author, so he waited in silence, not wanting to rush her. He did bite his nails at the window, a nervous habit he generally reserved for one of his play's opening nights.

"Ha!" Dottie exclaimed.

Jim whipped around, immediately relieved to see Dottie smiling, even if it was an ever-so-slightly crooked smile.

"Another ghost writer!" she quipped. "I swear, none of these famous male authors who churn out more than a book a year have written for themselves since the second or third bestseller."

"So you can read normally?" Jim asked, quickly adding, "I mean, normally for you?"

"I can," Dottie affirmed. "The extra bits came to me just fine, though I had to concentrate harder on the reading itself. My eyes wanted to skip lines, which I've never had difficulty with before. So I may be a slower reader, but I've still got it."

Taking off her reading glasses, she rubbed her eyes with a relieved laugh, which turned into a brief, stifled sob. Jim again came to her bedside and reached for her hand.

"Oh, Jim, I was so scared. I was lying there in the ambulance, thinking of all my unread books and of you and all my friends. I've had more time on this earth than many, but I'm greedy. I want more. I want to see your plays. I want to see Philip get married one day. I want to see Gail again in person. And I want to read and read and know all the secrets behind the words, but there's never enough time. I've been given a reprieve, but how much longer will I get? Another year? Two?"

Jim didn't know what to say, so he just held on to Dottie's hand for dear life.

Philip returned then, juggling a beverage holder in one hand and a paper bag in the other. "Caffeine and treats, just like you ordered! I may have panicked at the bakery counter and bought far too many things, but c'est la vie!"

Jim stood to help Philip free his hands, giving Dottie a moment to collect herself.

Even so, when Philip went to hand Dottie her coffee, he stopped short. "Okay, darling? Anything wrong? Did anything change?"

"No, nothing changed, thankfully. Just an old lady having a moment, dear."

"Oh, good!" Philip replied, sounding truly relieved.

Once all three drinks had been distributed and each of them had chosen a croissant or sweet roll from the impressive selection, Philip held his latte aloft in a toast. "To Dottie, the toughest old broad I know!"

"Here, here!" Jim answered with enthusiasm, though

he was mindful of how Dottie cautiously held her cup in both hands.

They all took a sip. Glancing at Dottie sidelong, Philip added in a lowered voice, "But you do need to stop smoking. I've been saying that for years."

That earned him a smack on the arm from Dottie. "Oh, you little nudnik!"

They all laughed and tucked into their pastries, and Dottie went back to holding her coffee with just one hand.

As he watched his dear friend, Jim realized that with all that had happened since finding out about her stroke, he'd forgotten to tell her that he'd learned about another reader like her. He couldn't tell her with Philip there, so he could only hope there would be time to tell her later.

Hopefully, there would still be more time for a lot of things.

Dig

Alexandria, Egypt, 2017

It was an unusual case, even for Elise.

Most clients brought her to clean, climate-controlled rooms in universities or museums, where everyone wore cotton gloves to protect preserved books and scrolls from their skin's natural oils. There would be magnifying lenses of all shapes, sizes, and strengths, as well as higher-tech devices, such as hyperspectral imaging cameras.

Elise would sometimes use the tech, but only after she had read the document with her own naked eyes.

To others, she probably appeared to figure out details slowly, each test and bit of research bringing her closer to the truth of a document's origins and author.

In reality, as soon as Elise read a manuscript, she knew the truth. Her real job, from there, was digging up evidence to support what she knew. After all, her colleagues would never accept her real explanation: "I read the scroll and had a vision of the author and his intentions. I know where the idea came from. I even know he was worried about his sick mother on the day he wrote it."

That kind of thing would never fly in the field of paleography.

So Elise took what she already knew and went digging. She tried to find records of the author or other surviving documents by them, and if there were any, use her expertise to point out stylistic, linguistic, and other similarities.

She was good at her job. The organizations and institutions that hired her were usually satisfied with the outcomes and answers she provided.

However, her job was frustrating at times. Occasionally, there was nothing to find to prove what Elise knew to be true. In those cases, she could tell people her theories, but she couldn't offer any evidence to back them up.

Elise had risen to a stature within her niche profession such that even her best guesses were respectfully regarded, but having her knowledge seen as only a hunch was not as satisfying as having others know what she knew.

Elise had never been one to take pleasure in keeping information to herself. In that sense, she was a true academic. Information not shared with the world was dead, or very close to it. Elise saw her job as raising memories and lost knowledge from the grave. Yet if those memories went no further than her—if she were the only witness to their last exhalation—then was the necromancy she performed worth the trouble?

Sometimes, Elise considered writing fictionalized accounts of some of her difficult-to-prove cases, a means of giving them new life in a different form. She'd had dozens of papers, journal articles, and even textbook chapters published throughout her career, so she had plenty of connections, especially with publishers.

Yet presenting the knowledge as fiction wouldn't be the same. People might read the words and be entertained, maybe even learn something in the process, but they still wouldn't accept the story for what it was: historical truth.

Also, writing for entertainment was not Elise's strong suit.

She wished she knew whether there were others out there like her. If there were, Elise would write about all the things she'd learned. Those like her would read her words and know the thrill she'd felt reaching back in time through the writings of someone long gone and often long forgotten.

Over the years, she'd felt that a few folks here and there might have had the same gift. An ex-girlfriend of hers seemed to really get things at times, but it had turned out Jessie was just empathetic and open-minded when it came to seeing cross-disciplinary connections. Jessie deeply understood what she read, but not with the extra level of perception and detail Elise received.

Her mentor from the lit department in college had also stood out. The excitement in Rebecca's eyes as she read had made Elise think more was going on with her mentor than she let on. Reading Dr. Steadwell's academic papers, Elise could feel that something existed beyond Rebecca's extensive knowledge of the topics she wrote about.

Whatever Dr. Steadwell experienced, though, was beyond Elise's reach, as if behind a firewall. Even as they grew closer as respected colleagues after Elise's graduation—a move marked by an insistent "Please, call me Rebecca or Becky; you're not my student anymore"—the older woman was always holding something back, whether or not she realized it. If Dr. Steadwell did have the same gift as Elise, she hid from it, never fully flexing it. Maybe the ability frightened her. What would happen if Rebecca ever stopped trying to push away the extra perceptions?

Elise had received word from Rebecca, in a round-about way, just a few months back. She'd received an email from her alma mater asking if she would be willing to take on one of Dr. Steadwell's classes, as the tenured professor had taken an "unexpected sabbatical." The person who'd sent the request had accidentally included Rebecca's email to the university with her list of recommendations. When Elise read Rebecca's email—a brief, professional letter to anyone else's eyes—Elise had sensed excitement, elation, and euphoria bordering on mania.

She'd still had difficulty getting a clear read on Rebecca but, this time, for different reasons. There was no longer a dam of restraint, only a dizzying flood.

Elise had had to turn down the teaching job so she could stay mobile for international consultations, and she'd never found out whether Rebecca resurfaced again. She had used her research skills to track down Dr. Steadwell's sister, reaching out via social media to inquire about Rebecca, but she'd had to keep her concern pretty general. She thought of Rebecca often and worried for her, but there was little Elise could do without someone directly asking her for help.

Beyond reading, Elise also wondered if others might have similar gifts in different modes of communication and artistic expression. Were there people who heard layers upon layers beyond the melody and bass line of music? Would they get an understanding of the person who wrote the piece, the person who played the instrument, or some melding of the two, as Elise did when she read something translated from a different language?

What about art? Or dance? Or people who said they could commune with animals? Could people really divine the location of water? Essentially, Elise heard the voices of those who were long dead and gone, so could those other claims really be all that crazy?

Elise *had* read works penned by people who were considered delusional or mentally ill, something she did with great caution. Regardless of the objective veracity of such works, when she read them, they rang true—because to the people who had written them, they were true.

For this reason, she had a ritual for reading such works. Before she began, she would write a few facts about herself on a piece of paper. Then as she read, whenever the conspiracies and fantastic elements began to make too much sense, she would stop and ground herself by reading her personal notes.

To be honest, Elise could probably have used those grounding notes right about now. Her current assignment was so different in so many ways that, for once, she had no idea what to expect.

For one thing, Elise was on her way to Alexandria, Egypt—*the* Alexandria, for which all others had been named!

To think, she'd be able to stroll down roads once walked by countless intellectuals and great thinkers as they discussed ideas that would shape the understanding of the world for millennia to come. Even the bittersweet knowledge that it had also been the location of one of the world's greatest intellectual tragedies couldn't dampen her spirits.

A few weeks earlier, during the construction of some high-rise apartments in Alexandria, a few older buildings had been taken down, revealing the filled-in ruins of even older structures. Experts had been brought in to examine the site and determine whether it held any historical or archaeological value before construction could resume.

While sifting the fill turned up no significant artifacts,

an inspection of the old walls themselves proved interesting. The walls were covered in carvings of words from all the different languages of the ancient world, pointing to a possible connection to the heyday of the Great Library, when Alexandria was an intellectual powerhouse.

Since the construction had only been delayed, not abandoned, the walls were going to have to be moved from the site, and soon. The land developers had been patient at first, happy for the publicity, but they were champing at the bit as their deadlines passed with no progress.

However, those working to preserve the walls were concerned about the removal and moving process. The writing was so small in places that the slightest disturbance could make it unreadable. Sure, they were making molds of the surfaces and taking pictures with all sorts of specialized cameras and digital graphing techniques, but they still wanted the foremost experts in the field, including Elise, to view the walls in person before they were moved.

Still recovering from the sleeping pill she'd taken before her flight, Elise's arrival in Alexandria and the process of checking into her hotel were a blur. Luckily, she felt better after a hot shower, just in time for her hosts—a consortium of state- and university-associated cultural preservationists—to take her to dinner. Though grateful for the reception, Elise was sorry she had to wait until the next day to even see the site.

The food and outside dining room, lit with hanging lanterns, distracted Elise from her anticipation. The restaurant was selected due to its menu, a fusion of modern and traditional Egyptian fare, with a focus on Alexandrian regional dishes.

They started things off with *molokhiya* soup made with fried jute leaves. The soup had shrimp, but Elise's waiter informed the table that, in other parts of Egypt, the meat could be lamb or fish. There were also a variety of flatbreads served with fragrant hummus and tabbouleh, and mouthwatering meatballs called *kofta*. The only thing Elise didn't much care for was the traditional, regional liver curry.

The main course was a stuffed pigeon dish called *hamam mahshi*. Elise was so full by the time it was served that she could only pick at the stuffing and nibble some meat. But even if she hadn't been full, Elise thought she would have had a hard time eating pigeon. She'd lived her life in libraries, and where there were libraries, there tended to be pigeons. They were like the mascots of libraries, and it felt almost sacrilegious to eat them.

After all the dishes had been cleared away, the waiter brought desserts laden with figs, plums, and seasonal melons. Elise settled in with a plate of *ghorayeba*, butter cookies that melted in her mouth, and a cup of *qahwascitto*, Turkish coffee without sugar. Although all her dinner companions were multilingual and Elise had spoken fluent Arabic throughout the evening, she was complimented on knowing exactly how to order her coffee, as specific names were used for how much sugar one wanted in one's coffee.

She raised her cup in a casual salute. "No matter where I travel and no matter how much or how little I know of the language, I always make sure I know how to order a cup of coffee."

It was over the relaxed coffee and tea service that would stretch long into the evening that Elises's dining companions began to share their theories regarding the wall writing. The content covered multiple academic disciplines, including math, astronomy, and philosophical and political arguments. There were also more mundane writings, such as records of religious ceremonies to please the gods and municipal planning records for cities across the Mediterranean.

"What's odd," said one man as he sipped his tea, "is that the sentences sometimes end midway, or appear to pick up halfway, through a thought."

"Is it possible the writings were carved into the stones before they were built into the wall?" asked a man named Farhad, lighting up a cigarette. "That would account for the broken bits."

He shook another loose from his pack and offered it to Elise, who politely declined, though she smiled warmly. Usually, only men smoked in Egypt, so it was a subtle acknowledgment on his part that he considered Elise to be a respected equal at the table.

She'd read Farhad's recent work, a deep dive into how ancient, lesser-known trade routes could be deciphered by the sharing of words and other linguistic tracking. It was insightful. She'd written him an email praising his work, and Farhad had written her back. Since then, they'd struck up a friendly professional camaraderie.

From his more recent emails, Elise knew Farhad was thinking about asking her out on a less professional basis. He was also probably the reason she had been invited to this nearly all-male project, but that had nothing to do with his romantic interest in her. He knew Elise was incredibly good at her job and trusted her expertise.

The conversation eventually turned to the dig site itself. The walls had once been part of a basement of sorts, but the original structure had not been much larger. According to the city's records, the area had been rebuilt many times over, but none of the buildings in documented history had had a basement mentioned in the records. It appeared that the rubble from the demolition of the original building, or one built soon after, had been used to fill in the basement and newer constructions were built on top of it over the next few centuries.

The debris had damaged some of the carved surfaces, but a good amount of detail had survived. Some of the filler material had also been analyzed and, to everyone's excitement, it showed signs of having been exposed to intense heat. That meant the original structure, and therefore the mysterious writings, could have predated the burning of the Great Library.

The theories would have bounced back and forth long past midnight, but the restaurant had to close and everyone remembered just how early they would be heading out to the dig site in the morning.

Elise, however, couldn't sleep that night. She kept flipping through photos of the walls. She could read most of the languages, but even when she couldn't, she could still get at least a slight reading from the writing. As she read, Elise got a sense of great concentration and respect but also some confusion and frustration. She thought the confusion could be attributed to the different languages used. The person who'd carved the walls didn't seem like a scholar to her.

The next day would be a different ball game altogether. Elise would be able to read the walls with her own eyes, maybe even touch them, if permitted. She'd always gotten stronger readings from people's handwriting, but the walls weren't written; they were carved in stone.

Eventually, Elise made herself climb into bed. She stared at the ceiling for what seemed like hours, running her fingers over the folds of the luxurious sheets, dreaming of what the walls would reveal to her.

The next day, there was a quick breakfast and briefing in a small conference room. Then they prepared to hit the road for the dig site.

While everyone was gathering their equipment, Farhad nervously approached Elise, and she worried he had picked that exact awkward moment to ask her out. Instead, he apologetically handed her a paper bag containing a few items of clothing: a hat with flaps that covered the back of the neck, as if to provide sun protection, and a bulky khaki work shirt.

"The construction crew is working on the land around the dig. The foreman requested that no women come to the site, citing that it would distract and 'corrupt' his workers and bring bad luck to the worksite. I'm so sorry, but this is what I could come up with. We need you there; we need your eyes and expertise. Linda from photography will be receiving the same kit."

He bowed his head and made an apologetic gesture with his hands.

"I understand," Elise assured him. "This is better than the receptions I got in some other places I've been to. Remind me sometime to tell you about the difficulty I had getting my hands on a book of Jewish poetry written in Ladino from the Sephardic Golden Age that was in the possession of an orthodox—and grumpy—rabbi who would only talk to me from the other side of a screen."

Taking the items out of the bag, Elise removed her head scarf and stuffed her hair up under the hat. She threw the shirt on over her university T-shirt and rolled her pant legs down from the capri length she had them folded to.

"How's this?" she asked, exaggerating the depth of her voice.

Farhad chuckled. "You look great, sir!"

Elise grabbed her backpack, and they hustled out to catch up with the group at the rental van.

"Maybe," Farhad ventured as they settled into the van, "you could tell me about your adventure with the Ladino poetry and the grumpy rabbi sometime this week? At a quieter dinner spot, perhaps?"

"Sure, that sounds lovely. But first, we have a date with a wall."

The site was noisy with the sounds of the nearby construction. A tent had been set up over the excavated basement walls, but it didn't so much block out the sun as trap the heat and nullify the slight morning breeze that might have helped. Sweat was already dripping down Elise's chest and back when the dig supervisor acquainted them with the procedures they were to follow.

Once Elise got close enough to view sections of the carved walls, all the heat, jackhammers, and horn-honking traffic fell away. She'd put on latex gloves just before entering the tent, and she traced the stone with her fingers. That particular section was in Greek and appeared to be commentary on the works of Euripides. The next stone switched between Hebrew and Greek, but the content was from the Hebrew scriptures, as if it were in the process of being translated from one to the other. A section above those carvings was a bit more damaged than the rest, and the writing itself wasn't as well executed as some of the other sections, but she could tell it was something like a hybrid Sanskrit.

Those around her spoke excitedly about the Sanskrit, and one of them confirmed the content was Buddhist, but Elise was already reaching beyond the words and theories surrounding them.

What she saw was . . . a little boy.

The boy understood some of the words he chiseled into the walls, but he longed to know them all. He was tired and hungry, and sometimes, the rock he used to strike his makeshift chisel slipped and hit his fingers instead, making tears run down his face, but he would always raise the rock once more.

A dented lamp provided light, and as the boy rushed to get more words onto the wall, Elise knew he feared that the lamp oil would run out before he was done. He strained to read as many words as he could, tracing his fingers over the carvings again and again, just as Elise was doing some hundreds of years later.

She returned to the Hebrew scriptures that transitioned between two languages. There, she experienced an odd sense of vertigo. She could read both languages, but the boy who had written it on the wall could only understand Greek and had figured out extremely little Hebrew.

Elise also picked up another echo behind the boy. That other writer had been in a hurry, translating as fast as he could because the source work needed to be returned to the original owner, whose ship was to depart from the harbor that same day. He made mistakes and used scribal abbreviations, which he planned to return to later and fix for the copy to be saved.

Even further back, even fainter, was another scribe and another before him.

Elise shook her head, almost hard enough to dislodge the odd hat Farhad had given her, trying to clear away the echoes. She was most concerned with the boy who'd chiseled the words. She felt his concentration. He'd tried so hard to make the letters right, to make them like he'd seen the scribes write them. He'd watched the scribes, fetched them water when they were thirsty, run scrolls back and forth as they told him to, and brought them new ink when they ran out, and the boy had loved every minute of it. He'd loved—

Elise gasped so loud, those around her turned to look. She didn't notice.

Spreading her hands on the words, Elise closed her eyes, and she saw a little boy running back and forth through the library of Alexandria. He had bare feet, toughened from the stone floors and streets. He ate what remained of the scribes' and scholars' meals when he helped deliver their food. His robe, tattered, had been given to him by someone who pitied the poor orphan who found work where he could.

The boy picked up scraps of broken and worn-out scrolls, or ones the tired scribes had made costly mistakes on. Sometimes, the patient and kind ones would give him the greatest gift of all, better than any choice fruits from their plates: they would read to him. Teach him.

When they didn't have time, the boy read over their shoulders, careful not to cast a shadow on their work. He sneaked peeks at the scrolls he carried from the storerooms to the academics who requested them. If he wasn't working, he would perch on ledges and watch the learned men discuss their theories about the stars and how to calculate the distance between cities. Their spoken words went so fast and so far into the world of numbers, whose secrets eluded him, that the boy had a hard time understanding them. But if he read the same words from scrolls they had recorded their thoughts on, he was able to peer into their understanding.

He wanted to read . . . everything.

He wanted to start by reading everything in the library, and in the secondary library located in the Serapeum, the daughter of the main library. After that, he wanted to travel and read all the works stored in the Library of Pergamum, where the words were written on stretched-thin animal skins instead of pressed papyrus. The boy had heard that the scribes could write on both sides of the page that way. They didn't even need to roll the pages into scrolls; instead, they bound them into codices. The scholars of Alexandria spoke of Pergamum in hushed tones lest they suffer the fate of the great librarian who had been sent to prison when the emperor learned that the competing library had been trying to lure the renowned scholar away.

What Elise got from the writing made her head spin. She pieced together the impressions she was getting from the boy with what she knew of the history of that time, trying to pinpoint when he'd lived. As she moved along the expanse of wall, Elise felt the aging of the boy. She saw how his writing and understanding of the words progressed. She saw when he was sick, almost too weak to keep up the chiseling but feeling he must to keep up his practice, as he was unable to run the library halls and tend to the needs of the scribes, whom he missed.

For days and days, he was stuck in the basement of the inn the walls had supported. The innkeeper's wife was kind, keeping him hidden and fed throughout his convalescence. When he was well, the boy worked for her in exchange for a place to sleep. He cleaned the floors after all the others had gone to bed, emptied the chamber pots, and killed rats.

That was his life: days spent working at the library, nights spent working at the inn, spare hours spent practicing his writing until he could no longer keep his eyes open and he fell, heavy with exhaustion, onto the sacks of rice that were his bed.

The writings showed Elise this, over and over, through language after language and month after month.

Then they stopped.

Elise took a moment to steady herself and organize the images in her mind. Taking out her notebook, she made a rough map of the walls and the individual stones, and she went over each again, attempting to put them in at least a loose chronological order, based on the age of the boy as he chiseled them. Farhad tried to engage her about what she was doing, what theory she was working on, but she dismissed him with an impolite mumbled grunt and dodged around him to get a better look at the next section of stone.

Eventually, Elise found what she felt with fair certainty was the last entry. It was nothing special, a later practice of translating Greek to Hebrew, since the boy saw Hebrew to Greek more often. He was more confident in his abilities and was experimenting. It was a day like any other for the boy, and then there was no more.

What had happened to him? Did one of the scribes get him a full apprenticeship? Had he found better lodging? Or did the innkeeper discover the carved-up walls and put him out on the streets? Was he run over by horses in the road? Was there an accident that had ended with him falling in the water at the docks and finding out he couldn't swim?

Elise realized she had been staring at the last stone for far too long. It held no answers for her, and she stepped back to review what she knew. The boy had knowledge of the "jailed librarian"—most likely Aristophanes, who had been imprisoned during the reign of Ptolemy V Epiphanes. But that didn't help her pinpoint much, as it could have been discussed for decades or more after the fact, as a legend of warning within the library halls. Elise could probably narrow down the time period more based on the content of the writings, but any of her colleagues could do the same. Maybe she could find mention of an inn in some municipal documents? Highly unlikely for the time period in question.

The real story was the boy himself, and Elise could never bring his story to light with any kind of proof to back it up. Over a thousand years ago, a hungry little boy had found hope, refuge, meaning, and family in a library. The library was seen as an important intellectual landmark and would always be remembered as such, but this boy, long dead, whose name and fate she didn't know, had just shown Elise a side of the library that no historical account ever could.

Elise's life was lived partly in libraries. She knew them to be living, breathing buildings. They were places of quiet study and contemplation, sure, but also places filled with song and gossip, clogged toilets, and on some very exciting days, babies being born and hearts being broken. That was exactly how the boy knew his library. He knew what foods the scribes preferred and which they would leave un-touched. Which scribes were in love with one another, and who was jealous of those affairs. Who of the scholars sought prestige, and which ones pushed their minds be-yond the limits of all that was known for the sheer joy of figuring out new things about the world around them.

And the boy knew that written words were more than lines and shapes that added up to a single idea.

Elise saw that he felt an inkling of what she did when she read. He understood that words contained a bit of the essence of those who wrote them, and if a person just read closely enough and were open to it, they could see so much more than just one word after another after another. This boy, who had carved walls with no thought of anyone ever reading them, understood that scribes and interpreters were conduits, each an important link in a chain that passed knowledge from hand to hand and, eventually, to the world. Without being told, he had grasped how each person forming the sum of the whole of the chain added a part of themselves to it, whether they meant to or not.

That boy was someone a younger version of Elise could have sat beside and read with, knowing he understood things at least slightly like she did. They would have been friends.

If that boy had grown into an adult . . .

But Elise would never know. Even if he had become a scribe and had gone on to write more in his lifetime, all of those works would have been lost by now, either consumed by the first great fire or destroyed during the Christian fury that ripped down the Serapeum. Or they would have just crumbled to dust due to time and decay. If Elise ever had the unlikely luck of getting her hands on a piece of writing the boy had been part of somewhere down the chain, he would be but a whisper of an echo and a grown man.

Hot, painful tears pricked the corners of Elise's eyes.

Separating herself from the group, she escaped the stifling tent and sat in the sun. Soaking in the warmth on her back, she caught sight of some boys playing ball in the mouth of a narrow alley down the road.

Elise watched them for a moment, then opened her bag and took out a notebook. This situation called for old-school, handwritten note-taking. In one column, Elise listed what she knew from the carvings, both from the content itself and from the impressions of the boy who'd produced them. In a second column, Elise jotted down ways she could look for evidence to support what she knew so she could present it to an audience of her peers in a way that would hold empirical water. She knew she was reaching with some of them.

> *Look into the stages of literacy children progress through as they learn to read/write, and match them up with mistakes, etc. made by the boy?*
>
> *Check with those handling artifacts found in the fill, and look for anything that could indicate the presence of a child living in the space?*
>
> *Are the makeshift chisel and rock in the rubble? Is the rock of a size more suitable for the hand of a child than that of an adult?*

"Who's 'the boy'?"

Elise snapped her notebook shut as Farhad sat down beside her and offered her a cold bottle of water. She shot him a dirty look but accepted the water. The heat was brutal.

Farhad lit up a cigarette. "I wasn't reading over your shoulder. Although I can't say I've never been guilty of that habit in my lifetime. You were talking to yourself. You kept mentioning something about a boy."

"Sorry, guess the heat is getting to me." Elise took a long drink.

Farhad took the dodge in stride, and to Elise's dismay, she found his polite but persistent curiosity admirable. "So, you have a theory about the writing on the walls, and it involves a boy? And you're not ready to talk about it yet?"

Elise had to smile. Farhad may not get from written words what she did, but he seemed to have a knack for reading her like a book. Though still cautious, she gave in a little. "I have the beginnings of a theory, but I'm trying not to have it lead to confirmation bias. It may or may not involve the writer in question being a child."

Nodding thoughtfully, Farhad smiled. Apparently assuaged by his victory, he got up to return to the tent, leaving Elise with her thoughts.

"When you're ready to talk about your boy, I know a great café off the beaten path that stays open late. They have excellent *ghorayeba*," he called back over his shoulder, clearly trying for an air of nonchalance.

"Sure." Elise opened her notes again. Only after Farhad had reentered the tent did Elise realize she'd possibly just agreed to a date.

In the days that followed, Elise grew more and more frustrated. Her expertise was an asset to the team of researchers and the work being done, but Elise couldn't reveal her "theory" of the boy scribe because none of the physical or contextual clues remotely pointed in that unusual direction. The boy was one of the most amazing discoveries she'd ever made in her professional and personal life, and she couldn't share it with anyone without sounding absolutely crazy.

Little by little, though, Elise found herself letting slip her "other" observations around Farhad. He had this way of listening when she spoke to him, as if he took the time to process everything she said and reflect on it before responding, which was refreshing. Too many of the academics Elise interacted with tended to start composing a witty one-up retort before she had even finished a sentence.

It didn't hurt that Farhad had the most amazing amber eyes Elise had ever seen, framed by long lashes. And when he was thinking hard, his mouth curled up on one side, showing off a deep dimple.

Halfway through the week, Elise took Farhad up on his offer to take her to the place with the good *ghorayeba*.

"Oh my god, how are they so light yet so rich all at the same time?" Elise covered her mouth so cookie crumbs wouldn't fall all over the embroidered linen *galabiya* she'd bought earlier in the day.

"I told you it was the best around. It wasn't just a line to get you to come hang out with me, though, I mean, here you are, so . . ." Sipping his coffee, Farhad looked off to the side, hiding his smile behind his cup but not quite hiding that dimple Elise liked.

"I know you're the one who recommended me for this project," Elise countered. "Now I'm wondering if it wasn't my expertise you were interested in at all. Maybe this whole thing was just a ploy to get me to go on a date with you in Egypt."

"Wow, yes, you figured it out," Farhad deadpanned. "I personally buried meters of ancient walls with archaic multilingual writing carved into them, then hired a construction company to try building on that exact spot, all so I could drop your name for the job of decoding the mystery."

"I think the filler debris showing signs of having been through an inferno was a nice touch," Elise volleyed back.

"It wasn't too much? I felt I might be overselling it, maybe."

"Well, I mean, I'm here, so . . ." Elise picked up another cookie.

Farhad put down his coffee and leaned across the table. The flickering candlelight reflected in his eyes, making them all the more golden. "Yes, here we are."

His hand may have started to edge across the tabletop toward Elise's. Clearing her throat, she suddenly found the need to fidget with her napkin. "In all seriousness, I am grateful to be here on this dig. The implications of all those different languages, the unique translations, the content itself—this is going to fuel dozens, if not hundreds, of papers in multiple disciplines for years to come. I'm excited to be one of the few to see it intact before it all gets moved."

"Hmm, I think we all feel extremely blessed to be here." Farhad leaned back in his chair. "And all kidding aside, I'm happy you're on the team. I've been a fan of your work for some time, Elise, and I've wanted to see your methods firsthand. Your ability to see connections and track down evidence that supports your theories is unparalleled. If I didn't know better, I'd think you were a time traveler who knows all the answers already and just has to uncover the artifacts to patiently explain to the rest of the world how it all went down. That's why I've been so interested in this 'little boy' theory you've been so reluctant to talk about. With your track record, I'm just waiting for you to suddenly have it all tied together with a bow."

Elise stared at Farhad. She blinked several times, stared wide-eyed, then blinked a bit more.

"Wait, are you actually a time traveler? Elise, I know you have two doctorates, but are you the Doctor? Is there a TARDIS hidden behind a tea stall in a back alley somewhere around here?" Farhad looked around, then peered under the tablecloth.

Elise didn't laugh, though. Instead, she took a deep breath, leaned across the table, and spoke in a hushed tone. "Farhad, I'm not Doctor Who, but what if I told you your guess about me knowing all the answers was closer to the truth than you think?"

Farhad leaned in, matching Elise's posture and taking her fingertips in his. He was smiling, but not in a mocking way. "First of all, his name isn't 'Doctor Who.' That's the title of the show. His name's just the Doctor. Secondly, I absolutely want to hear more."

Two coffee refills later, Elise had explained her gift and her experience with it and had given examples of how it affected her work. She'd also told Farhad about the boy in the library and how she could never bring this particular story to light the way she wanted to. True to his nature, Farhad asked insightful questions along the way.

By the end of her explanation, they were both practically vibrating, less from the caffeine than from the excitement of the conversation. Elise's leg jiggled under the table as she awaited his response.

"Wow." Farhad's lips pulled up into a warm smile. "Just when I thought Dr. Elise Borg couldn't possibly be any more brilliant or amazing, you hit me with all that."

Elise smiled in return and finally exhaled.

The waiter came by, pointedly dropping a check on the table. Only then did the duo notice how late it was. Farhad paid the check, and the two of them started to walk back to the hotel.

Elise thought maybe Farhad needed more time to process everything, but after only a block or two, he picked the conversation back up.

"So, what are we going to do about the boy? The world needs to know about him, one way or another. It's absolutely magical. He's like the ancestor of every reader who wanted to read all the books, isn't he? Have you thought about writing a fictionalized version of his story?"

"We?" she asked.

"Well, I mean, we are part of a team here on this project. I'm not saying we should loop everyone in on this, but I think you and I make a good team."

He was looking up at the stars as they walked, but he looped their hands together effortlessly, as if Farhad's hand could find hers anywhere.

"Yes, we do," Elise said, squeezing back. "But fiction writing is not one of my areas of expertise. I've dabbled before, but it all comes out sounding like it was written for a professional journal. And besides, would adults want to read about a little kid?"

"Well, write it for kids, then. If anyone needs to know this story, I think it's kids who are just starting out on their reading journey. And I did say 'we,' remember? I don't want to brag, but I am the favorite uncle in my family because of the amazing bedtime stories I tell. And you know what I tell my nieces and nephews stories about? My work. I don't even dumb it down for them. It's just a matter of giving kids a character they identify with, then weaving the facts around the character in an entertaining way. In this case, the character is already there. He *is* the story."

Elise nodded slowly. "You may be on to something. Do you think we could make it multilingual? Oh, and maybe have a section in the back with pictures from the dig site and explanations of the factual references made in the story?"

Farhad gently tugged Elise into a shadowed alcove and dropped to one knee. "Elise Borg, will you write a book with me about a boy who lived in the Library of Alexandria?"

"If I say yes, will you kiss me?"

And there was that smile, that dimple. Tugging Farhad to his feet, Elise kissed him.

Mother of Invention

San Francisco, 2019

Shion gulped down a tall glass of water in one go, even though the cold made their throat hurt. They hadn't drunk enough that day, and they needed a soul-shocking palate cleanser after what they'd just read. Submitted to the family press for the anthology about matriarchs they were putting together, the piece detailed a story a Black grandmother had told the author, her white granddaughter.

Adopted into a multiracial family at an early age, the author had gone to nursing school to follow in her grandmother's footsteps. The piece began with her confiding in her grandmother about an elderly patient who had used openly racist language in her presence, assuming she was of like mind due to the color of her skin. Her grandmother had answered with a sad, knowing laugh.

"Men like that—people say they don't know better because they're old. Well, I'm old too! All age means is that we've lived through all the same times. He simply resists changing his heart and mind at every turn.

"Remember how I told you I did some home care

when I was paying my way through nursing school back in the day? And that that's how I got in to see so many of the big, old houses in Atlanta that I would never have gotten a chance to step into otherwise?

"Well, one old man was real gentlemanlike to me. I was fond of him, and his family was nice. They always had his clothes laid out for him and all ready for me to get him into after his bath. They would have the cook set out two glasses of lemonade and some cookies for us after I had taken the old man around the neighborhood for a walk in his fancy wheelchair.

"One day, we got caught in a light drizzle, which turned into a downpour a block before we got back to the house. We were laughing as I pushed him up the ramp onto the porch, but I had to change him out of his dripping clothes and into something dry. There were no clothes set out for such an occurrence, so I had to go into his closet to get him something.

"Mind you, he had his wits about him; he was just lame from having polio as a child. He could have said something to try to stop me from going into his closet, but he didn't. And hanging there, next to his pressed plaid shirts, was a KKK robe."

"What did you do, Gran?"

"Well, darlin', my heart dropped into my stomach like a cannonball, and my skin heated so fast, it felt like those Georgia raindrops turned right to steam. I took out the robe, gripping the hanger as far from the fabric as I could, and held it out to that soaked old man.

"He calmly explained in his Southern drawl, 'Oh, honey, don't you fret about that. You're one of the good ones, so you've got nothing to worry about. Now, put that away and grab the blue shirt and the matching pants.'

"I walked out of the bedroom with the robe, leaving the old man shouting after me, sounding genuinely confused by my reaction. I left the robe hanging from the crape myrtle out front as my resignation.

"For years after that, every time I saw a picture of men in those damn robes, standing by burning crosses or posing under a hanging tree, I felt sick—sicker even than before I knew about him—thinking one of them hooded bastards could have been him. I drank lemonade with that man, lemonade that Black hands made for him. He probably thought the cook was one of the 'good ones' too. As long as we were under him and polite, he was fine with us living.

"The worst part was, he made me hate myself some. What had I done to be considered a 'good one' by that awful man?"

The grandmother could never bring herself to drink lemonade again.

Shion wasn't sure they'd be able to drink lemonade, either, for quite some time after reading that story. But what they were sure about was that they were going to accept the piece for the anthology—and that the granddaughter would have a future in writing if the nursing thing didn't work out for her.

Shion did a few stretches and then printed off two more submissions. Printing was an extra step that used up paper, but it felt right to them. Maybe it was all the stories Grandma G had told them about the thrill of sliding a stack of paper out of an envelope and holding someone's hopes and dreams, sweat and tears in her hands. Leafing through stories, page by page, and getting a sense of whether the words amounted to a book the world would want to read or, in some exciting cases, needed to read.

Grandma G had started out in the basement of a

famous publishing house in New York. To the chagrin of her wealthy Waspish family, she'd jumped off the corporate publishing ladder and thrown herself into independent, feminist publishing for the next several decades. Together with their cousin Freya, Shion ran GB Club, the most recent indie imprint. The name stood for Greek Bitch Club, and their symbol was a pomegranate pierced by a quill, all wrapped in the coils of a snake—a combination of references to Persephone, Medusa, and Sappho.

The next submission Shion picked up was sweet, but it contained nothing striking or memorable. They jotted some notes in the margin about some well-executed poetic imagery so they could include it in the rejection letter. If Shion had time, they would look up the submission guidelines for a college friend's online lit journal. With a bit of tweaking, the submission could find a home there in the journal's prose section.

The third piece showed promise. In the cover letter, the author talked about their great-grandmother, a real spitfire who "became more and more herself as the years went by." The story itself was a hybrid of the old woman's journal entries, memories from the author and other family members, and a question-and-answer interview with the great-grandmother herself, who "at ninety-eight, still remembers how we each like our maté and bugs all the school-aged kids to tell her what they learned each day."

The formatting—including pictures embedded in the text—didn't translate well during printing, so the narrative was annoyingly hard to follow at first. However, the woman at the center of the story was fun and clearly loved and admired by the family members who spoke of her. By the second or third page, Shion had gotten used to the formatting issues and found themself enjoying the read.

There was another factor at play, though. A nagging familiarity Shion couldn't put their finger on.

Most of the narrative took place in Argentina and focused on the woman's role in her family and her encouragement of their dreams. In the last few years, she'd studied field hockey when one of the author's cousins showed an aptitude for it. Their great-grandmother, whom everyone in the family called Bisabuela, also supported that cousin's rise in the sport—all the way through to her making the acclaimed Las Leonas team—by helping pay for equipment and sports camps.

But from there, the story moved backward in time, mostly through journal entries, to establish how Maria had become the beloved matriarch and independent woman who nurtured the dreams of her family.

She and her husband, a hardworking man named Tomás, had moved back to Argentina from the United States in the late 1980s. Upon their return, they found that the country had changed, somewhat for the better, somewhat for the worse. Tomás's favorite brother, whom he'd spent years trying to convince to move to the States, had disappeared in 1980 and was presumed dead. A vocal political critic and activist, the brother had become a victim of Argentina's internal Dirty War, swept up in one of the government's harsh crackdowns on dissidents.

Tomás had always been a quiet man, not one to rock the boat, but when he heard about his brother, he swore he would do all he could to make their corner of the world safer for their children and grandchildren. He also promised Maria that, since he was moving toward retiring from their agricultural export business, he would finally learn to tango, as she had always wanted him to.

One day, as Maria prepared to make pasta sauce for

dinner, Tomás stumbled in the garden while bringing in the tomatoes. Maria chuckled to herself, planning to tease him about his clumsiness when he came inside with muddy knees.

But he never came back in.

Maria found Tomás lying between rows of his prized plants. Somehow, even as he collapsed, Tomás had set the basket of tomatoes safely off to the side. She held him for his last few moments while he smiled through the pain of a heart attack.

After Tomás passed, Maria looked through his journals. She cried as she read about how much he'd loved her, and she cried some more as she considered everything he hadn't known about her.

Tomás had known nothing of Maria's dreams, which she'd kept hidden for no good reason at all—dreams of building machines and inventing contraptions no one had ever thought up before. Her husband's journals spoke of his wife fiddling with all the appliances in the house and how it amused him, and Maria wept with regret that she'd never told him that she understood, just by looking at the machines, how each of them worked and that she'd had so many ideas for making them work better.

Maria wept for how little she had known of Tomás's dreams. He'd watched tango competitions on TV with her and pretended to hate them, but only to hide how self-conscious he had been about his lack of coordination. He'd always thought himself too slow for his smart and charming wife, and he'd dreamed of taking secret lessons so he could one day sweep her, quite literally, off her feet.

After crying her eyes dry, Maria resolved never to hide herself again and to create an environment for her family where no one ever felt the need to hide their passions.

I enjoyed being the grocer's wife, but it was time
to become more Maria, to become my truest self.

The line was followed by a picture of young Maria and
Tomás, already surrounded by four children, standing in
front of a grocery store. The next picture was of a much
older Maria. Her dark hair was streaked with steely gray,
but she still looked elegant in her cap and gown as she
received her bachelor's degree from Universidad Tecno-
lógica Nacional.

Staring at the pictures, Shion felt an odd, rolling blend
of déjà vu, vertigo, and whiplash. Their first thought was
that the story of Maria had been previously published or
had been submitted to them in an earlier form.

Then the truth hit them.

"Holy shit! Grandma G's book!"

Shion dropped the papers and fumbled with their
phone, pacing the room as they waited for their grandmother to pick up. They could picture exactly where in
their grandparents' study the book of unfinished stories
lay. Shion had read that book more times than they could
remember—at least twice every summer during the week-
long vacations they and their siblings spent in the San Francisco row house. Amid an eclectic mix of antique rugs and
velvet-upholstered wingback chairs in the front rooms, ta-
tami flooring and sliding screens in the addition out back,
and heirloom silver candlesticks set next to Buddha stat-
ues, the book sat on a shelf under a reproduction of one
of Georgia O'Keeffe's New York skyscraper paintings,
which Shion's cousin had gifted their grandmother for her
eightieth birthday.

The book contained only a handful of pictures, depicting the specific locations Grandma Gail and her three
friends from Tandem Bike had been able to sleuth out,

back when the unfinished stories in the book were still being mailed in to Dottie. There were photos of a rail station, the deck of a ferryboat, the docks where the freighters came in, and one of a produce store called Silva's Market. In the final picture, a young Maria fixed a display of oranges, a child on her hip. Even with the blur of the candid shot, Shion had no doubt it depicted the same woman and store as their printouts did.

Actually, Grandma Gail had two copies of the book: one for herself and another for a member of the original foursome of junior editorial staff whom they had all lost track of years before. Grandma had always hoped, and half expected, the elusive Ted to pop back into her life—right up until she received what had felt like a goodbye postcard from him and, later, a call from New York informing her of his death.

Shion's call went to voicemail, and they growled at the phone's screen. Then the time display caught their eye, and they realized they had called smack-dab in the middle of Grandma and Jiji's midday meditation, during which they never answered their phones.

As Shion waited for the meditation hour to pass, they read the rest of the submission. Maria lived her dream of becoming an engineer, dabbling in a little bit of everything. She held several patents, none of which the author completely understood beyond the fact that one had been widely used in Formula 1 race cars from the midnineties to present day. Maria avidly followed the field of robotics and was especially interested in devices used by space programs. Whenever the Pierre Auger Observatory opened their doors to the public for special occasions, she never missed an event.

In essence, Maria had learned to dance the particular

version of the tango she'd always wanted to learn. And she made damn sure everyone else in her family, and beyond, would have every opportunity to dance their own desired dances as well.

Shion teared up, remembering the Maria from the unfinished story, the one who had existed before she orchestrated her own personal renaissance. That Maria was frozen in time, making her schematic drawings of battery-powered children, only to stuff her drawings into the pages of women's magazines when customers came into the store.

When Shion finally got through, Grandma G's response was incredulity. "Shion, it couldn't possibly be the same woman. I mean, what are the chances? Maria is an incredibly common name and . . ."

As Shion listed off more and more details, their grandmother grew quiet. Eventually, Shion heard Jiji speaking in the background. "Gail, what's wrong? Is our Shion okay?"

When Grandma G spoke, there were tears in her voice. "Shion is fine, Riku. It . . . it's Maria, from our book. The Mother of Invention. She's still out there."

Gail sniffed a few more times, composing herself. "Shion, can you email me the submission, please? And would you do me the favor of contacting the young person who sent it in to see if it would be at all possible to get me in touch with Maria directly? I think it's high time she read the original story written about her."

Mirror, Mirror

New York City, 2019

Elise was busier than she'd ever been, and she wasn't even doing her usual job. The book she and Farhad had collaborated on would be coming out in a week, and life was a whirlwind of interviews and promotional photo sessions. The advanced reader copies had been well received and reviewed. Several prominent authors had provided complimentary blurbs for advertising and the back cover. Preorders were pouring in, and there was talk of potential award nominations. The buzz had swelled to international levels, what with the novelty of an American white woman and an Iraqi man writing a book together and both open to interviews in English and Arabic. The marketing department had even put together swag-filled promotional packets, complete with stickers, bookmarks, and coloring books, for librarians to use at themed events.

The Boy in the Library was being billed as a multilingual middle-grade historical-fiction adventure book. The artist had depicted a few of the real wall writings in the illustrations at the start of every chapter, and though Elise and Farhad had played a little fast and loose with the timing of major events—making their main character present for both the imprisonment of Aristophanes and the burning of the library, which were more than a lifetime apart—the publisher had said it would be fine. The story was still educational, and they'd put a note clarifying the timing in the nonfiction section at the end of the book.

At the moment, Elise was packing for her and Farhad's trip to New York. Or rather, she was procrastinating packing for the trip to New York by checking her email. Clicking through her inbox, she would select whatever caught her eye and put it on voice narration while she packed a few more items.

Elise loved the voice-narration feature. A vaguely female computerized voice would read her the email, and she would just get the facts the sender wanted her to receive. No picking up invasive impressions about the status of the sender's marriage or their fears regarding the downsizing of their department.

Looking for the next email to listen to, she noticed a personal email from an address she didn't know. The subject read *Bookstore Personal Appearance Invitation.* That was odd, considering most invitations went through the marketing department of the book's publishing house. Elise looked at the name and address again. Nope, still no recollection of a James Lowry.

Selecting the email, she got the narration running and hit her sock drawer.

"Hello, Ms. Borg," the computer read. "My name is Jim Lowry. I'm a New York–based playwright, and I'm writing to you on behalf of a friend of mine, Dorothy Barber, co-owner of Flights of Fancy Books here in the city.

"But I'm getting ahead of myself. You see, you came

up in conversation, in passing, one of the first nights I had the pleasure of hanging out with my girlfriend, Jessie Blum. She told me you were able to see things about her, things she'd never voiced out loud, simply from reading her writing. As it happens, not long before meeting Jessie, I was graced with the friendship of someone with a gift similar to yours, though perhaps not to the same acuity. That friend is Dottie, the aforementioned Ms. Barber, who I had the fortune of meeting when I moved into her building.

"Dottie's retired now, but she used to be a significant name in the New York publishing scene. When I told her what Jessie had said about you, Dottie was intrigued. We looked you up on the internet together and saw in *Publisher's Weekly* that you and Mr. Mohammed had secured a contract for a book that stemmed from your work in Alexandria. Dottie still has connections in publishing, so she was able to obtain an ARC. She read the whole thing in one sitting and absolutely loved it. She said Mr. Mohammed seemed like a very sweet man, and she felt your admiration and your frustration on every page, 'a bittersweet taste.'"

By this point, Elise had abandoned her sock hunt. Still holding a half-rolled pair, she stared at the floor and listened as the digital, monotonic voice continued to read.

"So, Dottie is usually a pretty patient lady, but she thought New York would probably be on your book tour anyway, and she would very much like to meet you.

"Ms. Borg, if I may confide in you, Dottie's not doing well. She isn't getting around like she used to, and though she's still herself, her evenings are getting, well, a little dim. She gets frustrated by it. You see, she has all these books. Well, I'll let her tell you about that.

"The crux of it is, she would like to invite you to the

bookstore to read your book. Mr. Mohammed as well, of course, but she most ardently wants to meet you. I hope you find it in your heart, and in your schedule, to drop by. Please see the attachment I've included. It's a scan of a handwritten invitation from Dottie. She insisted you see it in her own writing.

"Thank you so much for your time and consideration. Sincerely, James Lowry."

Elise was at the computer and clicking on the attachment before the last of James's email was read off. The scan showed a personal letterhead in a vintage design. The handwriting was shaky at the edges but otherwise determined and focused.

Dear Ms. Borg,

My good friend Jim brought you to my attention. I have since read several of your journal articles and an advanced reader copy of your upcoming book. It's lovely. I agree with your editor's choice to market it toward the MG crowd. I think it will inspire many a young reader to continue their journey and see where it takes them. And I was very happy you had an editor who didn't shy away from your alluding to the same-sex relationships among the library scribes. It may get your book banned in some markets, but aren't banned books some of the best books?

I think we are alike, you and I. I would like to invite you to my bookshop, Flights of Fancy, to do a reading of your book. If I am being truthful, my invitation is not entirely unselfish on my part. I hoped you could read a little something for me and tell me what you think. And I may have some

*items in my personal book collection that would
interest you in return.*

Sincerely,
    Dorothy Barber

Elise had to sit down. The old woman's desire to connect with her—to meet someone who understood reading the same way she experienced it—was so palpably strong. And the unassuming request to "read a little something for me" held such tremendous weight, so many questions unanswered for decades. The woman was also holding back when she wrote of "some items in my personal book collection that would interest you." When Elise closed her eyes, she saw Dottie's soft, wrinkled hand running lovingly across rows and rows of beautifully maintained books, a collection tucked away from light, prying eyes, and the bids of other collectors.

Taking a moment to collect herself, Elise picked up her phone and googled the address of the bookshop. She then emailed the publicist she and Farhad were working with. Elise never made demands and was very cooperative and professional about all the requests the marketing department made of her as a new author, but when she emailed them about this bookshop, it was not a request. They were absolutely going to make Flights of Fancy a stop on the New York leg of the tour. She then followed up with a reply to Jim, thanking him for reaching out to her and enthusiastically accepting the invitation.

Next, she called Farhad. When he picked up, she could hear the bubbly laughter of his nieces and nephews, who were probably hanging all over their favorite uncle.

"Listen," she said, "we're going to add an extra event in New York."

A week later, Elise stood in front of Flights of Fancy alone. The official visit, with swag bags for the kids and a fistful of permanent markers for signing books, wasn't until the following day, but Elise hadn't been able to wait any longer. Farhad was taking a nap in their hotel room, and she'd left him a note saying she had an errand to run and would be back in time for dinner.

Elise's heart was thumping as she stood on the sidewalk. The old brownstone's facade had been converted to a storefront for the business's entrance. On the other side of the building, according to follow-up emails with Jim, would be Dorothy's apartment. The small squares of basement windows just above ground level would lead to Jim's apartment.

Looking at the dusty glass, Elise wondered how long he would continue living there. She'd googled him as well and found out he had a new play that had just opened and was getting excellent reviews. She'd read that the whole thing was set around one set piece: a thick, low shelf, packed with books. All the action took place with the shelf as the focal point. The most recent article indicated there was talk of the play getting picked up by a bigger theater.

Taking a steadying breath, Elise walked into the bookstore, setting off the bell above the door. A girl at the counter was on the store's landline, but she covered the receiver to greet Elise and ask if she could help her find anything in particular. The bookseller gave no indication of knowing why Elise was there.

When Elise said she was just browsing, the girl smiled, nodded, and directed her attention back to the phone conversation. "Philip, you still there? So, I got two messages on our socials and one walk-in customer all asking about a book called *Princess of the Pomegranate Moon*. I googled the title, and it turns out that Bookstagrammer you like so much—you know, the cute guy with the glasses who also reviews lots of tabletop games? Well, he recently gushed about it, so now we're getting requests. Cool. Nope, nothing else really. The rose isn't rotating again, and I'm not tall enough to reach it. Ha! Yep, you too."

Letting the conversation drift away behind her, Elise took a look around the place, an eclectic blending of old and new styles. The ceiling had incredibly intricate molding embellishments, but there was also vibrant graffiti art on the exposed brick behind the register. Some of the bookshelves were built-in hardwood and had probably been there since the store was a home; others were made of industrial piping and what could have been repurposed barn wood.

All the way at the back of the store, one entire wall consisted of floor-to-ceiling mirrors, and the lighting was as bright as daylight. Overhead, a fantastic mobile slowly spun. It depicted a fox, a biplane, a rose, and an array of stars, all rotating around a sphere atop which stood a little boy. Elise smiled as she caught on that the mobile's parts were all references to *Le Petit Prince*. As the girl at the counter had mentioned in her phone call, the rose was, indeed, not spinning.

Some shelves sat in front of the mirrors. While Elise looked over the store, she caught her reflection looking back at her between the books. She would be in the bookstore again the following day, wearing the title of "author" and standing next to Farhad. She already knew how his hand would instinctively find hers when she was feeling nervous, and she smiled at her reflection. This moment in her life looked good on her.

The girl from the counter came through the area carrying a stack of books to shelve, and she smiled at Elise. "Still doing okay?"

"Yes. I'm actually spending more time admiring the art and architecture here than I am looking at the books."

"Yeah, it's a cool space to work in. I guess it used to be a dance studio or a disco or something before it was a bookstore." The girl motioned toward the mirrors with the paperback currently in her hand. "The mirrors used to freak me out a little, honestly, but now I'm used to it. Like, I would get the feeling someone else was here and watching me, but then I'd realize I was just catching my reflection out of the corner of my eye. I've seen a few customers jump or do a double take sometimes, too, so I guess it wasn't only me."

Elise nodded and smiled, but her brow furrowed as the girl moved back to the counter to greet someone who'd just entered the store. Elise wasn't sure why, but the hairs on the back of her neck stood up.

She turned to the wall of mirrors, took a few steps back so she could take in the whole space, and looked for some sort of clue. Yet Elise didn't have the foggiest idea what she was looking for.

As she scanned the shelves, her eyes fell on a hand-written note card standing tented between some books. Stepping closer to read it, Elise immediately recognized the handwriting: shaky around the edges but otherwise determined and focused.

I hope you find what you are looking for. Read long, read closely, and read with joy.

Sincerely,
   DB, Proprietor

Elise looked up from the card, glanced at her reflection, and did a quick check to be sure the salesgirl was still at the register. Satisfied she was alone, Elise leaned closer to the mirror, sticking her head right in a space on the shelf, and cupped her hands around her eyes to block out the light of the store. Squinting past the shadowy reflection of her own eyes, she saw exactly what she expected to see—exactly what she'd seen in her mind's eye as she read the note card. A cozy library, an imposing desk, and a small, steel-haired woman in a comfy chair with a quilt wrapped around her. The woman was looking directly at Elise and smiling as if she'd just caught sight of a long-lost relative.

Elise smirked.

Walking back out the door with the bell, she made a U-turn on the curb and climbed the stairs one door over. When Elise hit the intercom, the voice that came through the scratchy speaker felt familiar, even though Elise had never heard it before in her life.

"Come in, girl! Come in! First door on your right; I left it unlocked for you."

Entering the apartment, Elise beelined to the back, where the room she'd seen through the bookshop's mirrored wall would be. There on the back wall, a hanging tapestry had been pulled away to reveal the observer's side of the one-way mirror and the bright back room of the bookshop beyond.

This was an idle observation, as Elise focused on the woman sitting in the middle of her well-appointed library. Ms. Barber seemed smaller than Elise had pictured while reading her letter, perhaps because the older woman still pictured herself in her straight-backed, high-heeled prime. As they looked each over, smiling, Elise knew neither of them felt like this was their first time meeting.

"I'm glad to meet you, Ms. Barber. Afraid I couldn't wait until the book signing, but you figured as much." Elise held up the folded note card she'd plucked off the shelf on her way out of the bookstore.

"I made a guess. And call me Dottie; all my friends do."

Elise pointed toward the one-way mirror. "The mobile is beautiful."

"It is, isn't it? I can't take credit for that, though. The mobile was brought in by Philip, the other owner of the store. I'm really more of a silent partner in the business than I may have given the impression of being. Philip and I meet only once a month to talk about book business. I may request certain titles be ordered or certain authors be wooed into appearing in person, but I don't talk numbers. I leave that up to my accountant."

Dottie waved to an empty chair. "Now sit! Or better yet, help me up, and we'll go to the kitchen. I think the coffee I made earlier is still presentable, and I make sure to always have cake in the fridge. I am determined to have cake every day for the rest of my life."

Elise crossed the room and held out her arm for Dottie, who took it without hesitation. As they passed the hanging tapestry, Dottie gave it a swift tug, closing off the view of the bookstore beyond. The move drew Elise's eyes to Dottie's hands. They were the same hands Elise had seen caressing rows of books, only these hands also had a few healing bruises spread across them.

Elise's concern must have shown, because Dottie patted her arm.

"My balance isn't what it used to be, but you needn't worry about it. I have a hired companion, a wonderful young nursing student from Senegal, who comes every day for a few hours. We go for a walk, and she straightens up the place and makes me a hot dinner. And of course, there's my friend Jim downstairs, who helped me find you. He came by a few weeks ago with his girlfriend, who I understand is a dear old friend of yours. She's how he heard of your special talent for reading."

"Yes, Jessie and I were a thing a few years back, right around the time she started at the Circulation Desk. I'm sad we grew apart with all my traveling, but we kept in touch. She's going to come to the reading with Jim so we can catch up."

Once in the kitchen, Dottie aimed for the coffeepot. "No, you sit," Elise insisted. "I'll serve the coffee."

Dottie would have none of it, batting Elise away with exaggerated annoyance. "You can get the cake; I'll pour the coffee. Once I'm up and moving, I'm fine. It's getting up that's the biggest hurdle. Jim tried to convince me to get one of those chairs that lift you up, and I told him I love my big chair and I'll be damned if I get rid of it. But between you and me, I'm strongly considering it more and more each day. I must look like a hobbyhorse with how much I have to rock myself back and forth to gain the momentum to get to standing! But I can still pour coffee."

Dottie demonstrated her pouring skills with pride, and they settled at the table.

Dottie ate a forkful of blueberry-filled cake and enjoyed a slurp of her coffee. Then she focused on Elise. "So, tell me about yourself. Read any good books lately?"

Laughing, Elise started talking about her reading life and how it had evolved into being her job and her life's work. She told Dottie how reading and her career had led her to Alexandria and the book she and Farhad had written together.

"It sounds both wonderful and wonderfully frustrating, to know such fantastic things about the world yet have no way of communicating them in a believable way. A blessing and a curse, yes?"

"Yes. But you understand the feeling well, don't you?"

"I don't get details like you do. I rarely 'see' through the pages as I read them. I get impressions of a writer's intentions and their feelings on the topic, and sometimes, I sense emotions overflowing from what was happening in the rest of their lives when they were writing. It's enough that I figured out I was getting more than the average person when I read—and enough that I could envision the next step in the evolution of the gift. I imagined the existence of someone like you, and now here you are, eating cake in my kitchen with me!"

Dottie held up her coffee cup, and Elise clinked hers against it.

After taking a sip, Elise stared down into her cup. "He was like us, you know, a little bit."

Dottie nodded. "The boy in the library."

"Maybe he was one of the first of us. He knew reading opened to him in a way it didn't for others, even those who knew more words and more languages than he did. He may have imagined the existence of you and me both."

"Have you ever met anyone else like us?"

"Mm-hmm," Elise answered through a mouthful of cake. She swallowed. "I had a professor at U of Michigan, and I got the sense from her writing and lectures that she saw beyond the words. Sometimes, I purposefully watched her reading something new to see if I could judge from her visible reactions. But Rebecca was so . . . restrained. It was like she knew she had a gift but consciously kept it in check. There was always a wall I couldn't see though, and

I often wondered what might happen if she allowed a crack to form in that wall. What if the crack split wide open and she was unprepared for how much would come flooding through because she'd ignored it instead of training herself to manage it? Then a few years back, she abruptly left the university, right before the start of a term."

"The wall crumbled, perhaps?" Dottie posed.

Elise nodded. "It did. A few months back, she got in touch with me. Turns out, she slid so deep into the flood, she almost drowned. She told me a street busker helped her surface long enough to reach out to her sister for help. Since then, we've been communicating by email and written letters. I've shared my grounding techniques with her, and she's processed her experiences with me. Rebecca's going back to teaching soon. We've made plans to meet up this coming winter."

Elise took another sip of coffee. "What about you, Dottie?"

"A long time ago, I had a friend who was into poetry who I thought, maybe . . ." Dottie paused, a faraway look in her eyes. "It turned out Ted was just a hippie. Eventually, he was 'feeling' lots of things, thanks to LSD. Last year, my friend Gail received word of his death, right here in New York City. Ted had been a wanderer, but last I heard, he was happy with his place in the universe, so I'm happy for him."

Dottie leaned heavily on the table to push herself up, which had Elise on her feet and ready to assist. Dottie made it up all right on her own and even cleared the plates into the dishwasher. She declared that she ran the dishwasher daily, even if there were only a few things in it. Then she looked a bit lost and sheepish, perhaps blushing.

"Did I tell you that already? About the dishwasher? I

feel like maybe I told you that already, or maybe it was someone else. I'm sorry if I repeat myself sometimes." She pulled her shawl tighter around herself, looking down at her feet.

"No, you hadn't mentioned the dishwasher yet," Elise assured her. "But I entirely agree with your philosophy. Who has time for dishes when there are books to read? Speaking of which, you had one you wanted me to look at for you?"

"I do indeed. Isn't it silly, though? Now that I'm so close to getting answers about it, I'm nervous. I've lived for so long not knowing, I'm not sure how it will feel to stop wondering. The book can wait a few more minutes, though. I'm on my feet and feeling like I can manage the stairs, so let me show you my library."

Elise didn't recall Dottie's library having stairs in it, aside from the rolling ladder. Perhaps there was a spiral staircase behind a false wall that opened at the pull of a lever disguised as a book.

Elise was almost down the hallway when she realized Dottie had stopped at the apartment door. The older woman leaned on a cane she'd retrieved from the coatrack and was sliding her feet into a pair of beaded, fur-lined moccasins.

"The library's downstairs in the basement, next to Jim's place," Dottie explained.

Elise nodded, and they walked down the stairwell together.

"Is Jim home today?" Elise asked.

"No. He grabbed a cheap red-eye flight to Chicago the night before last. There's a theater there that's interested in putting on his play, once its New York run is done.

"The play's good. You and Mr. Mohammed should

see it while you're in town," Dottie encouraged. "I'm sure Jim can get you tickets. I got to sit in the front row with him and his parents on opening night, an event followed by a wonderful party at the Circulation Desk. Jane wasn't sure about letting all those actors and theater people in, but it went fine.

"And Jim will be back in time for your book signing. The day after, he's going to be a featured speaker at the Main Branch of the New York Public Library, talking about how his time working there inspired the play. I'm so happy his career is taking off."

"You know Kodiak Jane?" Elise asked, having caught Dottie's reference. "I met her when Jessie first started working at the Circulation Desk. She's a character and a half and one hell of a writer. I wish she wrote more."

"So do I!" Dottie agreed. "I commissioned her debut novel, you know. It was the first time I really went out on a limb and pushed a book that others weren't sure would sell. A young one-eyed Black woman writing about life in Alaska in the early sixties? That was pretty damn niche. But her writing spoke for itself, and later, her account of the Anchorage earthquake of sixty-four was the best there was."

Dottie glanced at Elise slyly. "Did you know that before those books, Jane wrote quaint romance novels?"

Elise's jaw dropped. "Jane? Kodiak Jane wrote romance novels? Get out!"

"Well, they weren't smutty, if that's what you're implying, not that there's anything wrong with that. But yes, romances—complete with flannel shirts and wood fires. Though even then, Jane's voice and attention to details set her apart. She wrote about Alaska with such love."

Dottie stopped and steadied herself on the stairs long

enough to wag one moccasined foot. "These mukluk slippers are from her." Then she continued down the stairs. "I love that Jane made two homes for herself: one here in New York and one in Kodiak. She told me the night of the play, though, that she wasn't sure she was going to return to New York after her next trip to Alaska. If she takes her stuffed raven with her, you'll know she's not coming back."

Stepping off the stairs, they walked to a thick door in the basement, just down a short hallway from another, more common-looking door that Elise thought must lead to Jim's apartment. Dottie keyed in a combination, making no attempt to hide it from Elise. The door whirred as the electronic lock released, and Dottie leaned on the handle, opening the door. The room on the other side was dark, but Elise could already sense its size.

When Dottie switched on the light, Elise gasped. It revealed row after row after row of books. At the end of each stood a glass case displaying books horizontally, signaling their greater fragility. Taking up the only window was a large heating/cooling unit and several humidity-control units.

"I thought about getting some rolling stacks," Dottie admitted, "like what university libraries have in their lower levels to save space. But since I was little, I've had an irrational fear of getting closed up in them, like a fly in the fold of an accordion, so I didn't go that route. Still, I think I've done okay for myself over the years."

Elise had to agree. She strolled through only two rows before she stopped, too overwhelmed. "Dottie, I've been to some of the greatest library and museum archives in the world, and the curators would be drooling over what I'm seeing here. Why are you sharing these with me? Who the hell am I?"

"When you start opening them, you'll know why."

Elise retrieved a pair of white cotton gloves from her pocket and slid a book off the shelf, making sure to move the bookend over to fill the gap and support the missing book's shelf neighbors. She picked that particular book because it didn't appear to be terribly rare, compared to some of the others nearby. It was a nicely bound, and well-preserved, first edition of *The House on the Strand* by Daphne du Maurier.

She opened the front cover, and there it was: an inscription in the hand of the dame herself, addressed to Dottie. The words were simple well-wishes to 'a new friend,' but vivid images from the book came crashing into Elise's mind from the stylish script.

"You asked her about the book right as she was writing this. You captured her thoughts about it. Reading this inscription is like opening a time capsule of du Maurier's innermost impressions of her writing. It's incredible! Oh my god, are they all inscribed? But they can't all be like this. They can't all be inscribed to you; you're not *that* old!"

They both fell into a bounding laughter that bounced around the bare walls. Dottie had to hang on to both a shelf and her cane so she wouldn't laugh herself right off her feet.

"I'm so sorry!" Elise finally got out in between gasping breaths and more laughter. "That sounded absolutely horrible! Can we chalk it up to shock and excitement? I swear, I don't usually stick my foot that far into my mouth."

Dottie waved the words away. "It's fine! You're fine! I haven't laughed that hard in quite a while. But do collect yourself, dear, because I have been waiting to get a better peek into that woman's mind since I had her sign the damn book in 1969."

Composing herself, Elise read the inscription again, then told Dottie every detail that came through. After that, they picked another book, and another. Some were inscribed to Dottie. Throughout her years in publishing and bookstore ownership, she'd taken full advantage of every opportunity to pop an insightful question or two right as an author was signing a title page for her.

Older books, of course, were not personalized, but Dottie was an astute collector of inscribed copies. Her favorites were books addressed personally, from one author to another. In her early years of collecting, Dottie attended auctions herself, then later hired representatives to stand in on her behalf. She'd also been a shark on eBay in its early days, being able to tell a fake from an authentic signature just from a picture. The fakes were always laced with a dishonest feeling that made Dottie picture a stereotypical snake-oil salesperson on the other end of the pen.

With so many books, spanning decades and continents, Elise found herself swept away. She didn't even realize she had fallen into speaking the native languages of those authors who'd left unusually strong impressions until Dottie mentioned that she was speaking Russian.

"I could follow the French and some of the German, but the Russian is too much."

Only then did Elise notice how heavily Dottie was leaning on her cane. She still listened attentively, but her head was bowed and her eyes resting.

Elise slid the book she'd been holding back into place on the shelf. "You know, I've got so many of these authors roaming around in my head now, I think I may need a break and a tall glass of water. Would it be okay if we headed back up to your place?"

Dottie nodded, and they locked the door before making their way back upstairs, much slower than when they'd descended earlier. Elise offered her arm, and Dottie held it all the way.

Once upstairs, Elise planned on taking Dottie all the way to her chair in the library, but Dottie subtly nodded to the hall bathroom as they started to pass it, so Elise left the older woman to it. Meanwhile, Elise fetched them each a tall tumbler of ice water, putting them on coasters on Dottie's desk in the library.

Leaning over Dottie's desk, Elise noticed a short grocery list. Three out of the eight items listed were different types of cake. There was also a reminder Dottie had left herself about ordering birthday flowers for her friend Gail. Elise could read Dottie's fondness for Gail, whom Dottie pictured in her prime, the two of them circulating through a company Christmas party together. Intermixed with the images, Elise also read Dottie's feelings about needing to write herself such reminder notes and her fears of forgetting dates, forgetting her friend, and forgetting herself.

Dottie emerged from the bathroom slowly enough that Elise was able to take a few steps away from the desk and her snooping before the older woman was fully in the room. Dottie still looked tired but had clearly splashed some water on her face to refresh herself; there were water droplets clinging to the wisps of hair around her brow. If Dottie suspected Elise of poking around, she did them both the courtesy of not saying anything about it.

Once they were both settled and had had some water, Dottie asked, "Were you able to clear your head? Do you have a ritual for that kind of thing? How else do you keep yourself from getting overwhelmed the way your old professor did?"

Elise explained how she wrote herself grounding notes

when she knew she would be reading intensely, and how she always played her emails and texts aloud to distance herself from reading too far into them. Seeing behind people's messages sometimes felt like an invasion of their day, Elise noted, and she felt people deserved more privacy than that. Elise also talked about how she would get a book in audio form if she wanted to read it sheerly for the content or enjoyment. If she was intrigued enough by the story the first go around, she might bother to read it on paper afterward, to get more insight into it.

"But enough about me and my methods. Dottie, when I read the letter you had Jim send me over email, I felt how deeply you wanted me to read something for you, something in particular. That particular something wasn't with the other books downstairs. You keep it closer to you. I think it's time I read it for you and time you get your answers, don't you?"

Dottie smiled as tears brightened her eyes. She didn't even need to get up to get the book. Dottie merely opened a drawer in the side table next to her and pulled out the collection of unfinished stories. Dottie hefted it over to Elise, who closed her eyes, letting herself feel the weight of the book in her hands before taking a cleansing breath and opening it.

First, Elise read the inscription written by a man named Bobby. She quickly gathered that Bobby wasn't the author but had compiled the contents of the book and was someone who enjoyed a partner-in-crime type of playfulness with Dottie. And he loved her. Every word was laced with affection. Bobby looked up to Dottie and respected her strength and determination. He admired everything about her. Dottie was Bobby's best friend and one of his favorite people in the world.

"He passed away just a few years back, my Bobby," Dottie said softly, pulling Elise's attention from the page. "I so wish he was with us right now. Bobby wanted to know too. Read on, dear. I'm not getting any younger."

Elise did as she was told and soon found herself caught up in the words. The writing was good, amazingly good. The story and the images on the page were so engrossing that Elise honestly forgot at first to focus on the author. Also, the author was so in the moment as they wrote that it was difficult for Elise to get a read on them.

Just as she began to wonder why she'd never read anything by this person before, why Dottie hadn't championed this writer into getting published the way she had Kodiak Jane, the story ended.

Ended without an ending.

Elise flipped the page back and forth, thinking she'd missed something or that perhaps the pages were stuck together.

Dottie chuckled knowingly. "Tell me about it, honey!"

The simple words were an expression of understanding Elise's surprise but also an order, and Elise read on.

This time, Elise focused more on the writer, even as she allowed herself to get lost in the story. The second story also ended without a conclusion, though Elise knew the author was male before the words ran out. By the end of the third story, she could picture the author's hands on the typewriter he'd used, how he'd had to keep fixing the *S* key, manually flicking it back into place after each time he pressed it.

Over time, another image of the man's hands came into focus, gripping something other than the typewriter. Then his reflection in a mirror, wearing a uniform. But the author didn't just look into the mirror to see himself. He looked through it at others and made up stories about their lives.

There was something odd about the mirror; the shape seemed strange to Elise.

Then she had it. She knew the author's name; it was there on the tag on his uniform. Elise also knew why he never ended the stories and why he sent them to the publishing house where Dottie and her friends had worked. The information was there in front of her because Elise could see Dottie and her friends too. She could see a younger Dottie reflected in that oddly shaped mirror.

Looking up, Elise smiled. Dottie smiled back, but before either could speak, Dottie's phone rang, breaking the happy anticipation.

Dottie chuckled. "Of course I get a call right now! I better answer it, though. Not many people call me these days, as most who have this number are as old as I am. I always pick up, even if I'm reading, because you never know . . ."

Dottie pushed herself to her feet and made her way to the desk.

"Gail! Hello, dear! If this is a social call, I may have to call you back. I'm about to get some news I most definitely will want to share with you more than anybody. I've a guest and—"

Dottie stopped abruptly as the voice on the other end of the line cut her off. She listened intently, her eyes widening, and she appeared to have forgotten to breathe for a concerningly long moment.

Finally, she breathed out one long breath and leaned forward heavily onto her desk.

Elise instinctually got up and went to Dottie's side, ready to support her if need be. "Dottie?"

Dottie looked up at Elise as if she'd just remembered Elise was there, her smile from before the call returning, brighter even than before.

She sighed. "His name is Lenny?"

Elise's jaw dropped. "How on earth did you know?"

Bisabuela de la Invención

San Francisco and San Antonio de Areco, 2019

Not even forty-eight hours after the realization that one of the subjects of the matriarch anthology submissions was Maria Silva and she was still alive, Shion was setting up a video call between San Francisco, California, and the gaucho town of San Antonio de Areco, Argentina. Negotiating around a five-hour time difference, they'd aimed for the sweet spot between Maria's siesta and when she took pain medication for the arthritis in her knees and hands.

"Bisabuela is coming along in just a minute," Maria's great-granddaughter explained. "My cousin is getting married this weekend, so a bunch of my relatives are here at the house to help bake for the reception. Bisabuela is in the kitchen, telling them all what they are doing right and wrong with the Italian pepper cookies, the Italian anisette cookies, and the *alfajores*. She was brought up Italian, but Bisabuela learned how to make all the Argentinian sweets from her mother-in-law when she got married, and she swears she makes them better than her husband's sisters ever did."

The screen jostled, and there was some background talk in Spanish. Then the laptop was placed on a table, and Maria slowly lowered herself into the armchair in front of it. She put on the headphones and fiddled with the volume on her own, before greeting Shion and Gail in both English and Spanish with a warm smile and a twinkle in her eyes.

"So, I understand you are going to publish the nice story my little Juliana wrote about me. She did such a good job on it. Everyone said such sweet things about me; I was very flattered by it."

"Yes," Gail began. "The story's exactly the kind of piece we want for our matriarch anthology, and you are absolutely the kind of woman we want our readers to hear about. But we actually wanted to get in touch with you about a different story written about you a long time ago. This would have been back in the early sixties, when you and your husband had the grocery store in New York."

Before Gail could take a breath and continue to explain about the collection of unfinished stories and how Maria fit into them, Maria interrupted. "You mean the story the bus driver wrote about me? How do you know about that one? Oh! Are you the lady who dropped the flyer off in the store?"

The words were casual, spoken as Maria accepted a wooden cup from someone off-screen, but Gail's mouth dropped open and stayed that way.

Squinting, Maria leaned closer to the screen. "*Juliana, la pantalla de mi computadora está* frozen."

"No! Not frozen!" Gail coughed out. "A bus driver? You knew him, and about the story? Why didn't you tell Dottie when she dropped off the flyer at your store? For that matter, you remember the flyer?"

Smiling, Maria nodded. "I remember. Sometimes,

those days back at the store, or my days spent at *universidad*, seem more real to me than what I did before today's siesta. What would you like to know?"

Gail wanted to reach through the screen and hug the brilliant woman on the other side of it. "I want to know about the writer. He wrote a lot of stories like yours, stories that let the reader look right inside people's lives, elevating their experiences to something even more beautiful and real. But he never finished them. Any of them. What do you know about him, Maria?"

"When your friend came and posted the flyer, she said someone wrote a story that took place in or around our store, and she let something slip right before she left. She used my first name when she thanked me for talking with her and letting her post the flyer. When she'd first introduced herself, she asked if I was Mrs. Silva, as was displayed on the front window of the store, and I never mentioned my first name. So after she walked out, I reflected on how flustered she was and figured I was likely in the story. So naturally, I kept a close eye on the flyer."

Maria looked at someone off-screen. "*Marta, consígueme la caja tallada de mi dormitorio, en la que guardo mis papeles personales, por favor. Gracias.*"

She turned back to the video call. "I watched everyone who read the flyer. It was days, and no one took it or wrote down the information. When I was upstairs making dinner, I hoped I didn't miss someone coming in and picking it up. Tomás wanted to take it down, but I gently insisted it stay up. Then one day, several customers came in right before closing. More than one were filling paper sacks from our discounted bruised-fruit table. I always watched that closely to make sure they didn't try to slip in some of the good fruit. A man came up from the other side to have me ring him up. He looked a little familiar, but I didn't put any effort into trying to place his face, since I was watching the other people. After he left, when I was ringing up the other customers, something caught my eye. There was a bare spot where the flyer used to be. It must have been him, the quiet man, who took it."

Someone, presumably Marta, placed a box at Maria's elbow. Maria smiled her thanks and took a sip from the straw in her wooden cup.

"After that, I kept looking for the man to come in again, but I didn't see him. Then one day, I took the children to the library. I stepped on the bus, paid our fare, and jostled to find a set of seats for us all to fit. Only after I got us all settled did I look up and see him. He was looking at me in the mirror, but he looked away quickly. I knew it was him, the quiet man who took the flyer. He was our bus driver! He must have driven us to the library dozens of times."

Gail let out a breath, understanding running through her. All those different locations, all those beautiful details that were clearly written by someone who loved New York, all those carefully documented character observations cultivated through day-in and day-out encounters with the people he wrote about. Even when the author wasn't driving, people used to being invisible tended to know how to stay invisible.

Gail would have reflected further, but Maria continued her story.

"When it was time to get off at our stop, I made it a point to walk up to the front of the bus instead of out the side door. I stopped there long enough to prompt him to look up into my eyes. He was only able to manage a nervous glance or two, and I saw his ears getting red.

"'Tell the bus driver thank you for the ride here, children,' I said to the kids. They were confused by this change in our library bus-ride routine, but they chimed in with thank-yous, my youngest saying *grazie* instead. I'd always made it a point that the children could speak some Italian so they could greet their grandparents appropriately on our monthly phone calls with them. But anyway, the driver gave a little smile and nod but looked away.

"The next week, I got my neighbor to watch the children for me, telling her I wanted to go to the library by myself to attend a program about flower arranging. I let another bus go by first, waiting for him. When he pulled up and opened the door, I sat in the seat right behind him. I could see his ears getting red again. When we stopped at a traffic light, I handed him a paper sack of fruit, told him they were for him. He said thank you, barely above a whisper. Then I leaned in and asked him, 'So did you go to see the lady from the publisher about your stories?'

"His eyes went so wide! I almost felt bad asking him!" Maria laughed in remembrance.

"The light turned green, and he hit the gas with more gusto than usual. The bag of fruit on his lap almost rolled off. He gently put it to the side, on top of his folded overcoat, and gave it a pat, as you would a cat after placing it on the floor. He took two big breaths, then whispered that he did not contact your friend. 'I had to drive that shift,' he said. 'Drove right past, and I saw them standing behind the big windows in the lobby.'

"I asked him why he didn't just get someone else to take his shift so he could meet all of you or at least call in and ask for the lady on the flyer. I couldn't understand why someone would pass up an opportunity to have the work of their heart be acknowledged and shared.

"His eyes strayed from their straight-ahead vigilance, and he stole a quick, blinking look at me through the mirror before shifting in his seat in his discomfort."

Gail smiled at Maria's storytelling abilities, wondering, just a little, how much was excellent memory and how much was creative embellishment. She quickly decided she didn't care. Creative embellishment could sometimes paint a truer recollection of events than facts would have.

"He finally answered me," Maria said, "but with a question. 'Why don't you ever build the things you make drawings of in your notebooks?'

"Then it was my turn to be shy and struggle to find words! I clutched my big handbag to my stomach, knowing I had one of those notebooks in there at that exact moment. He got a little braver and said, 'Forgive me. I've seen the pages sticking out sometimes, and I see the books you check out and how you hold them so carefully. I see you turn your head whenever we pass a hardware store, and I see you, on my route, out under the hood of your store's delivery truck that you park in the alley.'"

Growing quiet, Maria looked down at her hands. "I had never felt so exposed. I just nodded. Then I rode the rest of his route with him, until it came back around to the store. As I got off, I thanked him. He picked up the bag of fruit and nodded his thanks to me in return, before putting the bag back down and giving it another pat. I was almost all the way down the steps when I turned and hurried back up. Leaning down by his ear, I squeezed his arm through the uniform shirt and told him I would be honored to read the story he'd written about me. And even if he didn't want me to read it, I was grateful he had written it."

Pausing, Maria opened the lid of the ornately carved box that had been placed next to her. She sifted through papers, sending a crinkling static through the video feed from Argentina to California. After a moment, she lifted out several sheets of thin, tri-folded paper tied with a piece of twine. She slid the string off carefully, rolled it in her fingers, and held it up to the webcam for Gail to see.

"The twine we kept in the store to tie up the bunches of carrots and beets!"

Gail nodded, and Maria opened the papers, smoothing them out over her knees. When she spoke, her words were aimed down at the papers instead of into the camera. "A letter came in the mail for me about a week after I took that bus ride. He included a handwritten note, along with the typed pages, apologizing for the typos. He said one of the keys always got stuck. I took the bus lots after that, but I never saw him again. I can only imagine he must have changed routes. There was no return address on his letter, so I never got his last name and never knew where to send my thanks."

Maria sighed heavily. For the first time since the start of the video call, every one of her ninety-five years showed in her face.

"He said such . . . he made me sound . . ." The old woman sniffed. "He saw me. He really *saw* me. He saw my dreams and my hesitations, and he wrote them all down in a wonderful, beautiful story. He didn't get all the details right, but that's okay. Every word he wrote was truthful, despite the little mistakes.

"I read the story many times right after I received it, but I read it less and less over the years that followed. Sometimes, I would forget it existed, until I looked in my box for something else. After Tomás died, I began to read it again. Tomás's regrets about not having learned to dance got me thinking, but this story"—Maria waved the pages at the camera—"helped me find the strength to apply to school, to show up every day among all those young people, to speak up in class and make mistakes and missteps and miscalculations. I thought of this story when I got my first patent, and I knew that the young mother in the story would be proud of the woman and engineer I had become.

"He never finished the story, but I think I know why. It was my job to write the ending, and I like the way it turned out."

Gail didn't notice she was crying until Shion handed her a box of tissues. Maria appeared to need a moment as well, and she took a long drink from the straw in her cup, until it made a slurping sound.

"Did you ever publish his stories?" she finally asked. "Were they a big hit?"

"Well, my old friend Bobby had a special printing made of them for me and our two other friends from Tandem Bike. Bobby even took pictures of a few places we tracked down that he wrote about. Your picture is in there, Maria, a snapshot Dottie took on her old Kodak. His stories were beautiful, but there was no market for his unfinished works, beyond us four fans and, later, the family members we shared the stories with.

"Your story, 'Mother of Invention,' was always one of my favorites, Maria. I think that story was partly responsible for the kind of work I decided to publish because I wanted to tell the stories of women who would otherwise be lost. Actually, I have one extra copy of the collection. The friend I was holding it for passed away recently. If you'd like, I'll send it to you."

Maria clasped her hands together. "Oh, I'd like that!" She then began massaging her thick-knuckled fingers, hissing through her teeth.

Gail recalled the talk of arthritis medication and knew Maria had likely been rolling dozens of cookies before she got on the video call. "I've kept you for some time, Maria. I'll let you get back to your family and the baking for the wedding. I hope it is a beautiful event. Later on, I'll have Shion and Juliana work out getting the book to you. And of course, you will get a copy of the anthology with your new story in it when it's hot off the presses. I was thinking we should title that one 'Mother of Invention' as well. Do you think that would be all right?"

"*Perfecta. Perfetta.* I think Lenny would approve. And I will send you a box of the cookies we made this weekend! Don't let the name of the pepper cookies fool you; they are not spicy, mostly chocolate."

Gail thanked Maria again, then asked, "But who is Lenny?"

"Lenny! You know, the bus driver."

"But," Gail sputtered, "you said he didn't leave you a name or return address!"

"He didn't, not on the envelope. But it was on his name tag; didn't I mention it? And here it is on his letter, see?" Maria held the paper up to the camera, which took a moment to focus on the writing.

Sincerely,
  Lenny

Chapter One

New York City, 2019

Jim had mixed feelings about moving out of the basement apartment. He was, of course, excited to be moving in with Jessie. She was brilliant, funny, and gorgeous, and he didn't think he would ever tire of being near her. When they curled around each other at night, it felt like home in a way Jim had never experienced before.

Jessie didn't know he'd nearly gone cross-eyed on more than one occasion from focusing intently on the lines of her tattoos and how, even with the most precise lines, there was blurring at the edges. Jim wanted to know every hard and soft edge Jessie had. Maybe he would tell her that one day. Maybe it would win him a smile or a laugh, maybe even a kiss.

Tiring of her biannual trek between Kodiak Island and New York City, Kodiak Jane had made the decision to move back to her beloved Alaska for good. Everyone at the Circulation Desk knew she was serious because she had carefully packed up her stuffed raven for the journey home. She had offered to sublet her apartment to Jessie for an extremely reasonable rate. The space was great, just the right distance from the bar and the Theater District. Jim was making enough from his plays that he would soon be able to quit his job at the library and dedicate himself full-time to playwriting, although that, too, was bittersweet. Jessie had assured him he would always be welcome at the Circulation Desk, and not just because he was sleeping with the manager and good at cleaning glasses, but Jim knew he would miss the library.

Leaving Dottie was going to be hard too. Sure, Jim would drop in once or twice a week and make sure Dottie got tickets to all his shows, but she would no longer be just a thump on his ceiling away.

He worried about her.

Dottie had a young woman who came by for a few hours every day, and Philip was right next door at Flights of Fancy, but what if something happened outside those hours? Jim was going to set her up with voice-activated smart devices around her apartment so she could call for help, if needed. That, or one of those old-school buttons on a chain that contacted a service.

Mostly, Jim worried about Dottie getting lonely. He knew she had her books and all those contacts in her address book, but it wasn't the same as being just a flight of stairs away from a good friend. Some days, Dottie was great. But sometimes, she seemed to carry the weight of all the books she would never get to read on her thin shoulders, and those shoulders got a little more stooped every time Jim saw her.

The thought plagued him as he boxed up his books and decided what furniture he would bring to Jessie's and what he would just leave on the sidewalk for someone to spirit away. Jim thought about it as he and Jessie drove out to Jersey to look at some furniture his dad's old friend, the building manager and apartment-building owner, offered to give him for free for the new place. He was doing renovations to some of his buildings and was replacing all the staging furniture in the model apartments with newer stuff. He said Jim could have his pick of the older items.

Once Jessie had navigated their borrowed van through downtown traffic and was no longer gripping the wheel with white knuckles while cursing under her breath, Jim started to tell her something of what he'd been thinking about. Sitting side by side in the van, both looking forward, instead of directly at one another, made it a little easier.

"I never told you this, but I almost didn't come to New York. The day before I was supposed to head out here, I was really close to chickening out."

"How come?" Jessie asked.

"Well, my parents—my whole family, really—they're very conservative people. Not politically speaking, but when it comes to making decisions about life, they take the safe route. Everybody went into career that were reliable and had retirement plans. They even married people who had the same safe mindset. No one had moved across the country before, and the fact that I went to college for something that had to do with the arts was about the craziest thing anyone in my family had ever done."

"Hmm, I can see the appeal of living in a nice, comfy safety net, but eventually, it has to feel a little like being trapped, right?"

"I don't know if I ever felt trapped. Maybe I would have if I'd stayed longer. But the thing is, I'm not a rebel."

Jessie gave a comically exaggerated mock gasp. "Are you kidding? Why, just yesterday you wore socks that didn't match when we went for coffee!"

"Ha-ha, very funny," Jim returned. "You know I was self-conscious about my socks the whole time because the cuffs of my jeans came up just enough when I sat down to show them to the world! I am a rule follower, like the rest of my family. I even had spreadsheets for my 'Move to NYC' budget plan. But then my play got picked up at the Cherry Lane, I found the basement apartment in Dottie's building that I could actually afford, and I decided to move early, completely off script.

"As I packed up the rented trailer with the contents of my childhood bedroom, there was quite a bit of space left, and I realized how very little I was bringing with me. I felt so unprepared. Scared. And then I felt stupid and naive. Like, who the hell was I to think I could possibly make it in New York? So many people were so much more talented and driven than I was, not to mention having better connections than I did."

"Ah! Imposter syndrome reared its ugly head!" Jessie said knowingly.

"Yeah. Big time," Jim agreed. "But then my mom came out to the curb. She told me she was worried because I'd been standing there staring into the trailer for about fifteen minutes straight. So I asked her, 'Do you think I should wait a few more months, write some more, and get a few more productions under my belt first? I could try building up more of a reputation in places closer to home, like Chicago.' I thought she was going to say that was a better idea than going off to New York, but she looked me right in the eye and told me I needed to go. So I asked, 'But what if I don't make it?'

"'Well, if you don't make it, you don't make it,' she said. 'That isn't the end. But here's the thing, Jim. You can't possibly get to the happy ending if you don't ever start chapter one of your story. Everything you've done so far in preparation for making this jump, it was just the prologue. You need to start the action now; you need to go. Be the main character in your life's story.'"

"Wow." Jessie dared to take her eyes off the road long enough to grab Jim's hand and bring it to her lips for a kiss. "I guess I have to thank your mom for that next time I see her. Because otherwise, my life's story wouldn't have such an amazing love interest.

"I'm happy you turned the page and made the move."

"Me too. I wouldn't have met Dottie or you or anyone from the library if I hadn't come. I wouldn't have written *The Stacks.* And you know what? I can't wait to see what the next chapter brings."

When they got to the warehouse, Brian, the building manager, met them at the door and welcomed them in. He apologized for the mess. The place had lumber stacked against one wall, countertops against another, and plumbing supplies squirreled away in cubbies along a third wall that reminded Jim of the card catalog at the Circulation Desk.

In the middle of it all, a couple of workmen discussed what supplies they would need for the day's jobs. One did a double take upon seeing Jessie, then nudged his companion and muttered something with a sneer. To his credit, the companion punched the crude jokester in the arm and pointedly went right back to discussing how much wood they needed.

Jim, Jessie, and Brian made small talk and caught up on family news. They discussed Jim's upcoming projects and the new apartment. The couple then picked out a plain-looking loveseat that would go with just about anything, something they could dress up with bright blankets or pillows. They also grabbed end tables, a chair for the bedroom, and a few floor lamps.

As they were loading up the last of it, Brian stopped them. "Hey, would you like a vintage typewriter? It's busted, but it could look nice on a bookshelf or something. It belonged to my dad's cousin. He lived in one of my apartments before he passed away a few years back, and I never had the heart to toss the typewriter."

Jessie shrugged. "Sure. If we can't use it in the apartment, I can always find a spot for it at the Circulation Desk. Hell, with all the wonderful nerds we have as patrons, you never know who might pull out a multitool while nursing a rum and Coke and get it up and running again."

Nodding, Brian led the couple to a back section of the warehouse that had storage cages.

"Sometimes, when my tenants die and they don't have anybody who comes forward, I put some of their more personal things in here. You know, just in case someone comes for the effects eventually. Photo albums, scrapbooks, military medals, handmade quilts, that sort of thing. I label them all with the name and the last address of the owner. The wife says I'm crazy, but I feel like some things are just worth saving, you know?"

Although the setup wasn't as organized as his friend Kate's archival process, Jim had to admit the landlord-turned-treasure-keeper didn't do a bad job. He found the typewriter after only shifting around a box or two.

Brian pulled out another box. "These were his too. He was a bit of an amateur writer, I guess. These legal pads are full of stories he wrote. I'm afraid I've never been much of a reader myself—take after my dad with that—but maybe there's something in here you could adapt for a play or something. Just make sure to credit old Lenny if you do, okay?"

Jim's head shot up. "What did you say his name was?"

"Lenny. Lenny Horowitz. Why? You ever heard of him? Is he famous or something?" Brian joked.

Jim was already reaching for the notebooks, hardly paying attention.

"It can't be the same guy, right?" Jessie asked, spying over Jim's shoulder. "I mean, what are the odds?"

"Brian, what did Lenny do for a living?" Jim asked. "He wasn't a bus driver by any chance, was he?"

The question caught Brian's attention. "Yeah, yeah, he was, in fact. Wait, *is* he a famous writer?"

Jim flipped through page after page of the legal pads. Although the handwriting was tough to read in places, it was clear the stories were all biographies, the locations were in New York, and the writing itself was Lenny's unmistakable style of very human yet wonderfully more.

Jim's eyes welled up. "Lenny Horowitz. I found you." He sighed, then looked up. "Yeah, Brian, he is famous. He has a small but intensely dedicated fan base. Thank you for saving these."

The Ending(s)

New York City, 2019

Dottie had been out and about most of the day. She'd met with her lawyer about making a few changes to her will. Though Dottie had long ago decided she would leave the building and her share in Flights of Fancy to Philip, she had never quite known what to do with all her books. When she met Elise, Dottie knew Elise understood their value the way Dottie did. Elise would give them a good home.

Following the meeting, lunch out, and a stop at a delightful bakery, Dottie was worn out, so she wasn't feeling her sharpest when Jim came knocking on her door. He was dirty and sweaty, grinning from ear to ear, and carrying a banker's box as if it were the Holy Grail. Breathlessly, he told her the story of the discovery of the notebooks.

Dottie knew she repeated herself several times as she asked Jim questions. Of course, she was sad to hear that Lenny had died, never knowing how much Dottie, Gail, Bobby, and Ted—and now so many others in their circle of friends and family—had loved his work. Dottie had thought she'd gotten all she was going to get when Gail connected with Maria and Elise read Lenny's work. It was hard to believe there was more.

But when she flipped open one of the legal pads, there Lenny was, loud and clear, after all those years.

Each yellow page was chock-full of the first, and only, drafts of Lenny's work, in his own handwriting. Dottie ran her fingers lovingly over the topography of his words. As she read, even though her vision was unclouded, she kept seeing the specter of a dark shadow in the middle of the page. When the writing strayed from the lines on the paper, Dottie felt Lenny's frustration with himself and his failing eyesight.

But the stories. Oh, the stories!

The first piece Dottie read was about a woman at a laundromat. Lenny captured every limping step she took and the pocketful of Hershey Kisses she kept just to earn smiles from children. This sometimes led to a conversation with their mothers about the perils, and exhaustion, of motherhood. The woman never had children, Lenny surmised, but she felt there was no harm in pretending she did with these strangers.

She would slip a few pairs of men's socks, undershirts, and boxers in with her things just before closing the washing machine. All the men's items were clean, still folded even. But she took great care in washing them, drying them, and folding them with her own laundry. Her husband had been gone for years. He had been a good man at one time. But as the bottle became an ever-present fixture in his fist, he grew distant. She lost him years before the liquor finished off his liver and kidneys.

She enjoyed pretending he was still waiting for her at home, sober, smiling.

Dottie read late into the night, well past her usual bedtime, with Jim sitting by her side. He made a pot of coffee for them both and kept warming Dottie's cup without her having to ask. They handed the notebooks back and forth, sighing over the beautiful writing. Dottie would tell him here and there about things she picked up from what she read, like Lenny's failing eyesight and how he missed typing on his typewriter.

It was late when Dottie turned the page and knew something was different. It wasn't a new story—or rather, not one Lenny had written about a new observation. The writing was just a snippet, not even a full page. It was something from his past, a glance through the big plate-glass lobby window of an office building from his driver's seat on the bus.

It was . . . her.

Dottie.

The day she, Bobby, Gail, and Ted had waited for Lenny to show up, solving the mystery all those years ago. Reading about herself from Lenny's perspective was akin to staring into a maze of fun-house mirrors. There young Dottie stood, feigning nonchalance. Yet Lenny, a well-practiced observer, could see her curiosity and hope, her eagerness to meet him.

The duality of perspectives, her own and Lenny's, made Dottie dizzy. She was reading Lenny writing about himself for the very first—and possibly only—time.

But even then, he couldn't bring himself to use *I*. Instead, he referred to himself in the third person. Lenny was "the bus driver," and he spoke of Dottie waiting for "the writer." He never called himself that, but he knew Dottie did. It stuck with him, to the point that Lenny finally tried to work it out on paper all those years later.

The young woman held herself tightly, even though she tried not to. She was waiting to meet the writer of the unfinished stories because she wanted to know their endings. She wanted to know who he was. With every drag on her cigarette, she thought to herself that by the time she exhaled it, he could be walking through the door. She could finally know. She dreamed of having the answers she sought when she laid her head on her pillow that night.

Yet she also liked the teetering tension of the moment. She liked being on the cusp. The smoke from her cigarette hung there, curling around the horned rim of her glasses, moving glacially slow in the still air of the lobby. She wanted to know, but she loved the magic of not knowing. It had become as much a part of each story as the words themselves.

She didn't know the bus driver—the writer—was watching her. Or maybe she imagined he did. Maybe that imagining was another layer of the story. She didn't know he wasn't mysterious at all. She didn't know he was just another New Yorker, making his way in the world, never knowing how the stories around him ended, and loving the magic of it all.

Dottie released the deepest sigh she ever had. Then she laughed at the cliché of it, as if she were the leading lady of a romance novel "letting out a breath she didn't know she was holding." Dottie laughed because she knew exactly how long she had been holding that breath.

She'd been holding it since the very first time one of Lenny's stories landed in her hands.

She had finally read Lenny himself.

Hearing about him from Elise had been wonderful, getting his first name had been exciting, and Gail's call with the news from Maria had been nothing short of a miracle. Even though they couldn't track down employment records for the bus service with only his first name, everything they'd found was more than Dottie had ever dreamed they would get.

Jim bounding into her apartment that night, telling her Lenny's full name and that he'd found Lenny's final stories was icing on the cake. Reading more of Lenny's stories, this time in his own handwriting, was transcendent.

It was practically a flood of impossible happenings after so many years of not knowing anything at all.

But in that passage, that half page of a strange memory, Dottie finally knew Lenny for herself. She finally felt what he felt about his writing, the way everyone's stories danced around and overlapped. They were threads in a woven masterpiece that changed and expanded from one moment to the next, an infinite tapestry with no endings.

Dottie laid the worn notebook down on her lap. She looked up from it to find Jim watching her worriedly.

"You okay, Dottie? You've been powering through stories for about two hours straight. I haven't seen you put down an unfinished notebook until now."

Dottie reached out, and Jim readily put his hand in hers. She squeezed it tight.

"Thank you, Jim, for everything. Thank you for bringing me Elise. For throwing books for me. For coffee and cake and for being my friend. Thank you for believing me and believing in me. Thank you for finding the notebooks."

"You're welcome, Dottie. I'm grateful for you being

my friend as well. Thank you for picking me out of all the possible tenants, for helping me get that library job. Thank you for reading every one of my published plays before you'd even met me and for trusting me enough to tell me about your gift. Did I ever tell you that when I wrote my name in your address book, I felt like I'd really made it?"

He paused. "Why are we doing this? Why does this feel so final? It's been a long day, and you probably need to get some rest, but I never thought you would put these notebooks down and leave them unread. You're kind of scaring me, Dottie."

She smiled. In that moment, she felt younger. The cloud of melancholy she had felt looming so often lately cleared, like storms parting to reveal the blue sky. The weight of unfinished business about her slipped away. She knew when she smiled at Jim, it still dipped a little on the one side. Even if he noticed—and even though Dottie expected he was still worried about this shift in her behavior—Jim still smiled back.

"Nothing is wrong, dear," Dottie assured. "I'm just . . . I think I'm finally content with the page I'm on. From the moment I first read anything, I kept wanting to get to the next page. I wanted to get to the end, so I could crack open the next book. And Lenny's unfinished stories, they confounded me, but you know all about that bit. Right now, I'm just right where I am. And Jim, I'm so happy to be here."

Jim's look of concern softened. When Dottie began to get up from her chair, he helped her without a word. He helped her load the dishwasher, and she walked him to the door, planted a soft kiss on his cheek, and went to bed. Dottie could hear Jim through the vents of the old building, shuffling around in the apartment below, where Jessie must have been waiting for him. She heard them murmuring, perhaps packing the last of Jim's things.

Dottie laid her head on her pillow and closed her eyes. Maybe she would dream of her younger self, with Bobby, Gail, and Ted all reading Lenny's tattered notebooks over burgers and beer. Maybe she would dream of riding in Lenny's bus. She might wake up tomorrow and finish reading the rest of Lenny's notebooks, with a steaming cup of coffee by her side.

Who knew; she might even come out of retirement, call in a few favors with the editors she had mentored over the years, and get *The Complete Incomplete Works of Lenny Horowitz* published. One more title after all these years would be a hoot.

Or maybe Dottie wouldn't dream, and she wouldn't wake in the morning either. It was all fine. There were no endings, after all. Not really.

Epilogue
Traveling

New York City, 2015

Lenny wasn't the kind of man to complain—he really wasn't—but he didn't like being in the hospital. He ended up there because he'd collapsed on the bus. It was his heart. He'd been experiencing the pain in his chest for a few days, maybe longer, and had known it meant nothing good, but he'd been managing.

He felt bad about the incident happening when and where it had, though. Lenny had never wanted to hold up anybody's day or make Cheryl, a new driver, pull over and wait for the ambulance. Cheryl took her job very seriously, and Lenny appreciated her commitment, but he kind of wished she could let herself have some fun with her job.

Lenny was ready to go, whenever his time came. If anything, he kind of welcomed it.

He could barely read the paper, or anything else, anymore, and doing the crossword puzzle was damn near impossible. Even if he could read the clues, getting the letters in the right boxes was difficult when there was a big black cloud in the middle of his vision.

Macular degeneration, he thought, was worse than going blind all at once. It tricked him sometimes into thinking he could still do the things he used to. He could see around the edges, maybe read, maybe see something he wanted to see, but only in his peripherals. And then, when he instinctively turned his attention to the words or whatever else he wished to see, his eyes swung the big black cloud right in front of it. His had become a life spent avoiding directly looking at the words or the beauty of the world so he could see any of it at all, yet he still never saw enough of it.

It got harder and harder for Lenny to think of a reason to get himself out of bed in the morning when he couldn't read anymore.

But he didn't mind the vision thing when he was riding the bus. Lenny had spent his life on buses, mostly in the driver's seat. He was always looking straight ahead, making sure no distracted tourists, wandering drunks, or reckless bike messengers were about to dart out in the bus's path. He prided himself on having never hit a pedestrian during his decades-long career.

Even with his eyes forward, Lenny could keep some of his awareness on his passengers. They were like his own private movie, playing on a long, rectangular screen over his head, reflected there in his mirror. He saw people fall in love, break up, pine for their sweethearts who sent them letters when they were overseas fighting in wars, or even pine for, say, their milkman.

Lenny saw young people determined to make names for themselves in business, fashion, the stock market, and publishing. Some of them made it; some of them didn't. Some of them found out that making it had never really mattered to them in the first place, and they discovered a different path that took them far away from Lenny's bus route.

When he rode the bus now, his eyes forward, he could still catch some of the city going by in his peripheral vision. It wasn't too far off from the old days; Lenny just didn't get to drive anymore. When he caught sight of a car running a red light at an intersection or someone stepping off the curb against the signal, his right foot still pressed into the floor in front of him. Some habits died hard.

He used to get so in the groove of his job—following the route, checking all the corners, looking for people waiting at the stops for him and his bus to come along—that he could let his mind go elsewhere. Lenny composed stories about the regulars on his route. He incorporated details he picked up about them from what they carried with them and who they traveled with.

That was one of the neat things about travel. When someone had to get from point A to point B carrying everything they needed, he got to see what kinds of things were really important to them. Lenny tried to keep his biographies as close to his real observations as possible, but of course, he had to make guesses and fill in the gaps here and there.

His story habit turned into something Lenny did on his vacations too. When he went to the Jersey shore to visit with his cousin's family, he made up a story of the people on the boardwalk. When he decided to take a train excursion to the Poconos in Pennsylvania during peak time for the fall leaves, he wrote about his fellow passengers. When he rode the ferry as something fun to do, he then wandered the docks and composed a tale about one of the sailors.

Lenny even bought a secondhand typewriter from a pawnshop to write his stories on. He liked the way it sounded and how the cylinder went back and forth, the way the words unraveled across the page. It felt like they were all going someplace, like the story itself was traveling and the words were just printed tracks as it passed. All the stories were based on what Lenny observed, but they were all in progress. He wrote and wrote, page after page, until, of course, he came to the end of what he knew.

As Lenny accrued a stack of stories, he found he would like it if someone read them. He didn't know many of his coworkers very well, only seeing them at the start and end of each shift. Lenny was a voracious reader but never much of a talker. His parents were dead, and he didn't have any siblings. He got along well with his cousin in Jersey, but his cousin didn't read. Well, he did when he had to, but it was very difficult for him. He worked with his hands building houses and hired other people to write up agreements and do his books for him.

Lenny remembered a nice bunch of young people on his bus during the evening route; they would pile on after clocking out at five o'clock. They talked about what they had read at their job that day and how they wished they could get something across their desk that they really loved, something that turned out to be the next bestseller or Pulitzer.

So Lenny sent them his stories. He didn't want them to feel obligated to write him back, so he never included a return address. He knew his stories wouldn't get published. People liked there to be neat little endings to things, but life wasn't like that. Granted, they probably liked neat little endings *because* life really wasn't like that.

Lenny thought he heard them talking about his stories once or twice on their way out for burgers on payday. He found out he was right when he read an ad in the *Tribune* that they had taken out just for him. They even posted a flyer of that same ad at Silva's Market. It was real nice of them to do all that, even though it did result in an awkward bus ride with Maria Silva. But he didn't show up for the meeting they requested. He thought about writing them a letter to explain, but explaining himself wasn't his strong suit when it came to words.

At least he had a name to send the rest of his stories to: Ms. Dorothy Barber.

Lenny wrote less after he retired. Soon after his last day driving a bus, he moved out of his humble home in the Bronx. Developers had been going door to door talking people into selling. He couldn't believe how much they paid him. Money wise, he was set for life. Lenny moved to Jersey, to an apartment building his cousin's son owned.

Brian gave him a good deal, and he stopped by sometimes to see if Lenny needed anything. He even sent his workers by to check on Lenny when Brian couldn't make it himself. Lenny got himself a library card for the local public library. He didn't throw out his old one, though, for sentimental reasons. And he still donated money to the Friends of the Library association for the Bronx Library Center, even after he joined the Friends association for his new library in Hoboken. The librarians there helped Lenny navigate the large-print books section and encouraged him to try audiobooks as well. Audiobooks weren't the same for him, though, not by a long shot. They didn't allow for the pleasure of rereading a great line over and over and seeing how it fit perfectly in the paragraph or on the page.

During the move, Lenny's typewriter was dropped; it never worked after that. Lenny figured there was no use in getting a new one. When he felt like writing, he just wrote longhand on yellow legal pads. As his eyesight got worse, he realized he would sometimes write one line right over the one before.

That's when he stopped. He found there were fewer stories roaming around in his head, anyway.

Lenny still liked to read the headlines and larger-print sub-headlines throughout the paper. The big color pictures were mostly visible. He trained himself to focus on one of the corners of the page so he could see the rest of it.

The hospital only had the *New York Post*, which was unfortunate, as he strongly preferred the *Times*. At least, he had ever since his beloved *Tribune* ended its run back in the midsixties. He used to read the *Tribune* cover to cover every day.

Why weren't there candy stripers anymore? He could have given one of them a few bucks to run out to a newsstand to get him a copy of the *Times*, maybe.

He felt a little woozy. That happened every once in a while since he arrived at the hospital, prompting a monitor at his bedside to beep and a nurse to come in and check on him. The nurses must have been busy with someone else, so he lowered the head of his bed, closed his eyes, and started composing a story about Cheryl in his head.

One quieter day, he had mustered the gumption to start up a conversation by telling her he used to drive the same route. She'd kept her eyes glued to the road, still not cracking a smile, but she did tell him she used to be a school bus driver and she worked construction before that. She had been one of the people who held the sign and counted cars to let through only so many at a time. He wasn't sure why she had left those jobs. Maybe she didn't like it when people didn't follow the rules; she seemed the type.

Lenny didn't even hear the loud beeping from the machine anymore or notice that there were several nurses in the room until one of them opened his eye and shone a bright light in it. He was real tired. His chest hurt, but distantly. He knew people were rushing around him and touching him, but he was too tired to worry about it all. Lenny just let them do their job.

In his mind, he rode the bus as Cheryl recited her life's story. As she talked, he typed the story on his old typewriter, which was somehow all fixed. Well, except for the *S* key; that had been a problem since Lenny bought it.

Then he was the one in the driver's seat, as he had been all those years ago. He smiled at the people in the mirror above his head, hoping they understood how happy it made him to drive them places, for however long he could.

Someone had taken over the bus route after Lenny retired. Someone would take over Cheryl's route when she, too, left it someday. Similarly, someone new would occupy Lenny's hospital bed after he left—which he realized was probably going to be soon. Maybe they'd be okay with the *Post*.

Acknowledgments

First and foremost, I need to thank my husband, Kris. His unwavering support started the moment I first shared that I wanted to seriously pursue writing. Whenever I get an acceptance, Kris is the first person I want to tell. When I got the email from Balance of Seven that they wanted to make *Bookstories* a reality, he was the first person I hugged. Kris also manages my website and helps me navigate new social media and writing software. Last Christmas, he gifted me a huge box of business cards and letterhead that proclaimed me an author. Kris makes me feel that I am already the person I want to be when I grow up.

Thank you to my boys, Ben and Sam, for being my biggest cheerleaders. Whenever they've bragged to their friends and teachers that I am an author, it has never not made me glow inside. Thank you also to Noel, my mother-in-law, for letting me go on and on about publishing and other book-world stuff. And thank you to Noah and Lexie, two of the kindest people I know, for sharing in my excitement.

To Angie, thank you for being one of the main characters in my life's story. I've loved growing up with you into the women we are today. I can't wait to see what hijinks we each get into in the next half century or so.

To my Ithaca girls—Maria, Melissa, Natalie, and Erin.

Thank you for listening all the times I went off on crazy tangents about writing, reading, and fandom lore. Thank you for reading my work. Since you are some of the coolest people on the planet, your generous encouragement and praise never fails to send me over the moon.

Tod Tinker, thank you for believing in the magic of reading and for believing in *Bookstories*. Every time I think about you texting Ynes, *I want this book,* during our initial video call, I gotta smile. Thank you, Ynes Freeman, for being with me every step of the way during this process, from initial meetings, the editing, the IndieGoGo campaign, marketing meetings, and so much more. This industry needs more amazing people like you, and you are destined to bring so many great books into the world as both a publisher and an author.

To the editorial team and my fellow authors at Balance of Seven, especially Leo Otherland, Charlene Templeman, Kat Seto, Emily Wynne, and Sarah Hines, thanks for sharing this journey with me. Looking back on the names in that last sentence, I am bowled over by the amount of talent and wonderfulness.

Thank you, Andrea, a.k.a. altocello, for creating cover art for *Bookstories* that captures the sacred communion of the transference of books and the sharing of stories. It's perfect. Thank you, Atlin Merrick, for introducing me to Andrea's art and for being an all-around phenomenal human being, mentor, fandom momma, and wrangler of cryptids.

To the magical movement that is NaNoWriMo, and especially the Winchester Nation WriMos, thank you for compelling me to bang out the first ten chapters of this book in thirty days flat in the middle of a pandemic. Yes, I have my winner's T-shirt to prove it.

And to all the writers, publishers, editors, librarians, and booksellers of the world, thank you for telling stories and making books. You build dreams. You wield magic. You bring us together, pressing books into each other's hands and hearts. And to the readers, of this book and others, thank you. Without readers extending their hands to receive the humble offerings of words, stories, and worlds, we would be nothing. Thank you for giving our stories a home. Remember to pass them on.

About the Author

Sarah Tollok lives in the beautiful Shenandoah Valley of Virginia with her husband and two sons. She refuses to choose just one genre to focus on in her writing or reading life, because she is having far too much fun. She has work featured in anthologies with Improbable Press, Alan Squire Publishing, and Clan Destine Press. She also is a contributing writer at Coffee House Writers, where she often shares about her love of reading. You can find out more about her work at SarahTollok.com.

Printed in the USA
CPSIA information can be obtained
at www.ICGtesting.com
JSHW012323210224
57590JS00006B/22

9 781947 012585